CW00338178

CHAINS OF DECEIT

'Now, down on the floor,' said Adrian. 'I want you to clean those boots.'

Scott got down on all fours and started licking the shiny black leather, beginning with the toe-caps and dragging his tongue over the eyelets and up the sides. His own cock was pressed against the white carpet, and his attention to Adrian's boots was causing it to rub backwards and forwards, sending shivers of pleasure through him.

He soon worried that he would have to stop in case he came: if he came without being ordered to do so, he risked Adrian's anger ... and that wasn't something he wanted. But stopping licking Adrian's boots would be just as bad: Adrian was his master, and Scott wouldn't dare to do anything without his express authority.

CHAINS OF DECEIT

Paul C. Alexander

First published in Great Britain in 1997 by
Idol
an imprint of Virgin Publishing Ltd
332 Ladbroke Grove
London W10 5AH

Copyright © Paul C. Alexander 1997

The right of Paul C. Alexander to be identified as the Author of
this Work has been asserted by him in accordance with the
Copyright, Designs and Patents Act 1988.

ISBN 0 352 33206 9

Cover photograph by Colin Clarke Photography

Typeset by SetSystems Ltd, Saffron Walden, Essex
Printed and bound in Great Britain by
Cox & Wyman Ltd, Reading, Berks

This book is sold subject to the condition that it shall not, by way
of trade or otherwise, be lent, resold, hired out or otherwise
circulated without the publisher's prior written consent in any
form of binding or cover other than that in which it is published
and without a similar condition, including this condition, being
imposed on the subsequent purchaser.

The Terrence Higgins Trust

SAFER SEX GUIDELINES

These books are sexual fantasies – in real life, everyone needs to think about safe sex.

While there have been major advances in the drug treatments for people with HIV and AIDS, there is still no cure for AIDS or a vaccine against HIV. Safe sex is still the only way of being sure of avoiding HIV sexually.

HIV can only be transmitted through blood, come and vaginal fluids (but no other body fluids) – passing from one person (with HIV) into another person's bloodstream. It cannot get through healthy, undamaged skin. The only real risk of HIV is through anal sex without a condom – this accounts for almost all HIV transmissions between men.

Being Safe:
Even if you don't come inside someone, there is still a risk to both partners from blood (tiny cuts in the arse) and pre-come. Using strong condoms and water-based lubricant greatly reduces the risk of HIV. However, condoms can break or slip off, so:

* Make sure that condoms are stored away from hot or damp places.
* Check the expiry date – condoms have a limited life.
* Gently squeeze the air out of the tip.
* Check the condom is put on the right way up and unroll it down the erect cock.
* Use plenty of water-based lubricant (lube), up the arse and on the condom.
* While fucking, check occasionally to see the condom is still in one piece (you could also add more lube).
* When you withdraw, hold the condom tight to your cock as you pull out.

* Never re-use a condom or use the same condom with more than one person.
* If you're not used to condoms you might practise putting them on.
* Sex toys like dildos and plugs are safe. But if you're sharing them use a new condom each time or wash the toys well.

For the safest sex, make sure you use the strongest condoms, such as Durex Ultra Strong, Mates Super Strong, HT Specials and Rubberstuffers packs. Condoms are free in many STD (Sexually Transmitted Disease) clinics (sometimes called GUM clinics) and from many gay bars. It's also essential to use lots of water-based lube such as KY, Wet Stuff, Slik or Liquid Silk. Never use come as a lubricant.

Oral Sex:
Compared with fucking, sucking someone's cock is far safer. Swallowing come does not necessarily mean that HIV gets absorbed into the bloodstream. While a tiny fraction of cases of HIV infection have been linked to sucking, we know the risk is minimal. But certain factors increase the risk:
* Letting someone come in your mouth
* Throat infections such as gonorrhoea
* If you have cuts, sores or infections in your mouth and throat

So what is safe?
There are so many things you can do which are absolutely safe: wanking each other; rubbing your cocks against one another; kissing, sucking and licking all over the body; rimming – to name but a few.

If you're finding safe sex difficult, call a helpline or speak to someone you feel you can trust for support. The Terrence Higgins Trust Helpline, which is open from noon to 10pm every day, can be reached on 0171 242 1010.

Prologue

—————

Leigh sipped his shandy and looked around the bar of the Collective hopefully. His watch said it was about nine thirty, but it seemed later – or rather it felt later: he'd been standing on his own all night, and it felt like an eternity. Why wouldn't anyone talk to him?

Leigh had only been in London for a few months, and the Collective and the Brave Trader were the only two places in which he felt comfortable. He'd tried a few of the other leather bars, such as the Harness and Vice, but they were a bit too heavy for him. It wasn't that he didn't like the leather scene and all that went with it – it was just that he preferred it in the more comfortable surroundings of someone's house, rather than the dark, stone anonymity of a back room or dungeon. He liked the more relaxed attitude of the Collective, and the homely, almost local feel of the Brave Trader. Even so, he hadn't made many friends – or found many lovers – in either.

He'd seen a couple of people in the Collective that night who he quite fancied: he'd caught a glimpse of a big leather bear with an impressive tattoo, but he couldn't see where he'd got to. The same was true for the other bloke he'd got his eye on: medium height, stocky, with a goatee beard. Leigh was sure that he recognised him from the Brave Trader, but there was something different about him tonight. Leigh had seen him when he first came in, but hadn't been paying close enough attention and appeared to have lost him to one of the dark corners of the bar. He took another swig and sighed. Just his luck – another lonely night.

'Don't you go into the Brave Trader?'

Leigh looked round and saw the bloke with the goatee beard standing next to him. Unable to believe his luck, he just smiled sheepishly. 'Sometimes,' he answered, trying to respond to the man's friendliness in a way that suggested that he was interested. 'I've seen you in there, haven't I?' He was sure it was the same person, even if there was something different about him.

The other nodded, and Leigh tried to work out what it was that was different tonight . . .

'That's it!' exclaimed Leigh. 'You're usually in a suit.' That was why he seemed so familiar. In a suit, he looked businesslike, professional – but still horny; in his leather waistcoat and jeans he was just irresistible. Leigh grinned with slight embarrassment. 'Sorry, but I was just trying to place you.'

'I'm off duty tonight.' The man laughed. 'You obviously know me, but I'm afraid that you've got me at a bit of a disadvantage. I'm Nathan,' he added, shaking Leigh's hand. 'Can I get you a drink?'

Leigh couldn't believe his luck. 'I'm Leigh. And a drink would be great.'

And that would herald Nathan Dexter's first direct experience with the Elective.

Leigh followed Nathan through the front door into the darkened living room, almost tripping over the doorstep as he did so. Both of them had had a little too much to drink, and Leigh was definitely feeling slightly unsteady. Unsteady, but determined.

'Want another drink?' asked Nathan. 'Or shall we . . .' He nodded upstairs.

Leigh laughed. 'You don't hang about, do you?' Having said that, he was as desperate to get to bed as Nathan was. As Nathan went up the stairs, Leigh took a brief look around the room and was intrigued: apart from the beige boxes of the very impressive-looking computer set-up in the corner, everything else was made of either polished dark wood or black leather. In short, Nathan clearly wasn't short of a few bob.

As Leigh climbed the stairs, he vaguely tried to remember what Nathan did for a living. They had talked about it, but for the moment it escaped him. Then again, it wasn't important: all Leigh wanted was a good night between the sheets, and, if he was any judge of people, Nathan was going to offer him just that.

By the time Leigh reached Nathan's room, Nathan was sitting on the bed, about to remove his ten-hole Doctor Martens. 'No – don't do that,' Leigh protested. For some reason, the idea of having sex while Nathan was in leather was starting to really turn him on.

Nathan looked at him with a curious expression. 'Why not?'

'Because I'd prefer it if you kept them on.' Leigh took off his green bomber jacket and tossed it into the corner of the room. 'I'd prefer it if you kept your leather jacket on as well.'

Nathan grinned devilishly. 'A man after my own heart. I'll take the jeans off, though.' Then he frowned in concentration, as if something had just occurred to him. 'Actually, it'd be good if you did the same.'

As Nathan quickly undid his boots so that he could remove his jeans, Leigh looked around the bedroom. It was less ornate than the living room, but still told of comfortable living. The bed, which stood against the far wall, was huge – far bigger than a double – with posts at all four corners, and Leigh could immediately think of a few uses for them. A bedside table stood next to the bed; a small lamp and an ashtray rested on top. But

Leigh's eyes were drawn to the floor next to the table: a set of handcuffs half protruded from between the table and the bed, and he realised that he and Nathan were going to be seeing eye to eye that night.

Seeing that Nathan had already removed his boots and boxer shorts, Leigh quickly unlaced his own boots and pulled off his jeans. Ensuring that his T-shirt covered his engorged dick – he didn't want to give everything away just yet – he pulled down his briefs and put his boots back on again, leaning against the wall for support as he laced them. He tried to catch a glimpse of Nathan's cock, but his denim shirt obscured it. Oh well, Leigh decided: something to look forward to.

Nathan stood from the bed and walked over to the enormous mirrored wardrobe. 'I've got a good idea that you might like this,' he called out. He opened the door and reached in, before pulling out what first appeared to be a tangle of studded black leather. Leigh recognised it as a body harness, and couldn't help grinning. It had been ages since he had last worn one of those.

'Put it on,' Nathan ordered. Suddenly, the atmosphere changed. Instead of Nathan and Leigh, there was now only Nathan and his servant. Leigh knew better than to argue: this was the way he liked it. He just wanted to obey. This was how he had wanted the evening to end, and it was a game that he most definitely wanted to play.

Pulling the harness from the bed, he stripped off his T-shirt. This merited a slap round the face from Nathan. 'Did I tell you that you could take off your T-shirt?'

'No.'

Another slap. 'No *what*?' Nathan bellowed. For a moment, Leigh had a dilemma: some masters liked *sir*, some preferred *boss*. Some just liked *master*. Leigh had to guess. Given what he had learnt about Nathan during the evening, he took his best shot.

'No, sir,' he said contritely, almost instinctively assuming the

4

compliant mindset he needed. Nathan Dexter was his master: at that point in time, he owned Leigh, body and soul.

'That's better. You know it's better when you're a good boy. Now, put that on.' Nathan was standing in front of him, hands on hips, still wearing his denim shirt. Leigh was desperate to catch a glimpse of his master's cock, but knew that would have to wait until he was ready. That anticipation alone was enough to ensure his complete obedience.

Leigh untangled the straps and started to fasten the harness around him. But he soon realised that he would need help; he'd worn harnesses before, but each one was slightly different, and he didn't want to disappoint his master by fitting it incorrectly.

'Sorry, sir, but I need you to help me.'

'That's all right,' said Nathan. 'When one of my boys needs help, they only have to ask.' He grabbed two of the straps and threw them over Leigh's shoulders; he then turned Leigh around and fastened the straps to the large metal ring which lay against the small of his back, the double of the ring that sat just below Leigh's firm pecs. Two more straps were snapped into place, linking the two metal rings together in a tight leather 'X'. He then turned Leigh around again so that he was facing him.

The next straps were thinner than the others; they hung down from the front ring and ended in a studded leather cockring. Firmly yet gently, Nathan fastened the cockring around Leigh's trembling dick, smiling at him as he did so.

'Thank you, sir,' whispered Leigh as he shivered at Nathan's touch.

Nathan said nothing; he just moved Leigh round again and hooked up the final straps – two more thin strips of leather that would pass between his buttocks and link the metal ring at Leigh's back to the cockring. Leigh let out a slight groan as Nathan's fingers stroked his arse as he pulled the straps through and attached them to the leather that squeezed the base of his

5

cock. After a few moments of adjustment, ensuring that all of the straps were tight, Nathan stepped back.

'There.' Nathan placed his hands on Leigh's shoulders and moved him in front of the mirrored doors of the wardrobe. 'How does my boy feel now?'

Leigh examined himself in the mirror – and liked what he saw. Since he had moved to London, he had spent his spare time at the gym, and the results spoke for themselves: he was broad-shouldered, with big biceps, a well-defined, smooth chest and flat stomach. His legs were just as firm, solid and muscular, covered with fine black hair. He glanced at Nathan and was honoured to see that he was admiring the V-shaped torso with obvious longing.

The black leather of the harness complemented Leigh's firm body: from the shining silver ring on his chest, sitting flat against his smooth solid chest, the studded black straps ran across his shoulders and his hips, and down to the ring that surrounded his thick seven inches of cock, now throbbing and red thanks to the tight pressure of the cockring.

Leigh felt so horny he could explode.

'Nice tattoo.'

Leigh looked at it in his reflection: a green dragon, its batlike wings spread across his left shoulder. 'Thank you, sir.'

Nathan pulled off his denim shirt and grabbed his leather jacket from the bed. Leigh was impressed: although Nathan was carrying a little extra weight around the stomach, he was almost as well muscled as Leigh was, with a chest covered in a thick rug of black hair which reached from just below his neck to the huge dick which stood proudly between his legs. Leigh had always thought that he was well hung, but Nathan's cock was both longer and thicker than his, the foreskin pulled back just far enough to reveal the glistening, deep red helmet. Nathan was wearing a solid metal cockring, only just visible in the mass of hair that surrounded his dick.

'On your knees.'

Leigh didn't hesitate: an order was an order, and all Leigh wanted to do was obey. Sinking to the floor, he waited. To take the initiative was forbidden, and the last thing that Leigh wanted was to upset his master.

'Suck my dick.' Nathan pulled on his biker's jacket and stood there, legs apart, his erection almost parallel with his stomach.

Leigh leant forward and took Nathan's cock in his mouth, guiding it in with his hand. He almost choked on its length, but wasn't going to let that stop him: he knew what he had to do. He moistened his lips and ran them up and down Nathan's cock, from the hairy base to the wet glans, his nose filled with the heady smell of fresh sweat. Leigh started to concentrate his attentions on the moist red helmet, pulling Nathan's foreskin back to reveal all of it.

Instinctively, his free hand reached down to grasp his own erection, but that wasn't allowed; a firm cuff round the ear from Nathan stopped that immediately. Leigh would be allowed to pleasure himself . . . but only when Nathan ordered it.

Ignoring the sharp pain, Leigh continued to concentrate on Nathan's helmet, which was now almost purple from the restraint of the cockring. Leigh's tongue probed the leaking slit, tasting the salty juice that was almost pouring from it. Leigh was sure that his master wouldn't be able to hold out much longer, and he couldn't wait for Nathan to fill his mouth with his hot load.

Risking another reprimand, Leigh started to finger Nathan's anus, stroking the hair that filled the crack between his buttocks, searching for the hot hole. As his mouth began to suck on Nathan's helmet with urgent, insistent tugs, he found Nathan's ring and gently inserted his finger. Nathan gasped, but didn't protest: if anything, he seemed to want more. It was hard to be sure, but it seemed to Leigh that Nathan was pushing himself on to Leigh's softly probing finger. Talking this as an unspoken command, Leigh pushed his finger further and further up the moist, warm passage. It wasn't long before it was in up to the knuckle; with his whole finger up there, he started stroking in time with his firm sucks on Nathan's cock.

'Good boy,' gasped Nathan. 'Good boy. You're gonna make your master come. You want that, don't you?'

Leigh said nothing – how could he, with eight inches of thick cock in his mouth? Instead, he looked up at Nathan and smiled. Nathan moved his hand from Leigh's shoulder and stroked his short hair, gently at first, and then more roughly, pulling and scratching. Leigh knew that Nathan was very close, and realised that he too was almost on the point of release, without even having touched himself.

He felt Nathan's balls contract; at the same time, his arse clenched around Leigh's finger. Leigh continued to suck, timing his rhythm so that it matched Nathan's. Within a second, Nathan let out an almighty grunt and seized Leigh's shoulders tightly.

Leigh felt the first spurt hit the back of his throat and he swallowed, relishing the hot salty taste of his master's come. Within seconds, his mouth was full – as fast as he tried to swallow, Nathan kept pumping, kept shooting. This was too much for Leigh; without warning, he felt himself come, his thick cock twitching and throbbing, shooting strings of white juice over the carpet and over Nathan's legs.

Nathan stepped away and looked down at the result. 'Clean up that mess,' he commanded.

Still shaking from the intensity of his own orgasm, Leigh inched forward on his knees and licked every drop of his own come from Nathan's muscular legs. His come tasted different from Nathan's: it was sweeter and less salty. He carried on licking, feeling his erection returning as he ran his tongue across the thick hairs of Nathan's legs.

'That's enough,' said Nathan, pulling Leigh to his feet. 'I didn't tell you to come, did I, boy?'

'No, sir. Sorry, sir.'

'My bad boy needs to be punished, doesn't he?'

Leigh nodded. 'Sorry, sir,' he repeated.

'Sorry isn't good enough.' Nathan reached down to the floor and pulled out the handcuffs. 'It's time you were taught some discipline.'

Leigh's erection was back before Nathan could even unlock the handcuffs. Leigh knew that it was going to be a long and demanding night at the hands of his new master.

He couldn't wait.

The room was pitch-black and smelt of fresh sweat and leather – the smell of men. As Scott closed the heavy metal door behind him, he could sense the jostling mass, all of them looking for the same thing. The same thing he was seeking.

Sex. Nameless, faceless, anonymous sex.

He lit up a cigarette, knowing that the flickering illumination from the match would allow the others to see his face and body for a second, to judge whether he was worth their time and effort. He knew he was; it was just a question of convincing them of it. And the fact that a number of the dark shapes were moving in his direction suggested that he had been successful.

Scott was feeling hot tonight – hot and horny. And it showed: in his face, in his attitude. And in the gnawing, desperate feeling that threatened to overwhelm him. He had to have someone soon – he just had to.

Seconds later, it paid off: one of the shapes was standing in front of him, and Scott immediately felt a hand roughly stroking the front of his leather trousers: hard, insistent strokes which quickly received the desired effect. This was what he wanted and his body knew it. His erection, already sizeable, now threatened to break free of its own accord. Throwing the half-smoked cigarette to the floor, he reached out and touched the shadow: all he could feel was solid muscle and cold leather.

Perfect.

The straining between his legs didn't last long; Scott didn't resist as the hand quickly and urgently unzipped his fly and pulled out his engorged cock, the foreskin withdrawn and the helmet smooth with wetness. And he didn't resist as the shadowy figure fell to its knees and engulfed his cock in the warmth of his mouth, pulling his trousers down as he did so.

Scott hadn't had sex for days – that was why he was in one of the back rooms of the Harness – and the insistence of the man sucking him off was proving too much. As the man's tongue flicked over the moist throbbing end and his fingers caressed Scott's balls and probed his arse, Scott couldn't help giving a quiet groan that broke the usual whispering silence of the back room and drew the attention of a few more people, looming towards him out of the dark. When the man slipped his hand up Scott's tight grey T-shirt and began to stroke his chest and stomach, his tongue teasing Scott's dick slit and his finger forcing its way up his anus, Scott couldn't help himself: within moments, he felt the orgasm building up from the base of his cock, and he had no intention of holding back. This was the whole point of the Harness and he longed for it, welcomed it.

The man kneeling before him wasn't alone in his attentions: other hands started to stroke Scott's face, his chest, his backside; unseen mouths nibbled at his neck and his ears. Almost instinctively, Scott reached out into the dark and found two huge dicks, one on either side of him, and grabbed them roughly. As he slowly wanked them with measured strokes, he relished the groans from around him, and relished the feel of the thick, moist cocks held tightly in his hands. Scott didn't want the moment to end: to at least three people, he was the most important person in the world, and he wanted it to continue for ever.

Obviously, it couldn't.

The person who kissed and bit and sucked Scott's neck was

ultimately responsible for Scott's orgasm. Scott couldn't hold out for another second: suddenly he felt the throbbing warmth explode outward and upward, building up and building up until it overtook him. Unable – unwilling – to control himself, he thrust his dick forward into the kneeling man's mouth, grunting with the release in time to the brutal pounding his was giving him. Somewhere outside the intensity of his orgasm, Scott was aware of other noises, other groans, from the men on either side of him, but he ignored them as he concentrated on his own enjoyment.

As Scott convulsed, the man swallowed every drop of his load, massaging his balls and rubbing his other hand over Scott's taut, hairy stomach. Finally spent, Scott sighed, and slumped against the cold stone wall of the dungeon-like back room. Even as the kneeling man licked the last drops of come from Scott's still-impressive dick, the others melted back into the shadows, the wetness on both of Scott's hands proof that they too had enjoyed themselves.

'Does it have to end here?' came the quiet words in his ear. The kneeling man was now standing next to him, his hand caressing the back of Scott's leather waistcoat. 'I only live a taxi ride away,' he said softly. 'Perhaps you'd like to come back with me.'

As he spoke, the door to the back room opened, momentarily casting a shaft of diffused light into the darkened dungeon. Scott was able to see the man clearly: taller than he was, with a muscular build, cropped blond hair and a short blond beard. He was wearing a pair of leather chaps, a leather jockstrap and a studded body harness, through which Scott could see two pierced nipples. Scott guessed that the man was in his mid-thirties, but his sculpted biceps and flat stomach suggested that he looked after himself. Scott was sorely tempted to take him up on the offer: it was still fairly early, and he wasn't in a rush to go anywhere else.

Besides, people who could give blow jobs like that weren't

that easy to find, and he could feel his erection threatening – no, promising – to return.

Without a moment's hesitation, Scott followed the man out of the dungeon.

One day, he would live to regret it.

One

Nathan Dexter stepped out of the shower and grabbed the towel from the rail. It was already eight thirty according to his Tag watch lying on the damp grey carpet, and he was due at the bar at half nine. He was cutting it fine – as usual. Then again, Paul and Neil were used to it. After twelve years, they ought to be.

As he towelled himself dry, he looked at himself in the mirror and, with a trace of conceit, was impressed with what he saw. He was about five foot ten, with dark, cropped hair and a well-trimmed goatee beard, and wasn't at all bad-looking, even if he did say so himself. Then again, he had had plenty of testimonials over the years. The slight thickening around his waist was currently worrying him a bit – he was definitely going to have to start watching his weight after he'd got the Christmas PR bashes out of the way – but the rest of him was fairly well muscled, thanks to his twice-weekly gym sessions. He'd just have a do a few more sit-ups, he decided. As he dried his thick covering of black chest hair, he allowed himself a grin: for a thirty-three-year-old man, he wasn't doing badly. *So why are you living on your own?* asked a cynical inner voice which he

13

tried to ignore, hurling an irritated growl at his reflection in the process.

Throwing the wet towel on the floor, he stomped into his bedroom and opened the wardrobe, trying to decide what he was going to wear. It was a Wednesday: that meant something smart but casual, rather than the head-to-foot leather or rubber of a weekend jaunt. The Timberland? The Ben Sherman? A plain white T-shirt? He chose the green and blue Ben Sherman: his favourite, even if it had been a gift from a less-than-fondly remembered ex-lover.

Five minutes later, he was ready. Ben Sherman, black 501s, brown Caterpillar boots: he looked the business. Grabbing his black bomber jacket from the coat-rack, he opened the front door and stepped into the chilly November night. Something told him that tonight had something special in store for him. Something . . . wonderful.

As usual, the pavement around Leicester Square Underground was packed with milling, aimless tourists, and Nathan found himself huffing and tutting as he forced his way out of the station and through the forest of rucksacks and foreign languages to get to the Crossed Swords, only a few hundred yards away. His earlier anticipation was now coloured with irritation: the whole journey from his house in Docklands had been a saga of missed trains and packed compartments, as if someone up there was trying to tell him something. He sincerely hoped not.

He reached the Crossed Swords with about a minute to spare, opening the smoked-glass door and walking into the dim interior. As his eyes adjusted to the reduced lighting, he tried to locate his friends among the throng of people. It wasn't difficult: Paul and Neil were standing in their normal spot near the DJ's booth, animatedly chatting away. They saw him immediately, waved and gestured for him to go to the bar. Two minutes later, all three were drinking lager and catching up on the latest gossip – a typical Wednesday night for them in one of the West End's busiest gay bars.

Paul, a thin but well-muscled man with short ginger hair, was telling them about the events of the previous Sunday. 'I couldn't believe it: he was the best-looking bloke in the club – we were all after him that night. And he copped off with the Slug!'

'You are kidding?' protested Neil, the same age as both Paul and Nathan, with wavy blond hair and a slight lisp. 'No one cops off with the Slug.' He shuddered, a look of distaste on his face. 'No, I don't want to know. Just the thought of it turns my stomach.' He took a swig of his lager. 'I mean: the Slug? There's hope for us yet!'

The three of them started laughing. Nathan sipped his beer and realised that, overall, he was happy with his lot. As a freelance journalist, he was doing very well: thanks to his extensive network of contacts, the commissions were pouring in, and his finances weren't just healthy – they were positively radiant. And, once the story he was working on broke, he'd be able to command his own price on the market. Then there were the friends like Paul and Neil, who he had known since they were at university together. There was only one thing really missing: someone to share his life with.

Sex wasn't the problem: Nathan knew he could still pull – in fact, like his writing career, his sex life had never been busier. But finding the right person, the person with whom he could forge a relationship, still eluded him. His last relationship had ended disastrously a couple of years ago, and it had taken him a long while to get over it, unwilling to open himself up and risk being hurt all over again. But now he was ready; it was simply a matter of finding the right person.

Except that he didn't seem to be able to find that person. He knew – or at least, he believed – that the right person was out there, somewhere. But he hadn't found him, and all that Nathan knew was that he was single. And he didn't particularly

15

care for it. Yes, he had his work, and he had his friends. But he wanted more: he wanted that close companionship that came with a relationship. Where was he going to find it?

Suddenly, Nathan realised that Neil was trying to attract his attention with clandestine winks and hisses, backed up by Paul, who was grinning broadly. 'What are you two on about now?' Nathan asked with a smile.

Neil aimed a subtle nod over Nathan's shoulder. 'Don't look now, but someone over there's paying you rather a lot of attention.' His voice dropped to a whisper. 'Can't see his guide dog, though.'

After nudging Neil in the ribs in revenge, Nathan nonchalantly turned round, scanning the bar for his mysterious admirer. 'Over by the stairs,' Neil added helpfully. Nathan frowned in mock annoyance: if there was one thing that Neil and Paul loved, it was a bit of intrigue. But when he finally located the object of Neil's comments, he was taken aback. The bloke was downright gorgeous.

The person in question appeared to be in his early twenties, and he was definitely showing a lot of interest. Nathan suddenly felt something that astonished him: he felt nervous. *Thirty-three years old and nervous!* Staring straight at his admirer, he smiled, and was delighted to receive a smile in return. And not a shy smile either – the boy grinned and raised his drink, indicating that Nathan should go over and join him.

At that moment, Nathan knew that his premonition had been correct: something wonderful *was* going to happen this evening. Taking his leave of Neil and Paul, he sauntered over to the stairs.

An hour later, Neil and Paul had gone home, having wholeheartedly approved of the match. Indeed, they had behaved more like a couple of maiden aunts than the hardened clubbers he knew them to be, fussing over the boy and welcoming him into their little social circle. As far as they were concerned, Scott James was 'a good one'.

Nathan spent a couple of moments examining the last dregs of warm lager in the glass before returning his attention to Scott, trying not to appear too eager – even though he *was* eager, eager to get the muscular twenty-year-old into his home and into his bed. But he could wait no longer; he looked up and caught Scott examining him with the same interest as Nathan hoped was written over his face.

By no stretch of the imagination could Scott be called handsome, but then again, Nathan was well known for having a thing for thugs: skinheads, bikers, truck-drivers were famous for being Nathan Dexter's stock-in-trade. Especially short, stocky hairy ones, and that summed up Scott perfectly. He caught Nathan's glance and smiled, a wicked bastard of a smile, and Nathan found his attention transfixed by Scott's blue eyes. They weren't so much come-to-bed eyes as shag-me-senseless eyes, a penetrating stare that immediately sent the blood to Nathan's cock. He wanted him so badly it hurt – and Nathan couldn't remember the last time he had felt like this about somebody.

Nathan looked up and down Scott's compact body as if weighing up a potential slave, imagining Scott's thickly haired arms around him, his big hands stroking his chest and pulling on his engorged dick. Nathan could see the telltale fur that poked above the collar of Scott's green polo shirt – it had been one of the first things he had noticed about the boy when he had gone over to talk to him – and wondered how far down it went, allowing himself to fantasise for a moment, hoping, praying, that the shirt hid a thick carpet of dark curls that he could run his fingers through, curls that would get entangled with his own chest hair as they rolled around on the carpet, on the bed – anywhere. His mind explored the possibilities, but he had to stop that particular chain of thought before the pressure in his jeans that the marvellous images were causing became too uncomfortable and too irresistible to ignore – although he couldn't help stealing a quick look at Scott's crotch, and was once again entranced by the bulging packet that awaited him when he could finally pull off Scott's jeans and take his, hopefully, thick cock in his mouth. He just hoped that the boy lived up to his promise.

'Well?' asked Nathan, and Scott grinned back at him. They both knew what he meant.

'Well what?' Scott teased.

'Your place or mine?' Clichéd, Nathan knew, but it served its purpose. An old writer friend of his had once claimed that, just as there were only a finite number of plots, there were only a finite number of pick-up lines. In his experience, Nathan had no reason to doubt it.

Scott drained the rest of his blackcurrant Hooch in one go, slamming the empty bottle on to the bar. 'Can we go back to yours? The halls of residence are a bit, well, awkward.' He smiled almost bashfully, and Nathan just wanted to hug him.

'I know what you mean,' said Nathan, unable to help laughing. He remembered his own time as a student, twelve years ago, and the precautions he'd had to take when bringing trade back. Especially since most of the trade hadn't even been worth all the trouble – as Paul and Neil had always been so keen to point out. At least they approved of this one. 'Mine it is. We'll get a taxi.'

Scott frowned. 'I haven't got a lot of money . . .' he apologised.

Nathan laughed. He had very few problems in his life, and lack of money certainly wasn't one of them. 'Don't worry about it – I just can't be bothered with the Underground.' Actually, I can't wait that long to get you into bed, he confessed to himself.

Getting their coats from the cloakroom – Scott pulled on an expensive turquoise bomber jacket – they made their way through the crowded bar towards the exit. As they pushed their way through the heaving mass of hopeful men, Nathan couldn't help noticing the admiring looks he was getting from both friends and strangers alike – although *envious* might have been a better word, knowing most of his friends. Old Michael, propped up against his usual leaning post, smiled and raised his lager, drunkenly slopping it over his sleeve – so, no surprise there – while Tall Ian raised an arch eyebrow and mouthed 'nice bit of rough' as they passed. Nathan smirked triumphantly, knowing that Ian would want a full account when they next met up.

Charing Cross Road was bitterly cold as they emerged into the November night, and Nathan saw Scott shudder in the biting wind, despite his jacket. Nathan couldn't wait to wrap him in his arms and run his hands over his strong chest and back, warming and exciting him as he did so, hoping that they wouldn't have to wait too long for a taxi. He turned to Scott and winked: 'Don't worry – it only takes ten minutes to get to Docklands.'

Even as he spoke, a black cab, FOR HIRE light on, appeared from around Shaftsbury Avenue and he stuck out his hand. The taxi slowed and stopped in front of them, and Nathan opened the door, glancing back at the black glass fascia of the Crossed Swords as Scott got in. He peered into the dimly lit interior, and thought back over the long, lonely evenings he had spent there. Even the nights when he had left with someone had lacked something – heart, or soul, or meaning. This time was different; he looked at Scott as he settled into the black leather seat and knew that this wasn't going to be another of those sort of nights.

Ten minutes seemed like ten hours as they drove past the floodlit grandeur of the Tower of London and over Tower Bridge. Nathan kept looking at Scott out of the corner of his eye, only to eventually realise that Scott was doing exactly the same thing. All Nathan could think about was Scott's massive cock in his mouth, pumping away as Nathan ran his hands through Scott's hairy chest. And then, later, Nathan's cock sliding in and out of Scott's arse with desperate thrusts, riding the boy as he groaned and bucked beneath him.

By the time the taxi pulled up outside his modern semi-detached house, Nathan's fantasies had all but taken control of him: he had an erection that just screamed out to be relieved, rubbing against his boxer shorts, its end damp with pre-come. His hands were unsteady and shaking as he handed the driver a tenner. Mumbling that he could keep the change, he virtually ran up the short path to his front door, pulling Scott along with him.

Was it the cold or the expectation that made his fingers fumble as he tried to open the lock? Nathan wondered. As he struggled to get the key into the door, Scott placed his hand on top of Nathan's to steady it, and Nathan felt a shudder go through him as Scott touched his skin for the first time. Normally, Nathan would have kissed him long before now – in the pub itself, probably, a rough kiss to make his mark, to prove his ownership to the others who hovered around – but there was something about Scott that had made Nathan know that he had to wait, despite his overriding urge to grab the lad and stick his tongue down his throat. Rushing it would spoil the moment, and that was something that Nathan just couldn't allow: it had to be perfect. He looked at Scott's huge hand resting on his, and imagined it gripping his cock, stroking and tugging . . .

With that image burning in his mind, Nathan turned the key and pushed the door open with almost unseemly haste, virtually falling into the darkened hallway. He turned to Scott and gave a bashful smile. 'Sorry – I'm a bit nervous.' Even as he said the words, he realised how nervous he really was; it was as if the other men – the one-night stands, the long-term relationships – had never happened. Why was Scott having this effect? he wondered. What was so special about this student? What made him stand out? He realised that Scott was talking to him.

'Oh come on,' said Scott, laughing. 'I bet you do this all the time.'

'True, but they're not usually like you,' he replied. Yes, it was corny, but that was how he felt. Like a virgin, he thought wryly. 'Cup of coffee?'

Scott nodded, but Nathan stopped in the doorway to the living room, unable – unwilling – to reach the kitchen. He couldn't wait any longer; in the enclosed space of the hall, away from the smoky atmosphere of the Crossed Swords, Scott's earthy, musky smell was too much to bear: he smelt of cheap aftershave and fresh sweat, an irresistible combination. Nathan turned and embraced him, kicking the front door closed with his Caterpillar boot and propelling the younger man into the living room with the weight of his body. Nathan rubbed his face against Scott's, cheek to cheek, feeling the boy's rough stubble collide with his own short goatee; the rasping sensation was glorious, and amplified Nathan's need even further. Forcefully, his mouth sought Scott's and found it almost immediately; his tongue pushed its way into Scott's mouth without resistance and began to explore the moist interior, while his hands stroked and caressed the taut muscles of his back. As Nathan kissed the boy ever more frantically, he imagined his tongue probing the pink stickiness of Scott's ring, and the thought drove him even more wild, more desperate. His grip on Scott tightened even more, as if he were terrified that the lad was a dream, a fantasy, that would escape. *What was it about this boy?* He just couldn't get close enough to him, and the thought of entering him, being part of him, became ever stronger.

Scott recovered from what Nathan guessed was surprise at his rough, demanding manner and responded, their tongues colliding and bruisingly massaging each other as Scott's kissing matched the rhythm of Nathan's. Still kissing, Nathan pulled at Scott's jacket, almost ripping it off him before throwing it to the carpet without looking, without caring. Scott mirrored his

21

actions, unzipping Nathan's bomber, pulling it away and hurling it on to the sofa.

Then they pulled away and paused for a second, staring at each other with undisguised longing: at that moment, Nathan knew that nothing else mattered. All he cared about, all he wanted, was the boy in front of him, and the expression on Scott's face told Nathan that this longing was totally, utterly mutual. Reaching out, he grasped Scott's hands and drew him towards him.

The buttons of Nathan's shirt offered no resistance; frantically, Scott unbuttoned them, although Nathan wouldn't have minded if the shirt had been torn off him — this was going to be worth it. As soon as he was free of his own shirt, Nathan tugged on Scott's Fred Perry and yanked it over his head, finally revealing a well-muscled torso without an inch of fat, and a thickly furred chest. Nathan couldn't help grinning: so far, Scott was turning out to be everything Nathan had hoped for, and the bulge in the boy's jeans suggested that Nathan wasn't going to be disappointed there either.

'Still fancy coffee?' said Nathan, standing without his shirt on. His erection straining in his jeans, coffee was the last thing on his mind, but he just couldn't think of anything else to say. Words were irrelevant.

Scott shrugged. 'Have you got a better idea?' But the smirk on his face clearly demonstrated that they were both on the same wavelength. Nathan reached out and took Scott's hand, pulling him towards him with an almost puppy-like eagerness. 'Upstairs is a bit more . . . comfortable.'

Scott shook his head. 'Later. I can't wait that long,' he said mischievously. He fell to his knees, and unbuttoned Nathan's flies, ripping the gap apart with a grunt. Nathan wasn't about to complain. He gasped as Scott's lips teased at the damp boxer shorts, his tongue flicking up and down Nathan's constrained erection. Nathan shuddered; normally, he could keep going for hours, but he could feel his orgasm growing within him at an unstoppable rate. Reluctantly, he tried to push Scott's head away, but he was having none of it – or, rather, he wanted all of it. Still just using his tongue, he hooked it under the flap of the boxers and released Nathan's cock. Eight thick inches of uncircumcised meat stood almost flat with Nathan's hairy stomach, and Scott wasted no time in running his tongue up its length until he reached the helmet, glistening and salty.

Nathan watched as Scott took the throbbing red end in his mouth and tickled it, eliciting a groan of pleasure from Nathan, who responded by thrusting his dick further down Scott's throat. Scott then started to suck, his lips wet and tight around Nathan's dick, and Nathan felt himself losing it.

'Stop!' he whispered. 'I'm going to come!'

Scott looked up at him, Nathan's dick still deep down his throat. He didn't say anything, but the expression on his face made it quite clear: *good*. He carried on sucking, and Nathan felt the familiar stirrings within him, a relentless surge of pleasure that started in his stomach and expanded until his whole body was shuddering. Scott didn't stop; his mouth took the rhythmic thrusting and played with it, his tongue licking at Nathan's helmet until Nathan couldn't hold back any longer. His breathing heavy, he tried to keep silent, but he couldn't manage it; the feeling was so intense, so overpowering, that he started to groan and grunt as his orgasm burst in his groin, and he grabbed on to Scott's shoulders for support as he shot his load into his mouth, pumping and pumping and knowing that he just *loved* this bloke and wanted to be with him for ever and keep doing this and, and, and . . . He abandoned himself to the feelings and the emotions that overwhelmed him, gripping Scott tighter and tighter as he almost screamed with release.

Scott didn't complain: as he swallowed every surge of Nathan's warm come, he stared up at him with a longing, a wanting, that intensified Nathan's orgasm tenfold. Finally, Nathan was finished, his cock drained dry. With a shudder and a whimper, he pulled himself away from Scott, drawing his still-hard dick from his mouth. He felt so drained, so exhausted, that he had to steady himself against the wall, realising that he was trembling with the exertion. It was a sensation that had been missing from his life for so long – he couldn't remember the last time that sex had left him feeling so ... well, so satisfied. Deep, deep down inside him, something unlocked.

'You should have waited,' he complained breathlessly – and needlessly. It was clear that neither of them had wanted to wait – even if they could have done. He gasped. 'You really are gorgeous.'

Scott looked up at him and grinned his bastard smile. 'That was only chapter one, Mr Journalist.' He jumped to his feet, chest muscles flexing beneath the mat of hair. 'Let's have that coffee, and then we'll get on with the story.'

Nathan put his dick back inside his boxers with some difficulty, since it was still virtually erect. 'I *do* have to go to work in the morning,' he complained, before realising how petty that sounded. Work was work, but Scott was ... magnificent. Everything else could take second place.

Thankfully, Scott took no notice. He winked at him and smiled, eyeing Nathan up and down as he did so. 'Then you're going to be late, aren't you? Anyway, I've changed my mind about the coffee. I'm more interested in the next chapter.'

Nathan didn't complain as Scott grabbed his arm and took him upstairs. Coffee had suddenly become rather irrelevant.

Nathan woke as soon as the alarm clock intruded on him, its insistent warble breaking into his dreams and rousing him from a fantasy that he couldn't quite remember the details of. It was something about a student ... Reaching out, he thumped the snooze button and thrashed around to make himself more comfortable – and immediately realised that he wasn't alone in the bed: there was a figure buried beneath the blue and gold duvet. Who the hell was it? Within seconds, that particular memory sprang into his mind – and solved the riddle of his

24

dream. It hadn't been a dream after all. The hot, sweaty hours that he and Scott had spent together, the levels of intimacy that they had reached that Nathan had forgotten existed . . . He pulled the duvet off the boy and grinned at the shocked and surprised look that greeted him.

'Morning,' he said cheerfully, relishing the bemused look on Scott's stubbly face. 'How are you feeling?'

Scott peered at him sleepily, blinking in the half-light that spilled through the black slats of the blind. 'Knackered,' he muttered. 'But randy.' He reached out for Nathan's hand, pulling it towards his crotch. Nathan resisted. Sort of.

'Didn't you get enough of that last night?' he protested vainly. But there was no sincerity in the protest: the lad was pure dynamite, and Nathan knew that he could no sooner resist him than he could stop the sun from coming up. *The Investigator* – the magazine for which Nathan did most of his freelance work – could wait.

'Whatever happened to my brave and fearless journalist?' said Scott, moving round so that his body was facing Nathan's. Nathan couldn't keep his eyes off Scott's huge erection, the thick, nine-inch dick which Nathan had sucked and wanked and allowed into him throughout the previous night. Scott had been everything that Nathan had hoped for – and more than he could ever have dreamt of. Deep, deep inside, Nathan could feel an aching void closing and healing, and yet there were alarm bells ringing: Nathan had been hurt before, and the last thing he wanted was to go through that pain again.

'Your brave and fearless journalist has got to get to work.' He tried to pull away from Scott, but the boy's mischievous grin and hand around his dick were persuasive arguments. He relaxed and made himself comfortable under the warm heaviness of the duvet as he hurled it back over them. 'But not just yet.'

Nathan's hand gripped Scott's dick, pulling the thick foreskin up and down over his moist helmet in a gentle rhythm. Scott

25

groaned softly, his own hand reaching out and stroking Nathan's erection. It was Nathan's turn to groan. 'My column can wait,' he whispered.

Scott sniggered. 'It sure doesn't feel like it,' he said, tightening his grip. 'It looks just about ready to me.'

Nathan cuffed him affectionately around the ear with his free hand, but didn't break his stride. Then, before he could help himself, he found himself whispering something that he'd been trying to keep to himself.

'I love you, Scott.' *Damn!* Nathan could have hit himself. That's it, Dexter, he thought: frighten the kid off. You only met him the night before and now you're virtually telling him that you want to marry him! No wonder you're still single – everyone you ever fall for runs a mile when you start telling them how you feel.

But Scott obviously didn't realise that Nathan had really meant what he had said; he simply winked and playfully tapped him on the nose with his fist.

'Flatterer. I can tell you're a writer.' Scott slid across the sheets to get closer to Nathan and put his free hand around his shoulders, massaging the sensitive region at the base of Nathan's neck.

How did he know that that was my soft spot? thought Nathan. But he didn't have time to think about that; hugging him tightly, Scott started to nibble at Nathan's beard, tiny sharp bites that started at his throat and continued upward, reaching his chin before moving round to his moustache, biting and nibbling all the time.

Neither of them was silent during this: Nathan grunted with each tiny bite, while Scott growled like a wild animal, low guttural sounds in Nathan's ear. It was as if words didn't matter: everything had been reduced to its lowest, basest level.

Nathan didn't know how long this moment lasted: it could have been minutes, it could have been hours. Scott was virtually clamped around his neck, kissing and biting, while his hand continued to play with Nathan's erection, and Nathan simply lay there, his hand around Scott's dick, allowing himself to experience levels of ecstasy that he had thought he had forgotten about. Any thoughts of love were lost in the sheer, primal pleasure of their being together.

Finally, after the feelings brought on by the combination of Scott's stroking, biting and wanking had reached almost unbearable levels, Nathan was left gasping and panting and so close to orgasm that he was sorely tempted to push Scott away. But Scott finally found Nathan's mouth and kissed him deeply, and Nathan responded immediately, his other arm around Scott's strong, smooth back, caressing him passionately. All the time, the two of them continued to wank each other, their strokes perfectly in time. Their grunts, groans and growls became louder and louder, their strokes in perfect time, their mouths locked together.

'I'm going to come . . .' gasped Scott, his body going rigid as Nathan continued to pull on his dick. Scott tried to pull Nathan's hand away, but Nathan didn't want Scott to hold off, and he wasn't going to stop. He carried on, increasing the speed with which he wanked the boy off, removing his arm from around Scott's shoulders and feeling his way through the chest hair, grabbing Scott's nipples and briefly squeezing each one in turn.

That was it. With deep, heartfelt groans, Scott came, his spunk gushing out in thick white gouts that went all over his already-matted stomach hair and covered Nathan's hand. But Nathan had other things to think about: even as Scott was shooting his load, he didn't stop playing with Nathan's dick; Nathan stopped holding himself back, and let Scott's frantic tugging take over. Seconds after Scott, it was Nathan's turn to come: as his cock flexed and tensed in Scott's grip, he pulled the boy towards him, feeling his wiry body hair – damp with mingled sweat and come – rubbing against and entangling with his own as he let Scott jerk the last few drops of come out of him.

Panting and gasping, the two of them lay on their backs on the damp sheets. Nathan looked round at Scott and smiled. Scott sighed.

'All right?' asked Nathan.

'What do you think?' Scott reached out and stroked Nathan's chest. 'By the way, I heard what you said earlier.'

'What was that?'

Scott wrinkled his nose. 'I just thought you'd like to know: I love you too, mate.'

Deep, deep inside, Nathan could feel the aching void close.

Two

―――――

Scott sat on the bed in his room, trying to concentrate on the thick book in front of him, but the deeper mysteries of computing somehow managed to elude him. All he could think about was the man he had met the other evening. Scott was a long way from being a virgin, but there was something about Nathan Dexter that was different from all of the other men he had had sex with. Something that told Scott that he would definitely be seeing him again.

Despite being a resourceful investigative journalist – according to one of Scott's friends who was studying journalism, Nathan Dexter had made quite a name for himself with some high-profile cases – there was a softness and a vulnerability about him that Scott couldn't resist. Scott knew that he should have been shocked by the speed with which they had both admitted the strength of their feelings for each other, but he still didn't feel any surprise: simply an unshakable knowledge that he and Nathan really had fallen in love.

Even the age difference didn't matter: Scott had always been attracted towards older men – usually even older than Nathan. Perhaps it had something to do with his less than satisfactory relationship with his father, leading him to seek out a father figure, an older person who could fulfil the roles of both lover and father.

Or perhaps he just liked older men, he thought. Sometimes, it didn't pay to look too deeply into these things: Nathan made him happy, and *that* was what counted.

But he did have doubts. Not doubts about Nathan: he was certain that they did feel like that about each other. No, his doubts stemmed from a very different part of his life, a part that had started months ago after a chance encounter in the Harness.

Despite his newly awakened feelings for Nathan, there were some areas of Scott's life which he knew he would never be able to discuss with him, areas which Nathan might not be able to understand, but which were very necessary to Scott.

The only solution was to lock that part of his life away, to keep it from Nathan and hope that the two worlds of Scott James never, ever collided.

He closed the book, giving revision up as a bad idea: his mind was too full of Nathan to concentrate. Looking at his watch he saw that it was still only nine o'clock: perhaps Nathan would like to go out for a drink. Or would Nathan think he was being too pushy, wanting to see him so soon after their last meeting? They had left things open-ended the other morning: they had parted in the centre of town, with Nathan late for a meeting with one of his contacts, and Scott dangerously close to missing a lecture. Scott had promised to phone Nathan, though . . .

A sudden warble made him jump. It was his mobile phone, almost buried in the soft folds of his duvet. He grabbed it and answered.

It was Nathan.

Ten minutes later, Scott was washed and changed and heading off to Soho.

★ ★ ★

Two hours later, Scott and Nathan were finishing off their coffees after a wonderful meal in one the gay restaurants in Old Compton Street.

Scott had expected a boozy evening in one of the local pubs, but Nathan had impressed him by reserving a table. The food had been excellent, and Nathan had chosen a bottle of wine which Scott knew he would never have been able to afford on his student loan.

All in all, Scott felt totally at ease in Nathan's presence: it was as if they had known each other for years rather than a couple of days.

Most of the conversation had been small talk, inconsequential chitchat about the food, the pubs and clubs nearby, Scott's course and Nathan's career. Both of them were steering well away from anything heavy, even though Scott wanted a re-affirmation of what Nathan had said to him the other morning.

By the time the coffees arrived, Scott decided that he couldn't wait any longer. As Nathan sipped his espresso, Scott said it. Just like that.

'Did you mean it?'

Nathan frowned for a second before clearly guessing what Scott meant. He grinned, and grabbed Scott's hand. 'Of course I did. Did you?' he added awkwardly.

'Yep. I haven't been able to think about much else apart from you. I was going to ring you, but was worried you might think I was being too possessive.'

Nathan laughed. 'That's why *I* waited till today to phone you. I didn't want to frighten you off.' He drained his coffee and indicated for the waiter to bring the bill. 'What do you fancy doing now? It's still quite early for a Friday night. We could go to a club if you want.'

Scott squeezed Nathan's hand. 'Actually, I wouldn't mind an early night.' And the grin on Nathan's face made it quite clear that he had the same idea.

★ ★ ★

Once more, the chosen destination was Nathan's house in Docklands: for some odd reason, Scott felt completely comfortable there – more comfortable than he would have felt in the halls of residence.

After the frantic hours of their first meeting, this night was proceeding at a measured, leisurely pace. Nothing was being rushed, from the drawn-out yet thoroughly enjoyable meal to the friendly conversation in the living room. Nathan had brought a bottle of wine from the kitchen, and the two of them were curled up together on the sofa, with Scott's head resting on Nathan's lap, and MTV on in the background.

'Thanks,' said Nathan.

'What for? Thank *you*. That was a brilliant meal. I'm not used to being pampered like that.' A faint twinge of guilt stabbed him in the stomach: that wasn't strictly true, but it would be too difficult to explain it to Nathan.

Nathan ruffled Scott's hair. 'Well, you better get used to it. Only the best for my boyfriend.'

Boyfriend. Nobody had ever referred to him as that before, and it had a ring to it, giving him a warm feeling of belonging, of being wanted, that he had never felt before. He reached up and kissed Nathan on the lips. 'I love you, Nathan,' he whispered.

'Love you, mate.' Gently easing Scott off his lap, Nathan got up and took his hand. 'Ready for bed?' he asked.

Scott got up and smiled. 'Maybe not bed,' he replied. 'Not yet, anyway.'

Scott removed Nathan's shirt with a gentleness that was light years away from their frantic needs of the first night. They could afford to wait this time, to take their time in exploring each other and find out what made each other tick. As Scott's shirt also fell to the floor, Nathan leant down and sought out Scott's nipple with his teeth, finding it in the thick chest hair and teasingly biting it with sharp yet playful bites.

Scott stroked Nathan's firm back, urging him to carry on biting, harder and harder. As the pleasure almost became too much to bear, Scott pushed him away and pulled him into a standing position.

Nathan embraced him, entering Scott's mouth with his tongue and finding Scott's tongue waiting to do the same. As they kissed, Scott's hands moved from Nathan's back to his trousers, unbuckling his belt and undoing the buttons, his hands gently touching the hard-on that waited inside. Nathan shivered at the touch, and began to remove Scott's jeans.

They stepped out of their discarded jeans at the same time, their erections revealed through the open gaps in their boxers. Moving as one, they reached out and seized each other's dick, squeezing gently at first, and then wanking with firm, constant strokes.

Still kissing, Scott used his other hand to pull Nathan's boxers off, leaving him naked: his solid body, covering of black fur and stiff erection exciting him even more than he thought possible. Dropping to his knees, he stopped wanking his boyfriend and took his cock in his mouth, relishing the hot warmth and salty taste of his helmet.

Nathan gasped, and put his hand on the back of Scott's head to pull him closer and put even more of his dick in his mouth. Scott responded by sliding his lips over the shaft, finding a rhythm that clearly excited Nathan.

Scott continued, trying to get as much of Nathan's dick in his mouth as he could, until Nathan, trembling slightly with the closeness of his orgasm, pushed him away.

Nathan guided Scott on to the soft blue duvet and urged him to lie down; once he had done so, Nathan pulled off his boxer shorts and allowed his erection to spring free. Getting on to the bed, Nathan knelt over Scott and kissed him full on the mouth, allowing their bodies to rub against one another. Scott could feel Nathan's hard cock sliding alongside his own, its motion lubricated by their juices flowing together, and the sensation suddenly brought him almost to the point of coming.

He tried to pull back, to make it last longer, but Nathan had other ideas. Clearly sensing how close Scott was, Nathan hurried down to Scott's cock, burying his face in Scott's body hair as he did so. Reaching Scott's dick, Nathan took it in his mouth and sucked it – hard, relentless sucks that took Scott's breath away.

As he did so, he moved his body so that one hand was squeezing Scott's left nipple; the other hand reached between Scott's legs and found his arse. A gentle finger began to stroke the hole, teasing strokes that were too much for Scott to bear. Within seconds of Nathan's all-out assault on his body, Scott's body exploded in orgasm, and he thrust his cock even further into Nathan's mouth.

Nathan didn't resist: he swallowed every spurt, every last drop of come that shot from Scott's hard, thick cock. Scott continued to shoot for endless seconds before the sensations finally lessened, accompanying the feeling with a yell of unrestrained pleasure.

He couldn't remember ever coming like that before; his whole body was shivering and tingling with the experience. He smiled at Nathan, and suddenly realised from the pool of white on the duvet that Nathan must have come at the same time as he had.

Nathan released his still-stiff cock and wiped a small droplet of spunk from the corner of his mouth. 'I take it you approved of that?' he asked.

'You bet. Although I would have liked to have taken care of that.' He looked down at Nathan's dick, only now subsiding, and the white stream on the duvet below it.

'Don't you worry,' said Nathan mischievously. 'You will.'

'I'll admit, it does sound like you're on to something, Nathan,' said Marcus without looking up from the stack of paperwork on his cramped and untidy desk. 'But you're going to need a lot more evidence than this if you want us to publish. We need hard facts, Nathan, not supposition. Surely you understand how *The Investigator* works by now.' The large, sweaty editor continued to leaf through the folders, but Nathan knew it was useless. Marcus was Marcus – an immovable and stubborn fact of publishing life.

Yes, Marcus, Nathan thought, I know exactly how *The Investigator* works. Heaven forbid that you'd do anything without making sure your corporate arse was completely covered. Nathan sighed: Marcus Moore's response wasn't unexpected, but neither was it welcome; things had been going so well over the last few days that he had half hoped that his editor's legendary caution might have abated somewhat. It looked like his luck had just run out.

'Come on, Marcus, be reasonable,' he protested, waving at the stack of folders which he had previously handed over. 'There's enough evidence there to blow this whole Elective thing wide open. I've got statements, witnesses –'

Marcus took off his glasses and rubbed the bridge of his nose. 'Nathan Dexter, you're probably the best investigative journalist I know. Look at your track record: the brewery fraud, the scandal over club prices, that bastard of a landlord – that's how you've made your name in this business. And, until now, you've always brought me articles based on meticulous research. Research – that's been your watchword. This, this –' he tapped the manila files '– isn't evidence. At best, it's hearsay and rumour. At worst, it's libel. And *The Investigator* isn't in the business of being libelled.'

Suppressing a growl of irritation, Nathan reached into the stack at random and extracted a folder. 'Rumour? Marcus, look at this.' He pulled out a sheet of paper and quickly scanned it to check which item of 'research' he had found.

'This documents twelve eyewitness accounts of people being

picked up in the Collective by the same man, all in the space of a week.'

'So?' Marcus shrugged. 'You've got evidence that there's a randy leather queen in the Collective. He's not the first and he certainly won't be the last.'

And you should know, Marcus, thought Nathan archly: you're there often enough, prancing around in your salopettes and Muir cap. Then reason intervened: So are you, Nate. He had to admit that it did sound rather feeble when put that way: Nathan had often picked up four, five, six people in a week, in the same bar. However, that wasn't all. He shoved another paper under Marcus's nose.

'None of them has been seen since. That was nearly six months ago.' At least twelve people, all fairly well known to the close-knit leather clientele of the Collective, just vanishing into thin air. It was too much of a coincidence – and Nathan didn't believe in coincidence.

Marcus stood up. 'Nathan, I don't disbelieve you. Too many odd things have been happening on the leather scene over the last two years for me to dismiss this. An ex of mine hasn't been seen in over a year – under exactly the same circumstances.' He squeezed his eyes closed and ran a podgy hand through his thinning hair. 'I want the story – I really do. But before I publish, we need proof.'

'Proof?' Nathan thumped his fist on the desk. 'How much proof do you want? Perhaps I should bring the Comptroller himself in. Would that satisfy you?'

Marcus raised an eyebrow. 'Yes, Nathan, it would. Keep digging: as soon as you bring me incontrovertible evidence – evidence that will stand up in court – that the Elective and this Comptroller really *do* exist, and that they *are* kidnapping people from London's leather scene, I'll print it. But until then . . .' His words trailed off, and Nathan knew that his audience was at an end.

'I'll bring you what you need,' said Nathan as he retrieved the files from Marcus's desk. 'Trust me.'

Marcus gave a predatory smile. 'I don't trust anybody, Nathan – that's how I became editor.'

Pulling his charcoal cashmere overcoat on over his box-cut, grey, three-piece suit, Nathan walked out into the cold November afternoon, and tried to resist the temptation to thump the wall in frustration. *The Investigator*'s publishers were based in Dean Street, near the heart of Soho's gay pub and club scene, and Nathan knew that he needed a drink. And he knew exactly where he was going to go.

Marcus's response had been expected, but Nathan had more than a professional interest in the story: that was why he was so eager – perhaps *too* eager – to bring the Elective to justice. Normally, Nathan wouldn't have dreamed of going to Marcus without the sort of proof that he required, but he was in a hurry: too many people were going missing from the leather scene – far too many. There wasn't any sort of discernible pattern: a couple of people vanish from the Collective, and then nothing. A regular down the Harness isn't seen for over a month. Nothing to link the events – except the Elective itself.

Nathan had first heard about the Elective one drunken evening in the Collective. He'd been standing at the bar, unwinding after a hard day in court, having watched with satisfaction as an unscrupulous landlord had been jailed for failing to maintain a collection of bedsits. Thanks to his negligence, five young gay men had died owing to inadequate safety precautions: and one of them had been a young Spanish guy called Paolo – a good friend of Nathan's. Nathan had trailed and stalked that bastard until he had enough on him to ensure that he was sent down for at least fifteen years.

He got twenty years for manslaughter.

Tired but jubilant, Nathan exchanged his formal suit for a denim shirt and jeans, leather waistcoat and leather biker's jacket, and headed straight for Earl's Court . . .

* * *

The Collective was the longest-established leather bar in London, and Nathan had been a regular there ever since he had moved to the city a decade before. It was the best place to go to have a few drinks and hopefully some casual sex; dark and slightly seedy, it suited Nathan's mood perfectly. With his happiness over the outcome mingling with his sadness over Paolo's death, Nathan himself was feeling dark and slightly seedy. He wanted a drink and he wanted a shag. In that order.

After three cans of Breaker, Nathan was feeling very dark and very seedy. OK, so the verdict wouldn't bring Paolo back, but Nathan felt that he'd made a difference. He deserved to celebrate.

We got the bastard, Paolo, he thought, mentally raising a glass to his late friend.

'I'm not surprised you look happy,' came a lilting Spanish accent. 'You nailed him.'

Nathan turned to see Chris standing next to him. Chris was one of The Collective's regulars, but Nathan knew him from his other usual haunt, the Brave Trader in Soho. Chris knew about Paolo's death – indeed, Chris had known Paolo for longer than Nathan had – and had been following the case almost as avidly as Nathan had.

As Chris bought him a drink to celebrate, Nathan momentarily wondered whether to ask Chris to come home with him, but quickly decided against it. True, Chris was a bit of a hunk – a short, tubby bear with a sweet face and puppy-dog eyes – and the two of them had spent the night together on quite a few occasions, but Nathan felt as though he owed it to Paolo to look for a challenge tonight. And Chris was about as challenging as a wet paper bag where accepting offers of sex was concerned. Besides, Nathan felt like a bit of rough stuff, and that wasn't really Chris's scene.

The conversation veered away from the court case, as Chris filled him in about the latest goings-on on the leather scene. It seemed that Big Jason's last 'get-together' – for 'get-together', read 'orgy', thought Nathan, having been to a fair few of Jason's notorious parties – had been another outrageous success; the owners of the Harness in Vauxhall were opening a midweek venue in Earl's Court, and was Nathan interested in an invite to the opening night party? Of course he was:

Nathan the party animal never turned down an invitation. And had he heard that another two leather guys had gone missing in the last month?

At the last bit of gossip, Nathan frowned. Chris's tone suggested that these disappearances were simply the latest in a series, but Nathan knew nothing about it. Then again, nailing that landlord had become virtually an obsession over the last year; any information he had received that hadn't concerned Paolo's death had gone in one ear and out of the other. Come to think of it, he did recall being told about the disappearance of Fat Mary, one of the Harness's most colourful leather queens, about six months ago, but he hadn't really given it much thought. Quite apart from his preoccupation with the upcoming court case, Nathan knew Fat Mary too well, and knew that a vanishing act was just the sort of attention-seeking device he'd employ if he didn't think enough people were paying him enough notice.

'I think you'd better start at the beginning, Chris,' he asked.

It seemed that Fat Mary hadn't been the first by a long chalk. The first person to vanish had apparently been a young leather guy called Keith. A new boy, up from Bristol, he'd been a bit of a loner. He'd started coming into the Collective about two years ago, but nobody could really claim to be friends with him, even though many people tried: the fact that he was incredibly handsome explained that, of course. One night, after he'd been frequenting the Collective about three times a week for six months, he'd been seen chatting to an older man, a leather-clad bear that nobody recognised.

And nobody ever saw Keith again. One of the few people who actually knew where he lived took the trouble to look him up about a week later, when his absence had been noted, but, according to his landlord, he'd moved out.

The day after he'd been seen with the mysterious bear.

Chris told Nathan of the others, in addition to Fat Mary and Keith. At least eight people from the Collective; three regulars at the Harness; two from the hard-core uniform bar, Vice . . . and those were just the ones that people had missed. Given the solitary, secretive nature of much of the leather scene, there could have been countless *others whose disappearances just hadn't been noticed. The only similarity among those who had disappeared was that they had all been observed in the company of people who were never seen either before or since. Then Chris mentioned the Elective.*

Nathan took a long swig of his Breaker. The existence of the organisation that people called the Elective had been rumoured for years: it was supposed to be the very highest echelon of the worldwide leather scene, a society that nobody could apply to join. If you were lucky enough, if you were visible enough on the leather scene and considered a suitable candidate, you might be asked, invited to join its ranks.

Like some kind of gay freemasonry, its members were forbidden from admitting that they belonged to the organisation, but the benefits it offered outweighed burden caused by the need for secrecy. There was the ubiquitous support network, ensuring that members always reached the very top of their chosen profession. There was complete immunity in cases where ambition or foolishness had led members to fall foul of the law, which, rumour had it, had been the saviour of at least two MPs. And then there were the legendary private parties, usually in exotic locations such as Morocco or the Caribbean, where each and every possible sexual pleasure was available amid unimaginable luxury and wealth. In short, membership of the Elective was the holy grail to which the more pedestrian elements of the leather scene could only aspire and never achieve.

But there was a catch. There wasn't a single shred of evidence to prove that the Elective existed. Everything was based on hearsay and rumour; an odd whisper here, a quiet word there . . . Nathan half suspected that the bloody thing was made up; it was probably just a fantasy put about by some bored old leather queens one night which had spread out of control and was now accepted as fact. But it had the ring of truth that Nathan just couldn't deny — like all of the best urban myths.

'What's the Elective got to do with it?' he said with a laugh. Forget The X Files; *London's gay scene was full of conspiracy theorists who'd make Fox Mulder look like the most trusting man on Earth.*

Chris shrugged. *'I'm just telling you what people are saying.'*

'The Elective's having a recruitment drive, is it?' He thought about it for a second before shaking his head. *'No, the Elective doesn't work that way.'* Then he laughed again. *'Listen to me: anyone would think I believed in the Elective myself. Anyway, assuming that the Elective is everything people say it is – and I'm keeping a very open mind about all of this – its members don't vanish. They stay on the scene and keep their mouths shut.'*

Chris leant forward. *'Slaves.'*

'What?' This was getting sillier by the second.

'The Elective needs slaves. It's kidnapping leather guys and shipping them abroad. That's what they're saying.'

'Who's saying?'

Chris frowned and bit his bottom lip. *'That's the problem. I got all of this from Fat Mary . . .'*

'Who's disappeared,' stated Nathan. It sounded ridiculous, but Nathan knew of countless investigations – by both him and his colleagues – that had started off on even more shaky ground, only to bear fruit somewhere down the line. Despite his earlier misgivings, Nathan was, if not hooked, very intrigued.

After the business with the landlord, he'd been looking for a new lead, and this one seemed ideal, especially since it didn't appear to offer the same personal angle – thankfully. Nathan didn't think he could go through such a vendetta again. Filing the information away for later – when he would be Nathan the journalist rather than Nathan the randy leather guy – he scanned the bar, peering into the dark corners that often proved so fruitful in the Collective; he'd had the few drinks he'd promised himself, so it was time to fulfil the second part of the evening's mission.

Chris grinned, reading his mind – or reading the expression on his face, more likely. *'I suppose you're about to go off on one of your grand tours of the Collective? Feeling lucky?'*

Nathan's scan had revealed something interesting lurking in the shadows at the far corner of the bar. *'Don't I always?'* he replied.

'Catch you later.' With that, he set off on a roundabout cruise that would take him to his destination without it appearing too obvious.

And that had been the night he had met Leigh.

Leigh had left around nine o'clock the following morning, leaving a satisfied but exhausted Nathan to nurse his hangover and contemplate what Chris had told him the night before.

Over a pot of very strong coffee, Nathan stumbled over to the corner of his living room and switched on his PC, watching through blurred eyes as the machine booted up. One of the perks of being a journalist was that his computer was permitted to link up to JournoNet, an exclusive, extensive and up-to-date library of all local and national newspapers and magazines, stretching back over the last ten years and across all of the States and Europe. With a couple of mouse clicks, he set JournoNet running, its little newspaper icon expanding into a full-sized window. It didn't look any different from dozens of other Internet news providers, but it offered Nathan access to all the information he could ever need. He just hoped that, where the Elective was concerned, it was enough.

Typing a whole slew of keywords into the powerful search engine, Nathan sipped his coffee and waited while JournoNet trawled cyberspace for any references that combined the disappearance of gay men with any reference to the Elective or something like it. The search criteria had been complex, but they'd had to be: what Nathan was looking for was extremely specific, and yet – if any evidence existed – would undoubtedly be submerged under a whole mass of unrelated and yet apparently similar cases. And, given Nathan's delicate constitution that morning, putting the criteria together had stretched his mental abilities to the limit.

He was fondly thinking about Leigh and trying to decide whether to ring the scrawled telephone number that had been thrust in his hand when his PC bleeped at him, telling him that JournoNet had finished its search. Squinting at the screen through his hangover, Nathan was surprised to see that JournoNet reckoned it had found nearly two hundred cases that matched Nathan's requirements. He reached over *and poured himself another coffee before settling down to wade through the results.*

What he read staggered him. Any doubts that he had entertained about Chris's story being dodgy or exaggerated evaporated as he discovered that the disappearances from the London scene were only the tip of a terrifyingly large iceberg. As he scrolled through the list, he could see that it contained reports from the New York leather scene, the Amsterdam scene, the Sydney scene . . . And all of them had one thing in common.

Across the entire world, from the States to Australia, leather guys were going missing.

That had been six months ago. As Nathan pushed open the door of the Brave Trader down Poland Street, he wondered where the time had gone – his conversation with Chris seemed only days ago. And then he remembered the stack of what he considered evidence under his arm and knew exactly where the time had gone. Nathan Dexter's watchword: research. When he got a case, he pursued it to the bitter end.

'Afternoon, Nathan. Pint?' Nigel, landlord of the Brave Trader of Queensland, was serving behind the bar, and was already pouring the drink as the door closed behind Nathan. Nigel was a tall, ginger-haired clone from somewhere 'up North', famed for his legendary rudeness to customers, both strangers and regulars alike. But, for all that, the Brave Trader was renowned for being the friendliest gay pub in London, with more of the atmosphere of a cosy local than a Soho gay bar. Perhaps that was why the Brave Trader had escaped the Elective's machinations; it was difficult for anyone to do anything without its being noticed and noted by the inquisitive bar staff. Indeed, much as Nathan loved the Brave Trader, he never brought his dates there unless he wanted the entire pub to know what he was doing.

As Nathan deposited his files on the bar and picked up his pint, Nigel started putting the tray of dirty glasses into the dishwasher. The Brave Trader was reasonably quiet: the lunch-time crowd had mostly gone back to work, leaving only the tourists and the hardened drinkers; Nathan waved at Eric, already three sheets to the wind, as he leant against the bar for support. Obviously it wasn't a busy afternoon in Eric's exclusive shoeshop.

'By the way, saw your little friend the other night,' said Nigel, his condescending manner suggesting he knew some-thing that Nathan didn't. Yet.

Nathan raised an eyebrow. 'Which little friend?'

'That little skinhead you used to knock around with,' he said with a sneer, closing the dishwasher door and switching the machine on. 'The one you brought to the Hallowe'en party.'

Nathan realised that Nigel meant Leigh, the skinhead he had met the night of the trial. Well, that was a coincidence. 'Really? How is he?' Nathan hadn't seen Leigh for about a month – long before he'd met Scott, actually, and that had been only a brief hello. He knew that he should have phoned him, but with the Elective case, and Scott . . .

'A busy boy, by the look of it.' Nigel gave a superior snort – his catchphrase. 'Copped off with a right hunk, I can tell you. You let that one go, didn't you?'

Nathan felt an odd pang that felt suspiciously like jealousy, and quickly tried to suppress it; his fling with Leigh had been wonderfully enjoyable, but it had petered out as Nathan had become engrossed in his search for the Elective. It wasn't surprising that Leigh had simply stopped phoning him. Nathan's nagging little conscience voice suggested that Scott would also be a casualty to Nathan's investigation, but Nathan silenced it immediately.

Even so, Leigh was still very special, and Nathan didn't really want Nigel revelling in his failures. But there was no one else in the pub that he felt like talking to, and Nigel offered a distraction from his irritation over Marcus. And Nathan did have a morbid curiosity about Leigh's actions. Almost masochistically, he decided to encourage Nigel. 'Go on then: what did this hunk look like?'

Nigel arched an eyebrow. 'Ooh, you would have loved him. Taller than you, big bear, bushy beard . . . then again, perhaps he wasn't your type: he had this really gorgeous tattoo.'

That caught Nathan's attention. 'What sort of tattoo?'

Nigel was removing the glasses from the dishwasher. 'What's it to you?' he sniped. 'I thought you'd moved on since then. Ivy saw you with some cute little thug down the Crossed Swords the other day. Mmm – very cosy, I gather.'

Nathan shrugged: Nigel could think what he liked. 'I'm just curious, that's all.' A quite horrible suspicion was brewing in Nathan's mind.

'He had a big black jaguar tattooed up his arm.' Nigel pouted at him. 'Anyway, I thought you didn't like tattoos. That's always been the excuse when I've tried it on.' He stroked his own tattoo, a teddy bear – just visible below the rolled-up sleeve of his checked shirt.

Nathan smiled, but he didn't feel it: all he could think of was Leigh's own tattoo . . . and the black jaguar tattoo of the man Nigel was talking about. Actually, he quite liked tattoos, but it had been a convenient excuse to keep Nigel at arm's length. Nigel's attempts to get Nathan into bed were the stuff of legend; everyone knew that Nigel had sworn to have sex with Nathan, and it had become an ongoing game between the two of them. And normally Nathan would have carried on the banter to liven up the afternoon. But a black jaguar tattoo . . .

'When was this exactly?' he said, a lot more forcefully than he would have liked to.

Nigel cocked an eyebrow. 'A bit keen, aren't we? Hoping to rekindle your lost love?' But he must have registered the serious expression on Nathan's face, because he answered him. 'It was Tuesday – I remember because Ivy and Patty were on that night.' Ivy and Patty – Ian and Patrick – were the Brave Trader's most productive gossip merchants. And, if Nathan's suspicions proved to be correct, he would need to talk to them. He just hoped to God that it wouldn't come to that.

Putting his half-finished pint on the bar, he picked up his files and headed out of the pub, calling out a hurried goodbye as he did so. Nathan, Mister Organised, had left his damned personal organiser at home – with Leigh's phone number in it. Getting back to Docklands had suddenly become his number-one priority.

If Nigel composed one of his trademark cutting replies, Nathan never heard it; he was through the door and on to Poland Street, pushing past dawdling shoppers to reach Oxford Street, his heart racing as he hailed the first taxi he saw. Despite the lack of detailed description in his files, there was one recurring theme: the bear with the jaguar tattoo. Two people claimed to have seen him in the Harness, and three in the Collective. And the end results had been the same: their companion for the evening had never been seen again.

If Nathan's suspicions were correct, two things had happened: Leigh had gone missing – and the Brave Trader had been compromised by the Elective.

Nathan paid the driver, bolting out of the taxi and running to his front door. As he unlocked it and ran inside, he realised that he was sweating. But why? Was it Leigh's disappearance? Or was it that the Brave Trader was no longer the safe haven that Nathan had always assumed?

Throwing the door shut behind him, Nathan hurried over to his desk and grabbed his electronic organiser. Leigh's phone number was definitely there, but it took a couple of endless moments to find and retrieve it, Nathan's fear making him fumble and mistype.

With trembling hands, Nathan picked up his phone and dialled the number, his breathing heavy. If Leigh had been taken by the Elective – well, Nathan didn't know if he could cope, after what had happened with Paolo. He'd been trying to distance himself from this case: having it intrude into his private life wasn't something he had planned on. To be honest, he hadn't even realised that Leigh meant that much to him.

Three rings, four rings, five rings . . . Nathan was on the point of hanging up and taking a taxi to Leigh's flat in Greenwich when it was answered.

'Is that Leigh?' Nathan stammered, trying to get a hold of himself. But the northern accent was unmistakable, even if he did sound a little tired and distant.

'Nathan? Is that you? Are you OK?' Even without the telephone, Nathan's sigh of relief must have been audible in Greenwich.

'I . . . I was wondering if you were going to be about at the weekend,' he said, as much for something to say as anything else.

After a few seconds' hesitation, Leigh replied. 'Not this weekend: I'm going to see my folks in Yorkshire for a couple of weeks. But when I get back? Fancy a drink?'

'Love to, love to. Anyway, I must dash. Give us a ring when you get back.' With that, Nathan put the phone down and sank on to the sofa.

You're getting paranoid, Nate, he thought seeing the Elective in every shadow. Recovering his breath, he reached for the phone again. He wanted to see Scott. Now.

Leigh replaced the receiver and turned to his companion, his eyes glassy, his expression fixed. The tall, chunky man with the thick black beard smiled at him. 'Mr Dexter, presumably?'

Leigh nodded. 'You were right: he is suspicious.'

'Of course I am,' he replied, stroking the distinctive black jaguar tattoo on his left arm. 'The Elective always is.'

Three

The Brave Trader of Queensland was packed solid, both the cruisy downstairs bar and the quieter lounge upstairs. It was busy, even for a Friday night, with a lot of strange faces among the regulars, keeping the bar staff on their toes and bringing a smile to Nigel's face as he counted the profits.

Scott and Nathan were crushed into the corner against the bar itself, chatting to Australian Mike, an amiable man in his mid-forties who many in the Brave Trader regarded as a cross between a father confessor and an agony aunt. Nathan included himself in that number: he'd just finished telling Mike about the incident with Leigh, having kept him informed about his suspicions regarding the Elective since he had decided to take the case. Mike had neither agreed nor disagreed with him about the Elective, but he had always offered an understanding ear. Nathan hadn't seen Mike since just before he had met Scott, the previous month, so he was filling him in with the latest results of his investigation.

'Have you seen Leigh since the phone call?' asked Mike. 'That was weeks ago.'

Nathan shook his head. 'No, but he did say that he was

going away for a few weeks. Anyway, I've got someone else to worry about now.' Nathan put his arm around Scott's waist and grinned, and winked as Scott smiled back. Scott was wearing a brand-new biker's jacket, almost the twin of Nathan's own, which Nathan had bought for him to celebrate the fact that they had been together for exactly a month. Leather suited Scott: it accentuated his thuggishness, and added quite a lot to their already brilliant sex life.

A month, he thought. It didn't seem that long since Scott James had entered Nathan's life, but it was. And since that chance meeting in the Crossed Swords, Nathan had never been satisfied. He realised now that his obsession with the Elective had been in danger of taking over his whole life: now Scott was around, Nathan simply wouldn't let that happen.

'I don't see what you saw in him,' said Scott. 'Seemed a bit of a wimp to me.' He shifted position as a very tall man — at least six foot five — with a ginger goatee beard pushed past to get a drink.

'Jealous, Scott?' Nathan was a little taken aback: this was the first time that Scott had ever shown the slightest resentment towards Leigh. 'You haven't got any reason to be jealous : I'm with you, aren't I?'

Mike raised an eyebrow. 'I seem to remember a certain Mr Dexter being rather put out when Paolo's ex walked into the Collective.' He picked up his white wine and soda. 'Or was I mistaken?'

Nathan almost spat his Coke out. 'That was different . . .' Then he laughed. 'I suppose you're right.' He tightened his arm around Scott's shoulder. 'Anyway, where do you fancy going after here, then?'

Scott frowned. 'I fancy going to the Harness, if that's OK.'

The suggestion was innocuous enough, but Nathan couldn't help feeling that there had been a change in Scott's attitude over the last week: his obvious — and new-found — dislike of Leigh was only one symptom; he was convinced that something was worrying Scott – as if he were hiding something. Dismissing it as more evidence of his own paranoia, he shrugged. 'I hadn't given it much thought.' Then again, both he and Scott were dressed for the Harness: leather jackets, leather trousers – another present for Scott – and biker boots. He looked at the clock above the bar: it was nearly eleven o'clock. The Harness got going about half-eleven; on the bike, the trip to Vauxhall took about fifteen minutes. 'OK – the Harness it is. What about you, Mike?'

'Oh no, not me,' he said, putting up his hands in mock defence. 'I fancy something a little more sedate, something more suited to a gentleman of my advanced years: I'm off to Vice tonight.' He nodded downwards to the canvas holdall at his feet. Nathan guessed that it held one of Mike's legendary collection of uniforms, all of them genuine, all of them with a tale to tell – if Mike was in the mood. And when he was in the mood, there was no stopping him. 'It's the Mountie outfit tonight,' he whispered.

Nathan laughed: the tale of *that* uniform was legendary. 'Somehow, you, Mountie outfits and *sedate* don't go together.' He finished off his coke and called over the bar, 'Ivy, can we have our crash helmets?'

Ivy – a tall, dark-haired clone – nodded and retrieved the two black helmets from under the bar. 'Off somewhere nice, girls?' he asked as he handed over the helmets.

'The Harness,' Nathan replied as he gave one of the helmets to Scott. 'What about you?'

Ivy reached over and struck the bell to indicate time. 'Time, gentlemen, please!' he bellowed, before returning his attention to Nathan. 'Oooh, I haven't decided.' He glanced over at Mike. 'I might go to Vice, though.' Ivy's preoccupation with the Australian was both well known and unrequited.

'You in uniform?' said Nathan. 'A nurse, maybe . . .' He stepped back as Ivy made to cuff him. 'Anyway, we're off – see you in the week. Give my love to Nigel.'

51

Giving Mike a peck on the cheek, Nathan walked out of the pub, with Scott just behind.

Neither of them noticed the extremely tall man with the ginger goatee beard following them.

Nathan's bike was parked just outside the Brave Trader. He and Scott put on their helmets and mounted the bike; Nathan kicked away the stand and turned the ignition key. Within seconds, they were off down Poland Street, towards Oxford Street and eventually Vauxhall.

The man with the ginger goatee watched them ride away. Seconds later, he hailed a taxi.

'Where to, mate?' asked the taxi driver.

'Vauxhall,' came the curt reply.

Nathan pulled the bike up just in front of the Harness, its understated, unimpressive brick façade belying its dark and intriguing interior. Although it was slightly early – as far as the Harness and its regulars were concerned – there were already another five bikes there. Scott recognised two of them: Peter K's red Kawasaki and Tom's black BSA.

'Look's like it's going to be a busy night if those two are here already,' he muttered, as they walked towards the plain metal door. Although Nathan had been there a few times, the Harness wasn't really what he would call one of his regular haunts. Indeed, he had been rather taken aback when Scott had revealed that he had full membership. However, once the initial surprise had faded, Nathan soon realised what this could mean to their sex life: rather than Scott being inexperienced in some of Nathan's favourite sexual fantasies, membership of the Harness suggested that he was as into them as Nathan was.

The last couple of weeks had proved Nathan's guess correct, putting his collection of leather and toys to full and lively use.

After ringing the discreet bell, they were briefly checked out by the doorman before being allowed inside. Nathan took

Scott's helmet from him and checked it into the little cloak-room, while Scott accepted a fiver off him and went off to get some drinks.

After depositing the helmets, Nathan wandered through the narrow black corridor into the cavernous main bar, one eye out for Scott, the other trying to see who else was in there. As he located Scott with the drinks, he realised that he was still overawed by the club; he'd only been there about half a dozen times, and the Harness never failed to impress him.

The first impression that anyone got of the Harness was of its sheer size: it was a converted warehouse, and the owners had done very little to hide its original function – save painting the interior black – claiming that it added to its ambience. Nathan had to admit that they were right.

Although the lighting in the main part of the club was dim to the point of being virtually nonexistent, it was sufficient to show off the high vaulted ceiling with its functional stone arches and occasional leaded window. The square room was about fifty feet wide, with a long bar occupying the left-hand side; about twenty people were clustered around it, including Scott.

The area straight ahead of Nathan was the dance floor, although the DJ didn't start until midnight: a bland mixture of taped high-energy and Europop was currently blaring out from the giant speakers, which stood like black sentinels on either side of the dance floor.

To the right were the 'doors'; that was all that anyone ever called them. Two were the toilets – male and female, although the men-only policy made them both equally available – but the other three led to the Harness's darker secrets: the main reason why the place was so popular. They were the back rooms: one was simply a large, unlit room designed purely for casual, anonymous sex. The second led to the 'playroom', a larger, better-lit room with manacles, ceiling harnesses, netting on the walls, and non-stop hard-core pornographic videos.

Nathan had been there once or twice, but the anonymity did little for him: he liked to know the person he was going with a little better than that. Then again, there had been nights when the anonymity had suited him perfectly, he though wryly.

As for the third room, well . . . Nathan had heard rumours, but nothing that could ever be confirmed. Unlike the others, this door was locked, with a bouncer on the other side. Nathan had never seen anybody ever granted admission, but there were enough people around who claimed to have seen inside – except that no two stories ever agreed. Some people even reckoned that it was exclusively for members of the Elective, but – despite his professional interest – that was one rumour that he soundly ignored. The Elective existed in private, in secret; a locked door in a busy S&M club was definitely not the Elective's style.

He walked over to the bar, where Scott was waiting with a can of Hooch for himself and a Coke for Nathan. Scott was chatting away to Peter K, another of the Harness's regulars: he was a compact, good-looking biker with a shaved head and a thick metal ring through his nose. His boyfriend, Tom, an older biker, was still waiting to be served at the bar.

'Hi, Peter.' Nathan accepted his drink. 'What's new?'

'I was just saying to Scott: no one's seen Noel for a while. Do you think . . .?'

Nathan knew exactly what Peter was getting at. Although Nathan hadn't initially wanted to publicise his researches into the Elective, he had soon realised that he had to make it known to a number of people. First, it was the only way to get information; secondly, it was his best chance of drawing the Elective into the daylight that it shunned: if the mysterious Comptroller who apparently controlled the Elective realised that Nathan was asking questions, he might be forced to show his hand. Unfortunately, it also meant that the moment someone dropped out of sight on the leather scene, everyone automatically assumed that they were the Elective's latest victim and felt compelled to report it to Nathan.

'Peter: Noel's in Australia,' Nathan explained patiently. 'He flew out last week. Anyway, I don't want to talk about work.' He sipped his Coke. Suddenly he realised that Scott's attention was focused on the far side of the bar. He was staring at a very tall man wearing a leather jacket who had just walked in.

'Wasn't he in the Brave Trader earlier?' Nathan asked.

'Who?' Scott replied with an innocence that was belied by his wide-eyed stare.

Nathan laughed – but it was a hollow, unfelt laugh. 'Who? That bloke that you haven't been able to keep your eyes off since he walked in.'

Scott looked slightly embarrassed. 'Are you annoyed?'

'Not at all.' But Nathan did feel a slight twinge of jealousy. In the month that they had been together, neither had discussed the parameters of their relationship; Nathan had been afraid of tempting fate if he had tried to pin Scott down, so the question of monogamy had never arisen. Now it seemed like the question definitely was going to arise: and not just theoretically. The tall man was walking towards the bar – if Nathan hadn't known better, he would have sworn that he was walking towards *them*. For a brief second, Nathan thought he looked familiar: he felt sure that he had seen him before – somewhere. But he just couldn't place him, and he was certain that he would have clearly remembered someone who was six foot five.

'Do you know him?' asked Peter as he got closer.

Nathan shrugged. 'He was in the Brave Trader – that's the first time I've seen him.' He dismissed the nagging feeling of familiarity and watched the man as he passed by them.

Now able to get a better look, Nathan could see why Scott had been so interested. He looked to be in his mid-twenties, with dark red – almost brown – hair, which looked like a crew-cut after a few weeks of growing out. He had a neatly cropped ginger goatee beard and long sideburns, which framed a slightly round face with a docile, almost dopey expression. The leather biker's jacket and denim shirt covered a solid, broad body; the black jeans showed off an impressive bulge between his legs.

Despite himself, Nathan could feel himself getting excited, his dick stiffening inside his leather trousers. He glanced down at Scott's crotch, and saw a similar bulge developing there. Whoever the stranger was, he seemed to be having the same, almost hypnotic, effect on both Nathan and Scott. A solution began to suggest itself to Nathan, but he wasn't sure . . .

'Bit of a hunk, eh?' whispered Peter as the man-mountain walked past to get to the bar.

Nathan had to agree – but there was a good chance that this situation would become awkward unless he made a decision. He made it. Beckoning Scott closer, he drew him away from the crowd at the bar. 'Do you fancy him?' he asked.

Scott shrugged. 'I, well, I suppose so. But I'm with you, aren't I?'

That wasn't quite the reassuring response Nathan would have liked, but it would have to do. There was a solution to their current dilemma, a solution that wasn't strictly infidelity . . .

He smiled. 'Have you ever had a threesome?' he said innocently.

Scott laughed. 'You mean . . .' He nodded over his shoulder towards the bar.

'Why not? We both fancy him – that's pretty bloody obvious.' He discreetly pointed downwards, towards Scott's noticeable erection. 'Have to make sure that he likes both of us, though.' Nathan had had a number of threesomes in his life, virtually all of them with couples. Most of them had been extremely enjoyable, but a few stood out as being complete disasters: disasters, because only one of the couple had really been into him. The unpleasant atmosphere between the couples

56

in those situations had been enough to ruin the evening's pleasure.

Scott frowned for a second, and then grinned. 'I'm OK – as long as *you're* OK about it.'

Nathan pulled him close and hugged him. 'As long as you don't run off with him.' It was meant as a joke, but Nathan immediately realised that he had inadvertently expressed what was worrying him – his own insecurity. The stranger at the bar – who, drink in hand, was transfixing both of them with an interested stare – was gorgeous, and Nathan really did wonder whether he would have competition.

Returning to Peter K and Tom, Nathan and Scott stood so that they could see the man. Nathan had already decided that he would do the talking: he had had more experience with threesomes, it seemed, so he stood the better chance of persuading the stranger to come home with both of them.

Rubbish, came the inner voice. *You just don't trust Scott not to go off with him on his own. Brave and fearless Nathan Dexter –*

Nathan surprised himself. *Shut it. I don't need you to tell me what to do.* Silencing his conscience, he looked over at the tall man and realised that he was smiling at him. Without hesitating, Nathan walked over to him.

'Hi,' he said by way of greeting.

'Hi ya,' said the other. 'Looks like it's going to be busy tonight.' And yes, in the fifteen minutes since Nathan and Scott had arrived, the Harness had filled up with its usual collection of guys in rubber and leather. 'I'm John, by the way. John Bury.'

'Nathan Dexter.' They shook hands, and Nathan couldn't help but find this amusing: the genteel veneer of civilised behaviour, when all he wanted to do was strip John's clothes off and suck his dick. But that was the gay scene: pure lust, bubbling away under the smooth cover of politeness. That was what the backrooms were for: to tap into that lust without having to bother with the preliminaries. But this was the main bar, and there were formalities to go through.

'Who are you with over there?' asked John, nodding over Nathan's shoulder.

'My boyfriend, Scott. He's the younger one. What about you? Are you with anyone?'

John shook his head. 'Nope – alone and lonely,' he said, sounding so forlorn that Nathan just wanted to grab him and stick his tongue down his throat. The inner voice started again – *and you were worried about* Scott *going off* – but Nathan took no notice whatsoever. He was sick and tired of his insecurity lecturing him. 'I don't come here very often,' John continued. 'I usually stick to the Courtyard.' He looked around. 'I just fancied a bit of a change.'

The Courtyard was similar in clientele to the Harness: a dark and atmospheric S&M club over in East London. Nathan had gone there quite a lot before he'd met Scott – he preferred it to the Harness – but he was sure that he had never seen John there: a six-foot-five hunk wasn't that easy to miss. He decided to let it pass. 'So why don't you come over and join us?' He laughed. 'We don't bite.'

John pouted, looking like a little lost boy as he did so. 'Oh, that's a shame. I was hoping you did.'

An hour later, Nathan, Scott and John were getting on like a house on fire, Tom and Peter K having retired to the playroom – after a couple of knowing winks from Tom.

John was a systems analyst for a computer company in Camden, so he and Scott had been able to chat away about computers: Scott's degree was in computer science, which gave them something in common, although he wasn't familiar with some of the courses that Scott was taking. John was also interested in writing – he was working on his first novel – which gave him and Nathan something to talk about, although Nathan made certain that Scott wasn't left out of the conversation: that was a perfect way to alienate his boyfriend, and that was one thing he really did not want to do. In this way, the evening passed enjoyably . . . but without direction, without a clear aim. Hopefully, that would come later, when Nathan could work out some subtle way of broaching what was foremost on his and Scott's minds – unless John took the initiative.

But as the evening wore on, the subject of threesomes had still not been raised, although the end result of the evening did seem inevitable – if Nathan had read John's body language correctly, that was. All that was left was for someone to *say* the damned thing.

John finished his beer and dumped the empty glass on the bar. Nathan's Coke was nearly gone, and Nathan noticed that Scott had almost finished his Hooch. It seemed that decision time was almost upon them.

'So, what now?' But Nathan hadn't said anything. He glanced round at Scott, taken aback that he appeared to be taking the lead. But it did seem clear that John's interest was with both of them, so Nathan decided to let Scott carry on doing the running: it seemed to be working. At the moment.

John shrugged. 'What do you suggest?' But his knowing smile made it clear that it was simply a question of getting it all out into the open.

Scott appeared to be an expert at this; Nathan was both shocked and secretly pleased. 'Do you fancy coming back with us?' he blurted out.

Oh, subtle, thought Nathan. John's going to jump at that. Second only to 'looking for a shag?' as a way of frightening them off.

John broke into a broad grin. 'I thought you'd never ask.'

Even though it was what Scott wanted, he couldn't help feeling a sense of unease as the three of them sat in Nathan's living room drinking wine from Nathan's lead crystal glasses. According to Nathan, it was a fine white burgundy, but Scott couldn't really tell the difference between the glass in his hands and Liebfraumilch: wine hadn't really featured much in his upbringing.

But it wasn't the wine that concerned him. Although John was extremely shaggable – indeed, he looked even better in the soft lighting of the living room – Scott wondered whether this was what Nathan wanted, or whether he was doing it for Scott's benefit. When they had been working out the mechanics of getting home – with Scott and Nathan on the bike – and John had got a taxi, Scott had had mixed feelings. When he and Nathan had reached the house in Docklands, Scott had half wanted John to arrive, and half hoped that he would have changed his mind and saved Scott the confusion that was going through his mind.

Scott braved a glance at his boyfriend, who was sitting on the two-seater leather sofa opposite the armchair in which Scott sat, and next to John's armchair. Nathan seemed at ease, chatting away to John and occasionally tapping him gently on the knee to reinforce a point. He didn't seem to have any problems with sharing Scott with someone else, and that felt . . . disturbing.

Is this going to backfire? Scott wondered. I thought I could handle it, but I'm not so sure. Nathan's done this before: he's used to it. But Nathan's the first man I've ever loved: am I going to lose him to John?

'Shall we go upstairs?' asked Nathan in a nonchalant tone of voice, as if this was something he did all the time. Perhaps it is, thought Scott. How much do you really know about Nathan Dexter?

'Suits me,' said John, rising up to his full height. He turned to Scott and grinned. 'Ready?'

They reached the door to Nathan's bedroom. John placed his hand on Scott's backside and rubbed it affectionately. 'I was hoping that tonight would end like this: two gorgeous blokes . . .' He leant down and gave both Scott and Nathan a brief kiss on the lips.

As Nathan opened the door, John walked in, urging Scott in with a slight push. Nathan switched on the bedside light and closed the door behind him, before turning to John.

He didn't say a word; he simply manoeuvred John towards the bed and sat him down. Once sitting, Nathan could easily kiss John on the mouth without having to reach. But he didn't just give him an affectionate peck: he placed both of his arms around John's broad back and kissed him deeply, obviously enjoying it.

For a moment, Scott didn't know what to do. Jealousy flared within him, a hot churning in his stomach that made him feel both sick and angry. If Nathan loved him, how could he do that with someone else? But another feeling began to rise, not in his stomach but lower down, both physically and emotionally. Seeing his boyfriend making the first overtures towards sex with someone else was beginning to turn him on. He felt his dick stiffen as Nathan unbuttoned John's denim shirt and tugged it out of his waistband, revealing John's broad, solid chest with its dusting of fine red hair.

Without thinking, Scott moved over to Nathan and pulled off his white T-shirt, almost feeling guilty as he forced Nathan's and John's lips to part to allow the shirt over Nathan's head: watching them kiss was exciting him, and something inside him didn't want them to stop. Rather than resume his passionate kissing, Nathan pulled Scott closer and indicated that he take his place. For a second, Scott hesitated; but it was what he wanted, it was the whole reason that the three of them were there, in Nathan's room.

John leant over and started kissing Scott, who felt the ginger goatee beard, softer and less bristly than Nathan's, tickle his lips and chin. One hand began to massage John's back, while the other stroked the equally soft hairs on his chest.

Meanwhile, Nathan had undone John's boots, pulling each

PAUL C. ALEXANDER

one off so that he could remove his black jeans. But he stopped for a moment when John's jeans were around his ankles and turned his attention to Scott. Gently pulling him away from John, he pulled Scott's grey T-shirt over his head and then kissed him deeply and sensuously, rubbing his hands through his thick chest hair.

'Don't forget,' he whispered in Scott's ear, 'I love you.' Then he unbuckled Scott's jeans and eased them over his thighs, his hands lingering for a second on the thickness inside his boxer shorts. He squeezed his dick firmly, and Scott felt it respond by hardening even further. Scott decided that it was time he took the initiative: the fears that he had had when this had started had gone, replaced by an excitement that was almost as intense as the feelings that always overwhelmed him when he and Nathan made love.

He pulled John's jeans off and threw them into the corner of the room. John was wearing a pair of white briefs, a damp stain at the waistband where the long bulge ended. Scott fell to his knees and began licking John's dick through the damp white cotton, tasting and enjoying his pre-come, while Nathan undid his own trousers and removed them.

All three of them were now down to their underwear, all of them displaying rock-hard erections through the tented fabric. Scott could feel himself getting more and more excited, caught in a situation that he had only ever read about before. He wanted to indulge himself, fully take part in it rather than just be a bystander. His licking became even more furious, soaking John's briefs and making them translucent, revealing the veined pink dick beneath them.

He was aware of Nathan kneeling down behind him, slowly pulling his boxers down. Then Nathan leant forward, and Scott felt a probing wetness between his buttocks, probing and searching through the thick hair. He gasped.

He knew what the feeling was, and knew that Nathan knew

62

how much it turned him on: it was Nathan's tongue, licking his arse, his tongue teasing his anus with brief, deep strokes.

Fuelled by this, Scott yanked John's briefs down, allowing his cock to stand free. It was as long as Nathan's, but not quite so thick, with a small foreskin that was already pulled right back over the red helmet. A bush of thick red hair sprang from around the base, framing huge balls. Scott virtually pounced on John's dick, taking the end in his mouth and licking every last drop of the clear, sweet fluid from the leaking slit. John let out a tiny yelp and shuddered, but this only made Scott even more eager. He began to slide his mouth even further down the shaft, but Nathan's hands on his shoulders made him stop. Nathan gently eased him away, his hands moving down to his fur-covered pecs.

'You can't have him all to yourself, you know,' Nathan said with a smile. 'Besides, I think it's time we let John decide what he wants to do.'

For a second, the three of them did nothing; Scott could see John looking between both of them, his eyes darting to their still-constrained cocks. Then, after fully taking off his jeans and pants, he moved round so that he was lying completely on the bed, his head on the pillows, naked with his erection stiff against his smooth, flat stomach.

'I want both of you,' he said. 'And I want both of you to suck my cock.'

Nathan stepped out of his briefs before pulling Scott on to the bed with him, indicating that they lie on top of John with their mouths against his cock. But it immediately became clear that John's greater height meant that they would be able to suck him off, but he wouldn't be able to reach their cocks. Scott was stuck for a solution, but Nathan raised his finger.

'Let's try this,' he suggested. Moving Scott and John as if they were chess pieces, he manoeuvred them around the wide bed so that Scott's cock was brushing John's mouth, while Nathan's own cock was against Scott's face. Nathan was nuzzled up to John's cock, his black goatee contrasting with the thick red hair.

'Right!' growled John, taking Scott's dick in his mouth and forcing it deeply down his throat. He started to suck it firmly, and Scott was surprised by how different from Nathan it felt. It was rougher, yes, but it didn't quite give him the same pleasure. Was this threesome going to turn out a disappointment? he wondered. Had all of this − all of the doubts and worries − been for nothing?

Two things changed that immediately: Scott guided Nathan's erection between his lips, and suppressed a groan of enjoyment as he tasted the familiar thick, salty dick in his mouth; and he felt a hand which he assumed to be John's stroking his arse, the fingers probing and finding his anus and gently penetrating it.

The three of them continued like that for timeless moments; all Scott could think about was the mouth around his dick and the dick in his own mouth, while John's finger went further and further up his arse, probing and reaching for his prostate gland.

He moved his hand so it was gripped around Nathan's cock and began to wank it, knowing the exact rhythm that would bring his boyfriend off. Almost simultaneously, he saw Nathan reach out to do the same to John, who was now writhing with pleasure. It was clear that John was very close, and Nathan found himself suddenly envious that Nathan was to be the recipient of the big man's load.

That envy dissipated as Scott felt himself coming very close; John's finger was stroking his prostate, making his orgasm both imminent and inevitable. He tightened his grip on his boy-friend's cock and increased the speed at which he was sucking him, aware of the light beading of sweat that was breaking out under the thick covering of black hair. Scott was only seconds away from coming, and guessed that Nathan was as well . . . but it was John who beat them both to it.

Shuddering and writhing, unable to cry out because of

Scott's cock filling his mouth, John spasmed, and Scott managed to move his head to watch him come. His huge balls virtually pulsed, and Scott could see Nathan struggling to swallow the load that was obviously flooding from John's throbbing dick.

Before he could observe much more, he felt himself losing control, and abandoned himself to it. As he came, he realised that Nathan was coming at the same time, and he was only distantly aware of his own come filling John's mouth with every brutal thrust as his boyfriend's hot, salty juice squirted against the back of his throat.

Before Scott could swallow, Nathan had disentangled himself from the threesome and pulled both Scott and John towards him. Their mouths joined, and the three of them shared each other's coming, kissing and mingling the white juices which dripped to the blue and gold duvet.

Seconds later, they all fell backward on to the bed. Scott felt Nathan's hand reach out and stroke his dick, then his chest, before finally touching his cheek warmly. John raised his head from the pillows with obvious difficulty and grinned at both of them, a small dribble of spunk trapped in his goatee.

'That was . . .' He laughed. 'That was unbelievable,' he whispered.

Nathan winked at him, squeezing Scott's hand as he did so. 'We aim to please.'

Nathan woke up with a start, instinctively reaching out and looking at the red numerals on the alarm clock next to him. It was five o'clock in the morning: far too early for him to normally be awake, so why was he so alert? He glanced at Scott, but he was still fast asleep, so it wasn't him who had woken him. Then he heard it.

A noise. Almost nothing, but Nathan immediately realised that someone was moving about downstairs. Whoever they were, they were trying to be quiet, but Nathan knew every sound in his house. It could be burglars, but there was a much more obvious answer: John. And it sounded like he was tapping away on Nathan's computer.

After they had had sex, Nathan had shown John into the spare room. Nathan's bed was big enough for the three of them, but he had been acutely aware that Scott had shown signs of unease both before and after the threesome, and knew that the boy needed to be reassured.

As it turned out, Scott had been fast asleep by the time Nathan had returned from showing John the spare room, but, as always, it was the thought that counted, he decided. But this noise . . . John could have gone downstairs to get himself a drink, and then decided to have a play around on the Internet, but Nathan suddenly had an uneasy feeling himself: as he had dozed, his mind had done what it always did in that twilight before sleep, sorting and rationalising the events of the previous day – a useful, even vital, skill for a journalist.

There were too many inconsistencies in some of the things that John had mentioned: his claim that he was a regular at the Courtyard, when Nathan had never seen him before; his unfamiliarity with aspects of computing that even Nathan knew about, even though John had said that he was a systems analyst . . . If he was a systems analyst, why would Nathan's computer be of interest?

Trying not to wake Scott, Nathan slid from under the duvet and tiptoed towards the door, grabbing a pair of shorts as he did so. Thankfully, he had left the door ajar – partly to let some air circulate, but mainly in the hope that John would want to join them again and would see it as an invitation. He pulled on the shorts and slipped through the gap in the doorway without making a noise.

He crept down the stairs, well aware that he would have to avoid the fifth stair down with its giveaway creak. As he reached the hall, he could see that the living-room door was open, and a distant light was on: the light above his computer.

'Everything all right?' he announced, striding into the room.

Then he fell silent when he realised that his stack of files – the ones that he had shown to Marcus the previous day – were scattered over the floor, their contents strewn around like overgrown confetti.

John was sitting at Nathan's computer, which was switched on.

For a moment, John – who was fully clothed, even to the point of having his jacket on – looked like a rabbit caught in headlights. Then he leapt from the chair, ran across the living room, and pushed Nathan against the wall.

By the time Nathan recovered from the twin shocks of John's violation and the shove in the chest, John was gone, the front door open to the December night. Nathan pulled himself to his feet and looked at the mess. His feelings had been right. But what had John been looking for? More importantly – what had he found?

Four

Scott opened his eyes and winced, immediately knowing with an all-too-painful certainty that he'd had far too much to drink the night before – his head was throbbing as if someone had hit him with a baseball bat. Even the soft light through the half-open bedroom door was sufficient to make him want to hide back under the duvet. With a low moan, he shifted round to Nathan for reassurance – but Nathan wasn't there. Puzzled, he sat up – and regretted it immediately as his head began to spin: he froze and waited for the world to stop, swearing that he would never touch another drop. Finally, after what seemed like hours, the room came to a standstill. Through blurred eyes, he picked up the alarm clock and checked the time: although it was a Saturday morning, he'd told a friend that he was going to meet him for lunch, and he didn't want to be late.

It was half past five in the morning. He wondered whether Nathan was in the bathroom, but the partly open door showed that the bathroom light was off. Gingerly raising himself from the bed, he grabbed Nathan's dressing gown from the back of the chair, threw it round himself, and made his way downstairs.

He hoped that Nathan *was* downstairs: the thought that he might be in the spare room with John wasn't one that he felt very comfortable with.

The door to the living room was open, the light on. Scott walked in and saw Nathan sitting on the sofa, wearing only a pair of shorts, staring at the floor. All of his files – his research into this Elective business – were opened, the countless sheets of paper scattered around.

'What's the matter?' Scott sat down next to Nathan. 'Had enough of the Elective already?'

Nathan looked at him, and, even in his befuddled state of mind, Scott could see that he was worried. No, *worried* wasn't strong enough to describe the devastated look on his boyfriend's face: Scott had never seen Nathan look so . . . so despondent.

'I didn't do this,' said Nathan quietly.

'Have you been burgled? Have you phoned the police?'

Nathan shook his head. 'No burglars, no police. It was John.'

'John?' Scott found that very hard to believe. 'Why?'

Nathan jumped to his feet. 'Isn't it fucking obvious?' he yelled. 'Why else would that bastard do this? He's part of the Elective.' He grabbed Scott by his sleeve and virtually dragged him over to the computer. 'Look at that,' he commanded.

Scott peered at the screen through hungover eyes. The only thing on the monitor, besides the image of a really hunky bear which Nathan used as computer wallpaper, was an error message:

INCORRECT PASSWORD. ACCESS DENIED.

'He was trying to hack into my private files, Scott. There are things in there which I've never committed to paper: interviews with people too terrified to even give me their names; sightings of the Comptroller; even a blurry picture of the Comptroller. John knew exactly which file to hack into.'

Scott was shocked; what had started off as a bit of fun was now a nightmare. He knew how much Nathan's investigation into the Elective meant to him: he also now knew that Nathan loved and trusted him enough to share this information with him. Despite his guilt at being the instigator of the threesome that had directly led to John's violation of Nathan's computer, he was touched by Nathan's openness.

'Wasn't the file encrypted?' Scott remembered a particularly boring set of lectures about encrypting files, putting them in code so that nobody without the password could look at them. He also remembered Nathan taking delivery of a software package which was designed to do exactly that. He hadn't asked why at the time; now it was obvious.

Nathan nodded. 'The encryption program is one of the most sophisticated on the market.' He slapped his forehead. 'What am I saying: it's not even on the market yet! I got it from one of my contacts in the industry.' He shrugged. 'Didn't seem to bother John, though: by the look of it, he was about five minutes away from cracking it.'

'He did say he was a systems analyst –'

'He said a lot of things – but how many of them were true?' Nathan reached down to eject a disk from the computer. 'You'd have to be a damned sight more than a systems analyst to break through this level of encryption: you'd have to be a professional hacker.'

Scott shook his head. 'Are you saying that John came back with us because of your investigation? Isn't that a little far-fetched?'

'Far-fetched? Far-fetched?' Nathan shoved the liberated floppy in Scott's face. 'I went through this disk a little while ago: it looks like it contains a program specifically designed to break through this particular type of encryption. This disk –' He threw it to the floor. 'That disk contains a program which the manufacturers claim shouldn't exist!' He slammed his fist on the table next to the computer. 'We've been set up, Scott. We've allowed the Elective into our home!'

Scott didn't miss Nathan's use of 'our', but those feelings were overridden by the twin emotions of fear and guilt. Fear that the Elective really did exist and that it had found them – and guilt that his desire had let them in. 'I'm . . . I'm sorry,' he whispered. 'If I hadn't been so keen on a threesome . . .'

Nathan's anger, which was almost tangible, subsided immediately. He pulled Scott towards him and hugged him tightly. 'It wasn't your fault. How could either of us have known what John was up to? He must have followed us from the Brave Trader to the Harness.' Nathan let go of Scott and sat down in front of his computer. 'Of course, the Harness . . .'

'What are you doing?'

Nathan shrugged. 'It could be nothing. But there's something about John that rings a bell.' He tapped away at the keyboard for a few seconds, before stabbing a finger at the screen. 'There – I knew it. I knew I recognised him!'

Scott leant over Nathan's shoulder and looked at the image Nathan had brought up. Obviously, it was a photograph from the encrypted files, because Scott hadn't seen it in the stack of printouts. It showed a very tall, red-headed man standing in the Harness with a short, cute-looking bear. The former's expression made it quite clear that he didn't want to be photographed.

'That's John,' said Scott redundantly.

'Exactly,' said Nathan. 'This picture was taken about three months ago for one of the freebie gay papers, but it was suppressed by someone so high up that the editor had no choice but to pull it – but he was able to give me a copy before the negatives mysteriously vanished. The man he's with is called Jonathan.' Nathan looked up at Scott. 'He's not been seen since this picture was taken.'

Scott sighed. 'What do we do now?'

Nathan chewed his bottom lip before replying. 'It's time to go on the offensive. Until now, I've tiptoed around the Elective, not coming completely out into the open, but making myself sufficiently visible in the hope that they might show their hand.' He nodded at the scattered files to his right. 'I'd say that they've shown their hand all right, wouldn't you?'

'How do we go on the offensive?' asked Scott. From what Nathan had told him, the Elective was faceless, formless: an almost unbeatable enemy. Indeed, until now, Scott had seen it as something of a complicated game of Nathan's, like chess or backgammon. The events of the last few hours made Scott realise that the Elective was far, far more dangerous. It wasn't a game any more.

Nathan picked something off the table and held it up. 'John wasn't as careful as he should have been. He left his wallet behind.' Nathan opened the brown leather wallet and started leafing through the contents. Scott could see credit cards, some money – and a driving licence.

Pulling it out, Nathan unfolded it and read the name and address out loud.

'John Paul Bury, 11, Lexington Road, Maida Vale . . .' He placed the wallet and the licence on the desk and looked up at Scott. 'That gives us something to go on.'

'So, what do we do now?'

Nathan stood up and smiled wearily. 'It's almost six o'clock in the morning. Neither of us have had much sleep, and there's nothing I can do until a friend of mine starts work in about four hours. So we go to bed.'

Nathan walked into the bedroom after Scott, feeling slightly less disturbed than he had done three-quarters of an hour ago. Having checked all of the doors and windows, Nathan was satisfied that the house was as secure as he could make it – although what was security to something like the Elective? Still, if they wanted to get him, they could. It was now a matter of outmanoeuvring, outthinking the Elective. He pulled off his shorts and laughed as Scott dived under the duvet, yelping with the sudden cold of the sheets.

He climbed into bed next to Scott, turning the light off as

he did so. Despite the lack of sleep, Nathan didn't feel that tired: the anticipation that he was about to take on the Elective face to face was flooding through his brain, filling him with a heady mixture of both fear and excitement. He turned on his side so that his face was only inches away from Scott's, feeling his warm breath against his cheek.

Nathan wasn't sleepy – but he was as horny as hell. He gently moved his hand so that it rested on Scott's solid, hairy stomach, and started to stroke him. With each stroke, he moved gradually downward, until he could feel Scott's dick, as hard and as eager as his own, it seemed. Moving even closer, he began to nibble at Scott's neck, allowing his mouth to reach further upward, so that his tongue licked at Scott's ear. Scott's voice was quiet in the darkness.

'So, you're not tired either.' As he said it, Nathan felt Scott's hand brush past his cock and he shivered with the contact.

'No point in wasting the opportunity, is there?' He kissed Scott on the mouth, his tongue and Scott's caressing each other. At the same time, their hands grasped each other's dick firmly, wanking with slow but forceful strokes.

Then Nathan stopped. Pulling himself away from his boy-friend, he slid further down the bed, his tongue passing through the wiry tangles of Scott's chest hair. He reached Scott's stomach, and then further down, feeling the warmth of Scott's cock against his cheek. His tongue sought out the hot sweaty crease between Scott's thigh and his balls, and licked more forcefully, knowing that this was one of Scott's big turn-ons. He continued for a couple of minutes, listening to Scott's increasing groans with mounting excitement, before turning his attention to his big balls. First one, then the other, Nathan took each one completely in his mouth and sucked it softly, breathing in the musky, sweaty smells that came from all around him.

Once Scott's breathing was hard and panting, Nathan moved on to the thick cock, its helmet fully exposed. He greedily took the whole length into his mouth, tasting the sticky, sweet moisture that was almost pouring from Scott's tight slit as Nathan's tongue slid over it. Scott gasped, and Nathan knew from their month together that the boy was getting very close. That was the way with Scott: it was quite easy to bring him off the first time, but this simply prolonged events: he was always just as keen to continue afterwards. Nathan, on the other hand, liked to draw the experience out, and this was the best way of doing it.

As he continued sucking, he moved his hand round, sliding it under Scott's firm arse so that his fingers could stroke the boy's ring. This was another party trick of Nathan's: it hadn't taken him long to realise that he could bring Scott off without ever touching his cock – but what was the fun in that? He loved sucking Scott's cock, he loved the taste of it, the feel of it as it filled his mouth. And, most of all, he loved it when Scott shot his load, the thick shaft expanding and contracting, delivering hot salty jets of come down his throat.

Suddenly wanting that more than anything, he forced his finger into Scott's anus, shoving it roughly into the warm, wet hole. Scott gasped, but whether that was with pain or pleasure, Nathan just didn't care. All he cared about was the result, and that took only a few seconds to achieve. With a deep, rising shout, Scott came, his hands grabbing the sides of Nathan's head so that he took every drop, bucking and writhing as he did so. Not that there was any chance of his not doing that: Nathan relished every hot spurt, feeling it hit the roof of his mouth in rhythmic bursts. As Scott's orgasm subsided, Nathan's tongue eased the last of the salty juice from the slit, eliciting an even deeper, more guttural groan from Scott that gradually died away into a heartfelt sigh.

Finally sure that he had swallowed all that Scott had to offer, he pulled his mouth away from the dick, still rigid, still thick. He looked up in the darkness, just able to see Scott's satisfied grin.

'Did that meet sir's approval?' said Nathan, softly stroking his dick.

'You were desperate to swallow that, weren't you?'

Nathan moved up the bed and snuggled up close to him, putting his arm around him and drawing him close. 'I just needed . . .' He shrugged.

'Reassurance?' Scott put a hand on Nathan's thigh and squeezed. 'That business with John must have really shaken you.' A bit of a turn-up for the books, thought Nathan: Scott had a lot to offer, but sensitivity wasn't his strongest suit. And yet he seemed to know exactly what Nathan was thinking.

Nathan was about to agree with Scott's analysis, before he suddenly realised that he still felt that same exhilaration he had felt earlier: that feeling of direct action. After months of fighting shadows, they'd shown their hand – as far as Nathan was concerned, it demonstrated that he had finally become a threat to their activities. And that pleased him.

He was vaguely aware that his physical needs still required gratification, and Scott's warm, hairy body against his was keeping his erection hard against his stomach, but sleep was irresistible – he was exhausted, worn out, and somewhere deep inside he knew that he needed his strength for what lay ahead.

The battle against the Elective was about to begin.

With that thought echoing around his mind, Nathan fell asleep.

Nathan woke with the weak winter sunshine bleeding in through the thin black slats of the blind. He stretched and yawned, his mind worryingly blank: there was something important to do, something about last night . . . Then he remembered what it was. He looked at the alarm clock: nine thirty. His friend Graham would be at work in about half an hour – then he could make a start. But he wasn't going to do anything without a few cups of coffee inside him.

He jumped out of bed and grabbed his dressing gown, briefly

wondering where Scott had got to. Probably watching the TV, knowing him. Nathan tried to remember whether he had been so carefree when he had been a student, and his mind drifted back to his days at university. Then again, he had never had a well-off boyfriend with a house to look after him. He knew that a few of his less-than-genuine acquaintances had made unpleasant noises behind his back: that Nathan should know better; that Scott was on the make, only after Nathan's money; and, perhaps worst of all, that Nathan should look for someone of his own social standing. As far as Nathan was concerned, they could keep their mouths shut and keep their poisonous opinions to themselves.

True, Scott came from a very different background to Nathan's, but what did that matter? Nathan loved Scott, and whether he spent his money on the boy or on himself was his business, and his alone. He'd worked hard to get where he was today, and he fully intended to make the most of life. The incident with John – and the greater fear, that of the Elective – showed that you could never be too careful. Nathan was determined to enjoy every second of his life, and Scott was now a very important part of that life.

The wonderful smell of freshly brewing coffee greeted him as he opened the bedroom door, wafting up the stairs and giving the day a sense of normality that reinforced his earlier thoughts. Bless you, Scott, he thought, walking downstairs and into the living room.

'Just in time!' came a yell. 'I was just about to wake you up.' Scott appeared from the adjoining kitchen, carrying a tray with a full cafetière and two mugs. 'After last night, I thought you deserved to be pampered.'

'Who's this friend, then?' asked Scott, sitting down next to Nathan on the sofa having poured them both coffee. Scott was wearing his T-shirt and his boxer shorts, and Nathan couldn't help stealing a glance at the thick cock and dark bush of hair through the partly open gap.

'What? Oh, Graham. The solicitor.' Nathan sipped his coffee and remembered when they had first met, about five years ago. Nathan had been on the south coast on business, and had spent his dull evenings in the local gay bar. One night his attention had been grabbed by a hard-looking skinhead standing next to him. Eventually, he had engaged him in conversation, and had been quite shocked to discover that he was far from the uneducated thug that Nathan had either expected, or, indeed, hoped. Graham had then been studying for a law degree, but his extracurricular activities were light years from taking the silk: unlike many of the so-called 'gay skins', who Graham would often describe as 'queens with crops', he was a proper skinhead, hanging around with some of the straightest, roughest skins in town.

Nathan had been hooked immediately.

He spent three days with Graham, never venturing out of the hotel in which he was staying. There was no need, and definitely no desire to. Nathan and Graham had each other to occupy themselves.

There was nothing they didn't try, no position they didn't explore. Work was briefly forgotten for those three days, and, when they parted at the end of the week, it felt to Nathan that he and Graham had somehow fitted a lifetime of sexual experimentation into that short but unbelievable period.

Both of them knew that it couldn't last: those three days had been a dream, suspended from the humdrum and the mundane, but they both had real lives to get back to. They swapped phone numbers, but that was the last Nathan expected to see of him. Until circumstance intervened.

Two years ago, Nathan had been in court after one of his investigations had led to the uncovering of a brewery fraud. Not one of his most exciting cases, but one that had brought him the gratitude of a number of pub landlords who had been ripped off. Standing in the public gallery, he had been surprised to see a familiar face next to him, although it had taken him a few seconds to recognise him in a suit and tie: Graham. He was in London with one of his senior partners, who had briefed the prosecuting lawyer.

That night they had got to know each other all over again, and the next morning they both agreed to make it a more regular occurrence. Over the last few years, Graham and Nathan had spent a number of nights – and days, and one memorable weekend – together: enough to keep the excitement there, but not enough for it to become bored or jaded. But there was another side to the relationship: a more mercenary one. Graham's legal knowledge had proved invaluable in a number of Nathan's recent cases, and his contacts meant that Nathan had access to information that other journalists could only dream of.

Which was why he needed to speak to him this morning.

Scott frowned. 'That skinhead one that you've mentioned?'

Nathan could detect the faint trace of jealousy in Scott's voice, but there wasn't time to pacify him. And he also knew that now wasn't the right time to explain his complex relationship with Graham to Scott, deciding that the more intimate details could wait for another time. Besides, he hadn't had sex with Graham since before meeting Scott, so there wasn't any point in making him even more jealous for no reason. 'At the weekend, he's duty solicitor at a police station near Portsmouth. I want him to use his connections to check out our friend John.'

'What good will that do?'

Nathan shrugged. 'I'm not sure. Perhaps he has a criminal record; perhaps there's something to connect him to the Elective. At the very least . . .' He hesitated, not sure whether what he was about to say would make Scott feel even more guilty. Nathan could tell that Scott still felt that he carried some of the blame for the previous evening, but it needed saying, if only for Nathan's peace of mind.

'At the very least, we can get the bastard arrested,' said Scott.

Nathan smiled. 'My thoughts exactly. Anyway, I'll give Graham a ring – see what he suggests.' Nathan got up and picked up his mobile. He caught Scott's puzzled expression. 'Less chance of the Elective tapping a mobile phone,' he explained.

A couple of minutes later, he switched off the phone. 'He's busy at the moment. They'll get him to phone me back.' He laughed. 'Probably up to his neck in paperwork, knowing Graham: work always comes first.'

'Get on your knees and suck it.' Graham stood over the young police constable, his impressive cock hard against his white shirt. The policeman, kneeling on the floor, looked up at him.

'Go on – suck it!' Graham ordered. In the dim light of the station darkroom, the policeman's eyes registered a mixture of shock and longing. After a moment's hesitation, he edged forward on his knees, taking the end of Graham's dick in his mouth and running his tongue around the engorged end. For a second, he seemed reticent, but his desire overtook him and he began to suck greedily.

'That's it, there's a good boy. Take it further – you know you want to, don't you? You want all of that skinhead meat in your mouth, don't you?'

The policeman nodded, straining to swallow all of Graham's seven-inch dick, but his movement was restricted by the handcuffs that chained him to the large developing table. Graham accommodated him by taking a step forward, before brutally forcing his dick even further down the policeman's throat, reaching down and grabbing his short ginger flat-top to make his meaning clear.

When Graham had arrived at the station half an hour ago, PC George had been hanging around the front desk, nervously waiting to speak to him before he went off duty. Graham had had no idea what it was about, and was a bit surprised when the policeman had suggested that they go into the station darkroom to talk about something that was bothering him.

Now Graham knew why. The darkroom could be locked from the inside, and the red light outside ensured that no one would come in and disturb them. And PC George, innocent, chunky PC George, had made it quite clear that he wanted what was inside Graham's trousers. When Graham had suggested using the handcuffs, the policeman had become visibly excited, his big packet straining against the blue of his uniform trousers.

PC George – Hugh – was about five nine, and built like a brick shithouse. Graham knew that he played rugby for the station team, and he had once caught a glimpse of him in the station locker room getting changed: he was solid muscle, and covered all over with a thick thatching of ginger hair. The bulge that Graham had seen in his briefs that time had intrigued him, but he had resigned himself to Hugh being nothing more than a fantasy to wank over – something he had done many, many times.

Now he knew that Hugh felt exactly the same way about him. He glanced down, but the sight of the uniformed man, his mouth full of Graham's thick, blue-veined cock, was nearly enough to make him come. Being sucked off by a policeman was the stuff of fantasies, of books; when he had set off for work that morning, he had never imagined that he would have a hunky cop chained up, begging for sex.

Graham pulled away, feeling his cock spring back against his stomach. 'Get up!' he barked. Hugh got to his feet, his left wrist still chained to the table. Graham unzipped the man's trousers, and stroked the damp cotton of his briefs, feeling the solid, pumping cock beneath them. Graham could see how eager Hugh was for it: apart from the erection, his briefs were soaked with pre-come.

Kneeling down, Graham nuzzled the policeman's groin, drinking in the musky sweat and the salty smell of him. He grabbed Hugh's crotch roughly, pulling at the cotton until the cock was released. And what a cock! Although it wasn't as long as Graham's – about six inches – it was much thicker. Hugh was circumcised, and the big red end was wet with the evidence of his excitement. Graham opened his mouth as widely as he could, but he couldn't manage to get more that the wet, red glans down his throat.

This was enough to satisfy Hugh, though; as Graham's tongue flicked over the warm salty dick, the policeman shuddered and let out a whimper. Graham guessed that Hugh had been telling the truth when he said that this would be his first time: if Graham carried on, even for another few seconds, the policeman would come. And there was no guarantee that he would stay around for a rematch. It was time to slow down the pace.

Letting Hugh's cock slide from his mouth, Graham got to his feet.

'That was good for starters, but I think you need breaking in.' He took a step closer so that his face was only inches away from Hugh's, close enough to feel the hot breath. 'Is that what you want?'

'I . . . I . . . I want to feel you inside me,' Hugh whispered. 'That's all I've been thinking about for weeks.' He gave a shy grin. 'I can't help thinking about you, about doing things with you . . .'

He stopped as Graham grabbed the policeman's belt with both hands and urgently undid it. As soon as it was free, he pulled the uniform trousers to the floor, followed quickly by the white briefs. Hugh's legs were thick and muscular, covered in ginger hair, and his thick cock bobbed between them, unable to rise much above the horizontal because of its weight. Graham gave it a quick wank, but stopped before Hugh could come. He knew that this wasn't going to last very long, but he was determined to draw it out as long as he could.

Moving behind Hugh, he put his hands between the muscular shoulders and pushed him down on to the bench so that his square, stubbly jaw was pressed against the dark wood. Thrusting his hand into his pocket, he pulled out a packet of condoms and a tube of lubricant before pulling down his trousers and pants.

Hugh said nothing; he lay bent over the bench, his whole body taut with anticipation. Graham ran both his hands over the hard, hairy back to relax him, and felt the tightened muscles begin to loosen.

Graham rolled the condom over his dick, aware that it was now so sensitive that it would take only a couple of strokes to bring himself off. Then again, he doubted that Hugh could hold out for long either. He smeared the white lube over the condom before squeezing a sizeable amount over his fingers; he then rubbed it into Hugh's hot, hairy arse, before pushing his finger into the hole. Hugh gasped, but didn't move; Graham continued, thoroughly lubricating Hugh for what he was about to do.

Moving forward, he put one hand on Hugh's back once more, and used his other hand to manoeuvre his dick so that the end just touched Hugh's arse. Then he began to ease himself inside, gently at first. The first inch went in without resistance before hitting the tight muscles of Hugh's sphincter.

'Relax,' he whispered. 'It won't hurt if you let yourself relax.' He pushed a little harder, and felt the opening widen. Within moments, half of his dick was inside Hugh. For a second, Graham wondered whether Hugh would be able to fully relax, but he soon realised this wasn't going to be a problem: the inner muscles opened, and he slid all of his cock inside the policeman.

Hugh growled, but Graham could tell it was with pleasure, the pleasure of feeling another man inside him for the first time. Graham withdrew slightly before plunging in, more roughly, now. Then he pulled out so that only the end of his cock was still inside Hugh.

'Enjoying it?'

'Oh yes – keep going!' Hugh hissed.

Needing no further urging, Graham once more pushed his cock all the way into Hugh, and then assumed a smooth, regular rhythm, placing both hands on Hugh's back to steady himself. He knew that it would only be a matter of minutes before he cold no longer contain himself, but he didn't care. Beneath him, Hugh's breathing was heavy and panting, and his free hand was furiously pulling on his cock.

'Don't stop!' he gasped. 'I want you to come inside me!'

There wasn't any danger of that *not* happening. Only seconds later, Graham felt himself coming, the urge building up from his stomach, causing his balls to clench and his dick to become unimaginably sensitive. His fucking became even harder, even more insistent, and he heard himself grunting in time to his cock thrusting into Hugh's willing arse.

As Graham came, he fell forward on to Hugh's back, which was damp and beaded with sweat. After four hard strokes, he was drained, both physically and mentally, and was only vaguely aware that Hugh's come was splattered over the table.

He pulled his softening dick out of Hugh's arse and removed the condom. Hugh looked round at him, his face red with exertion.

'Was that OK, Constable?' he asked with a smile.

Hugh grinned. 'Better than I ever expected. I . . . I . . .' He suddenly looked embarrassed.

'Go on, what it is?'

'Can we do it again?'

Before Graham could reply, there was a knock on the darkroom door. 'Mr Wilson? Are you in there?' It sounded like WPC Sawyer.

Trying to keep the mixture of amusement and exhaustion out of his voice, Graham answered. 'I've just finished. Is it important?'

'There's a phone message for you,' came the reply.

Once the footsteps died away down the corridor, Graham returned his attention to Hugh. 'I'm tempted to keep you chained up here all morning, but I think that might be what you want.' He leant down and unlocked the handcuffs. As Hugh rubbed his chafed wrist, Graham pulled up his pants and trousers and made himself look presentable.

'If you want to do this again, you know where to find me.'

Hugh nodded. 'Perhaps we can take a bit longer next time?'

Graham laughed, hoping – no, *knowing* – that this was only the beginning. 'Perhaps.'

The moment that Hugh had dressed himself and was back to being PC George, Graham opened the darkroom door and checked his watch. Who was phoning him at ten o'clock on a Saturday morning?'

'Sorry to disturb you at work, Graham, but I need a bit of help.' Nathan was sitting on the sofa with another cup of coffee while Scott showered upstairs. Nathan knew that Scott was due to meet his friend Adrian for lunch, and the events and aftermath of the previous evening had threatened to make him late. Scott had offered to stay, but Nathan was reluctant to involve him any further: the Elective was dangerous, and the less chance they had of getting their hands on Scott the better.

Once he had got through to Graham, he briefly explained what had happened, while the television whispered in the background, the sound turned down. Graham's initial trace of envy when Nathan had described the threesome turned to genuine concern when he spoke about John's subsequent actions.

'So what do you want me to do?' Graham asked.

'Can you find out all you can about John Bury? I've got his address . . .' Nathan trailed off as his eyes caught the television. He grabbed the remote and brought the sound up:

'– has not yet been identified, although this picture – found in the deceased's pocket – has been released by the police. The

85

body was found under bushes in Hyde Park early this morning by a man walking his dog.' The newsreader's voiced droned on over a photograph of a goatee-bearded man standing in a garden. John Bury.

'Nathan? Nathan, are you all right?' Graham's voice seemed to come from a great distance away.

Nathan's voice was quiet as he answered. 'I . . .' He trailed off.

Nathan closed his eyes, unable to separate the images of John in his bed and John as a lifeless body, carelessly hidden so that he could be found. It was a warning. But Nathan knew that he wouldn't call off his crusade.

In some strange, bizarre way, he now owed it to John to bring his murderers to justice. 'They've killed him, Graham,' he whispered. 'The Elective killed him. But why?'

Five

By the time Scott came back downstairs, showered, and dressed in one of Nathan's shirts, Nathan had both regained his composure and decided not to tell Scott about John's death until later. Knowing Scott, it would only increase his feelings of guilt, and there was no point in spoiling the boy's lunch — he was already crucifying himself over what John had done, and to burden him with knowledge of the murder as well seemed almost cruel.

Graham had promised to get back to Nathan as soon as he could, but it had now become a waiting game: waiting for the Elective to make another move, or waiting to find another lead. Nathan had already decided his next step: more research.

'Where are you going for lunch, then?' Nathan asked as Scott put on his jacket. Food was the last thing on Nathan's mind, but he didn't want Scott to suspect that anything more was wrong than he already knew about. He was very glad that Scott would be out of the way for a few hours — just in case.

Scott shrugged. 'I'm not sure, yet. I'm meeting Adrian at twelve.' Nathan had never met Adrian, but he gathered that the two of them had been friends since well before Nathan had met Scott. It would do Scott good to get away from the shadows and the conspiracies for a while, he decided; he wasn't exactly a bundle of fun to be with at the moment.

Nathan got up from the sofa and gave Scott a hug. 'Have a nice time – I'll be thinking of you.' Good words – but Nathan knew that his mind would be elsewhere that afternoon. Somewhere considerably less pleasant than Scott's lunch with Adrian.

'What are you going to do today?'

Nathan gestured towards his computer. 'Nothing as fun as lunch, I'm afraid: some more detective work. There was obviously something specific that John was looking for; something that's very important to the Elective which I must have overlooked.' *Something so important that those bastards killed him for failing to find it.*

Scott kissed him on the lips. 'Well, don't work too hard: I don't want you to wear yourself out. We're supposed to be going out tonight, remember.'

For a second, Nathan didn't remember. Then he recalled that he and Scott had planned to meet up with Neil and Paul in the Crossed Swords. 'I hadn't forgotten,' Nathan half lied. 'I'll see you there about eightish.' After a few drinks, the four of them were planning to go out for a meal.

'Anyway, I'd better go or I'll be late,' said Scott, checking his watch. He reluctantly pulled away from Nathan's embrace and left the house; Nathan watched him through the window before sinking back down on the sofa and burying himself in his thoughts.

Think about this logically, Nate, he thought. He looked in your folders first, but nothing's missing. Then he checked the computer, so it must have been something that you *only* have in electronic format . . . Nathan suddenly realised what it could be – what it *had* to be.

He virtually leapt over to his PC – which was still switched on – and accessed one of his encrypted folders. The folder contained a collection of e-mails that one of his contacts claimed were from the mysterious Comptroller of the Elective to some of his operatives in the field. Only six e-mails had been intercepted before the contact had suddenly fallen silent; originally, Nathan had assumed that the silence was due to the Elective's plugging the electronic hole in their systems. After John's death, he was beginning to think that he'd been a little too naive.

Most of the e-mails were innocuous: invitations to various lunches, functions and speaking engagements. It was clear that the Comptroller led a very busy life in his dark and clandestine world, meeting and greeting some of the most important people in business and commerce. Unfortunately for Nathan, gatecrashing such events was completely out of the question: all of them took place behind locked doors, in exclusive clubs and member-only bars.

But a couple of the e-mails stood out: they seemed to contain nothing but gibberish, strings of numbers and letters in no recognisable sequence. At first, Nathan had dismissed them as errors, computer-generated junk mail proving that even the Elective wasn't perfect. But what if that wasn't the case? What if the e-mails were actually in code?

For a few minutes, Nathan squinted at the seemingly random characters, attempting to see some sort of a pattern, but he soon gave up: code-breaking wasn't among his strong points. Then it hit him: he might not know anything about code-breaking – but Scott did. His degree course definitely included cryptography, because they had talked about it before.

Although time was of the essence, Nathan knew that he wouldn't get a chance to discuss it with Scott until the evening: even if he had wanted to interrupt Scott's lunch, he didn't have the faintest idea where Scott and this Adrian were going after the Crossed Swords.

Shutting down his computer, Nathan decided that further research would be counterproductive: he needed to relax before his head exploded. He knew that he should contact the police about John, but he wanted to hear what Graham had to say first. No, unwinding was the first order of business, and he knew exactly where he wanted to go: for a swim. It might be boring, but from what Scott said, he wasn't expecting his lunch to be a thrill a minute either.

Scott was on his knees, Adrian's cock firmly in his mouth.

'Go on, boy, take it all,' Adrian ordered. 'I want you to take that cock all the way down your throat.' Scott pushed his face further into Adrian's crotch, swallowing as much of the thick uncut dick as he could.

The tall, blond man was wearing his heavy leather harness with a biker's jacket over the top: the harness showed off his muscular body, with his well-defined pecs, pierced nipples and smooth chest. He wasn't wearing trousers: the only other item of clothing was a pair of black leather biker's boots, polished until they shone. Scott was wearing an identical harness to Adrian's and nothing else. That was all that he deserved to wear.

'That's enough for now.' Adrian pulled his dick out of Scott's mouth, and it slapped against his firm stomach. 'Now, down on the floor. I want you to clean those boots.'

Scott got down on all fours and started licking the shiny black leather, beginning with the toecaps and then dragging his tongue over the eyelets and up the sides. His own cock was pressed against the white carpet, and his attention to Adrian's boots was causing it to rub backward and forward, sending shivers of pleasure through him. He soon became worried that he would have to stop in case he came: if he came without being ordered to do so, he risked Adrian's anger – and that wasn't something he wanted. But stopping licking Adrian's boots would be just as bad: Adrian was his master, and Scott wouldn't dare to do anything without Adrian's express authority.

But Adrian was too familiar with Scott's body. Even as the feelings of orgasm started to grow in his cock and balls, Adrian grabbed him by the back of the harness and pulled him to his feet.

'You must be very close now, boy. Don't want to you to come too quickly, do we?' Still holding on to his harness, he dragged him over to the white leather couch.

'Kneel down.'

Scott knelt on the sofa, grabbing the back for support. His cock felt like it was going to explode, but he tried to hold back the feelings. The trouble was, he knew what was about to happen – and he didn't know how long he could hold out once Adrian's thick cock was inside him.

Adrian didn't ease himself into Scott – he forced himself, grunting as he pulled Scott's arse apart and pushed his cock into Scott's waiting hole. Scott groaned with both the pain of entry and the pleasure of having his master inside him.

'Good boy,' Adrian whispered, sliding his cock further and further in until Scott felt his balls slap against his arse. Adrian was never gentle – that wasn't his way. But Scott accepted that, Scott wanted that: that was the arrangement they had.

Once Adrian was completely inside Scott, he tightened his grip on Scott's shoulders and began to withdraw his dick until it was almost out – then he thrust it back in roughly, causing Scott to grimace. Even Adrian wasn't normally this brutal, this . . . unfeeling. Scott guessed that his master was worried about something, but Adrian's life outside of their regular afternoon sessions was a forbidden subject.

'That's it, take it all!' Adrian said gutturally, forcing his way into Scott. Despite the pain, Scott could feel his erection rubbing against the leather of the sofa; he could feel his master's balls hitting his arse; he could feel the thickness of Adrian's cock reaching right up inside him. Adrian's groans became deeper, in time with each thrust, and Scott guessed that his master was as close to coming as he was.

Taking a risk, he abandoned himself to the feelings that were welling up inside him, and actively rubbed his stiff cock against the soft white leather. As he did, Adrian fucked him harder and harder, the rhythm quicker, more urgent, his groans more and more insistent.

'That's it, boy, go on!' he yelled, before fucking Scott deeper and harder than he had ever done. That was all that Scott needed: with a groan of his own, he felt his orgasm explode, and saw the creamy gouts of come spurt over the leather of the sofa.

At the same time, he sensed Adrian's cock shooting inside him, felt his panting breath in his ear. Two more deep fucks, and Adrian slumped on to Scott's back, exhausted.

'I needed that,' he whispered. 'Thanks.'

Scott was puzzled: normally, even after they had both come, their master–slave relationship would continue until Adrian said the code word. It was clear that he was really worried about something.

Well, if Adrian was prepared to break with tradition, so was Scott. Moving round from underneath Adrian, he sat cross-legged on the floor, the end of his dick just touching the carpet.

'Is everything OK?' he asked.

Adrian sighed. 'Business problems, Scott. I'm having trouble with one of my . . . my business rivals, and it's bothering me.' He shrugged. 'Still, business is business, and this is pleasure. How are things going between you and this Nathan?'

Scott smiled. 'Fine . . .' For a second, he considered confiding in Adrian, telling him about the incident with John. But Adrian was one part of his life, and Nathan was another: Adrian was sex, and sex alone, and Nathan offered the emotional support that he needed. 'No, things are fine.'

Scott had met Adrian about three months previously at the Harness, and what had started out as faceless sex in the back room had developed into a regular sexual relationship. When Scott had started seeing Nathan, he had considered stopping his sessions with Adrian, but Adrian – and his chequebook – had proved very persuasive. Initially, Scott had felt a little guilty, but he reasoned that his time with Adrian was purely physical; besides, they were separate parts of his life, and he intended to keep them that way. Adrian knew all about Nathan – indeed, he had actually heard of the Elective, and showed quite a keen interest in Nathan's investigation – but had assured Scott that he wouldn't interfere. And the money that Adrian gave him did mean that he didn't have to rely on Nathan as much as he might.

Adrian got up and wandered over to the huge mahogany desk which dominated the lounge. 'I'm going to give you a bit extra this week. There's something I want you to do.'

Scott joined him at the desk. 'Like what?'

'I need to go on a business trip next week: to New York. And I'd like you to come with me. It's only for a week.'

Scott couldn't help grinning. The furthest he'd ever been had been a weekend trip to Amsterdam and a week in Spain: but New York! Then the practicalities took over: a week in New York meant a week off his course, but that wasn't really a problem. The problem was Nathan: how could Scott explain that he was spending a week in New York with his weekly sex master?

'You're worried about what to say to Nathan, aren't you?' said Adrian.

Scott shrugged. 'It's going to be awkward.'

Adrian raised an eyebrow. 'Actually, it won't be. Nathan won't be in the country either.'

Scott was confused. He wasn't aware that Nathan was planning to go away, so how was Adrian? 'I don't understand.'

'You've told me that Nathan is trying to find information about this mysterious Elective. As it happens, I've managed to find out a few things about it myself.' He shuddered. 'Nasty organisation – too secretive for my liking. Anyway, I'm about to send Nathan this information – from an anonymous site, so he won't be able to trace me. After he receives it, I can assure you that he'll be catching the next available plane to Amsterdam – and that's only the start. I guess he'll be away for about two weeks – which leaves you free to come to the States with me.'

Scott was uneasy. Weekly sex sessions were one thing, but going on holiday? That was a level of deceit about which he wasn't sure he felt comfortable.

Adrian must have sensed his unease. His poise, his body language, changed. 'On your knees, boy: I've told you you're coming to New York with me, and you don't want to let your master down, do you?' Scott could see that Adrian's erection had returned, and felt his own doing the same. Suddenly, his guilt over going to the States evaporated: Adrian offered him something that Nathan couldn't.

Sex without responsibility.

Without prompting, Scott sank to his knees and took his master's cock in his mouth.

Nathan pulled himself out of the pool and wiped the water from his eyes. The forty lengths had been just what he needed to clear his head slightly, and he was feeling, if not relaxed, then more prepared to deal with the machinations of the Elective.

He stood on the poolside for a few moments, catching his breath, and looked around. For a Saturday, the pool was remarkably quiet, with only about four other people sharing the water with him. Although Nathan had been somewhat preoccupied, he couldn't help noticing the man who had entered the pool about ten minutes after he did. He had gingery-brown hair, cut quite short, and a well-kept but bushy ginger moustache, and Nathan found that he couldn't help staring at him. Each time that Nathan had passed him, his sweet-looking face had been rapt with concentration, but he had always smiled if he noticed Nathan swimming towards him.

Nathan was suddenly aware that the man was climbing out

of the other side of the pool, allowing him to get a much better look. He must have been a couple of inches taller than Nathan, and slightly broader, with a wide, solid chest, and a small amount of gingery-brown hair around his nipples. Nathan guessed that he was in his late twenties.

As he walked past Nathan on his way to the changing rooms, his smile became a broad grin, wrinkling his nose and making his eyes sparkle. Nathan could feel the beginnings of an erection in his trunks, and decided that he didn't really have much choice but to go into the changing rooms as well. The sensible part of his mind explained it away rationally: *You don't want the others in the pool to see you with a hard-on, do you Nate?* But there was another, more persuasive voice: *Hurry – you might get to see a little more of this hunk!* Thankfully, both voices were in agreement that he should get to the changing rooms as quickly as possible: and who was he to argue with his better judgment?

When he reached the changing rooms, he was delighted to see that they were empty, apart from the man and himself. Nathan made his way to his locker and opened it with the key that was attached to the rubber wristband he'd been wearing, trying to see where the hunk's locker was. Unfortunately, he was right behind Nathan, so Nathan had no choice but to retrieve his clothing from the locker and turn round.

The hunk was about three feet away, his massive hard-on thick inside his green trunks. The grin on his face made it quite clear that he was thinking the same thing as Nathan was.

Except that Nathan was suddenly unsure. Although he and Scott had never spoken about the boundaries of their relationship, Nathan hadn't had sex with anyone else since they had started seeing each other. Whether Scott was, Nathan didn't know: it wasn't something that you could gently bring into a conversation, was it?

But instinct was stronger. He knew that his own erection was as obvious as the hunk's, and, before he could even really think about what he was doing, he reached out and grabbed the firm cock through the thin fabric of the trunks. The man grinned.

'You obviously had the same idea,' he said in a quiet Irish accent. His hand began to stroke Nathan's dick, making his erection even harder. 'Nice big dick: can't wait to get my mouth round it.'

Nathan didn't say anything; he just pulled the Irishman's dick out of his trunks and was very pleased by what he saw. It was about six inches in length and thick, with a red helmet almost completely covered with foreskin. Nathan gave it a slow, tentative wank, pulling the skin back to reveal the shiny head.

'What d'you want to do?' asked the Irishman, taking Nathan's cock out and rubbing a finger over the helmet, still wet from the pool. Nathan gasped with the sensation. What he wanted to do was get down and suck the man until he shot in his mouth or turn him round and screw him, but neither seemed very sensible in the far-too-accessible changing rooms. Then he remembered the rarely used communal area at the far end of the room: a throwback to the old days of school expeditions to the pool. Now there were no school expeditions – there weren't any schools nearby – but the communal area was still there.

Motioning for the Irishman to follow him, Nathan made a vain attempt to hide his erection in his trunks before treading across the wet tiles towards the blue-painted plasterboard which separated the communal area.

He opened the door and peered inside: as he had expected, it was empty. In fact, it didn't look as if anyone had set foot inside it for weeks, with its dry and dusty floor.

He urged the other man to come in after him, before closing the door and quietly pulling the bolt across. The walls of the communal area were thin, but they stretched from floor to ceiling without a gap for prying eyes.

'I'm Nathan,' he whispered.

'Brian,' said the other, reaching out and pulling Nathan's trunks down without hesitation. Nathan's hard-on, which had temporarily subsided, took seconds to come back to attention, standing stiffly against his stomach.

'My, that's a nice cock you've got there,' said Brian, sitting down on the low bench which ran round three sides of the room. He pulled Nathan towards him so that his cock was level with his mouth, before leaning forward and licking Nathan's helmet with the tip of his tongue.

'That feels good,' said Nathan, 'really good.'

Brian continued licking, moving his tongue around so that it flicked over the whole head. At the same time, his hand reached up and sought Nathan's right nipple through the thatch of damp black hair and squeezed it tightly. Nathan gasped with the mixture of pain and sheer pleasure, and returned the favour, stroking Brian's chest until he found both nipples. He ran his fingers through the light dusting of hair before grabbing both nipples and squeezing, gently at first, trying to gauge how much Brain wanted. As Nathan continued to squeeze, Brian groaned softly, and Nathan wondered whether he was being too rough. But the look in his big green eyes made it clear that he enjoyed the action as much as Nathan did. Obviously Brian could take a lot of this.

As Brian carried on licking, Nathan began to feel impatient: even though Brian's blow job was really turning him on, Nathan wanted to take the big Irishman's cock in his mouth and return the favour. Brian began to take more of Nathan's cock, filling his mouth with the thick shaft until it was touching the back of his throat. Nathan knew that he wouldn't be able to last out too long if Brian deep-throated him, so he gently pulled his cock out, feeling the bristles of Brian's moustache tickle him as he drew his shaft past it.

'My turn,' he muttered, lifting Brian to his feet and taking his position on the bench, taking off Brian's trunks as he did so. Brian's cock was even thicker than it had been earlier, and, for a second, Nathan wondered whether he would be able to accommodate it. But his desire to do so outweighed his worries, and he slipped his mouth over the large head, tasting the salty pre-come as he did so. Carefully, he eased his lips further and further over the shaft until he couldn't swallow any more of it, before slowly moving his mouth backward and forward, ensuring that his lips and tongue caressed the helmet.

From the sighs and gasps that came from Brian, Nathan could tell that he was enjoying it. Nathan's hand slipped between his legs and grabbed his dick, which he started to wank in time to the blow job; he knew that this couldn't last for long.

This time, it was Brian's turn to pull away, leaving a string of clear fluid between his helmet and Nathan's mouth. Nathan licked his lips and swallowed it.

'I want you to fuck me,' hissed the Irishman.

Nathan shook his head. As much as he wanted to, it was clear that neither of them had any condoms on them, and Nathan was unwilling to shatter the moment by going back to his locker. 'Not now.'

Brian shrugged: obviously it wasn't too big a deal to him. 'OK, let's try this.' He lay down on the bench, and gestured for Nathan to lie next to him. The bench was just wide enough to take both of them – especially if Nathan lay with his head to Brian's cock, and Brian reciprocated.

After a couple of seconds of manoeuvring, they were in position. Nathan took Brian's cock in his mouth once again, and could feel Brian's warm mouth and bushy moustache surround his own. Nathan moved his right hand so that his fingers were stroking Brian's anus, the hot ring almost lost in a forest of damp hair. He extended a finger, and pushed it into Brian without any resistance. The Irishman tensed slightly, and Nathan was sure that his cock became even harder in his mouth. Then Brian started to suck Nathan harder and harder, his rhythm increasing until Nathan knew he was close to coming.

But so was Brian: Nathan was concentrating on Brian's helmet, licking and sucking it, well aware of the tightening of Brian's balls. Just as Nathan knew he couldn't stop himself, he pushed his finger even further up Brian's arse and felt the Irishman's body go rigid: as his arse muscles gripped tightly on to Nathan's finger, Nathan's mouth was suddenly full of hot salty fluid, shooting against the back of his throat. Even as Nathan struggled to swallow it, he allowed himself to let go, and thrust his cock violently into Brian's mouth, pumping his load down his throat. Three, four spasms later, and Nathan knew that he was drained, but Brian made no move: he just lay on the bench, his tongue gently stroking Nathan's softening dick. Nathan did the same, running his tongue around the ridge of Brian's helmet, drinking every last drop of his spunk. He felt so relaxed, so calm. The swim had started the job, but Brian had managed exactly what Nathan had wanted: he had taken his mind off the Elective.

Just before Nathan started to doze, he pulled himself away from Brian and sat up on the bench.

'You're good,' said Brian, throwing a hairy arm around Nathan's shoulders. 'Fancy coming back to my place?'

The offer was tempting — perhaps too tempting. Nathan estimated that it was about three o'clock, and he wasn't due at the Crossed Swords until eight. But he wanted to hear from Graham, and that meant he really had to go home.

'Sorry, Brian — I've got to get home. Things to sort out.'

'Fair enough: d'you want my number, though?'

Nathan grinned. 'You bet.'

Nathan was shattered by the time he reached his house; the swim had been demanding enough, but the added exertion of Brian had been an unexpected and exhausting bonus. He had taken the Irishman's phone number, but wasn't exactly sure what to do with it. His mind had already started to justify his actions to assuage the slight pangs of guilt that he felt.

You were screwed up over John, he thought, and your judgment was off-centre; you needed sex without responsibility.

Somehow, it didn't make him feel any more comfortable with what he had done. Should he tell Scott? He was sure that the sex-without-responsibility approach wouldn't go down too well, but how could he explain that he had spent the afternoon sucking off some big Irishman?

With these thoughts battling away in his head, he let himself into the house, aware that he suddenly felt uneasy. Nathan had always been an Englishman's-home-is-his-castle type of guy, and John's violation the previous night had hurt him deeply. He stood in the living room and studied it carefully, noting the position of every piece of furniture, every ornament, everything. For a full minute, he made a mental comparison between the room now and the room when he had left it a few hours earlier: only when he was certain that nothing had moved did he allow himself to relax.

There were no messages on his answering machine, but the expected message from Graham wouldn't have been left there; Graham knew as well as he did how insecure that would be. Nor had there been a message on his mobile phone: so when was Graham going to get back to him?

Come on, Nate, he thought: what do you expect – miracles? Graham's good, but you've effectively asked him to hack into the police central computer. Be reasonable – give him a chance.

Realising that his impatience was going to wind him up he carried on thinking in that vein, he wandered into the kitchen and poured himself a beer from the fridge.

He had only just sat down when the doorbell rang. Looking through the spyhole, he was both surprised and pleased to see that Graham was standing there.

Opening the door, he invited Graham in. 'I didn't expect a personal visit,' Nathan said, hanging up Graham's green bomber jacket.

'Some things are too important to say over the phone,' Graham replied. 'And besides, I thought you might want some company.' Graham had obviously changed out of his working clothes – somehow, the suit and tie that the police expected their duty solicitors to wear never looked right on him. But his current outfit, well . . .

Graham was wearing a white Fred Perry polo shirt, with red braces holding up a pair of bleach-splashed drainpipe jeans. The jeans stopped at his ankles, revealing twelve hole cherry-red Doc Martens. Graham smiled. 'So, here I am.'

Nathan grabbed him and hugged him tightly. 'I'm really glad to see you. Looking as sexy as ever.'

'Flatterer.' But there was definitely something about Graham that never failed to turn Nathan on. Whether it was the very short crop – virtually stubble – or the big, dopey-looking eyes, or the fact that sex with Graham was undoubtedly some of the best Nathan had ever had, Nathan didn't know. He did know that it was all he could do not to get down on his knees and start licking Graham's boots.

After pouring Graham a beer, Nathan sat down on the sofa opposite him.

'How are you feeling?' Graham asked.

Nathan shrugged. 'Not sure. I think I'm still slightly in shock.'

'That's hardly surprising.'

'I know: an attempted burglary *and* a murder.'

Graham raised an eyebrow. 'No: I meant that someone would want to have sex with you in the first place,' he said with an evil grin.

'Bastard.' Graham's gallows humour was legendary among his friends: legendary and necessary. Some of the cases he had had to deal with had been quite horrific, and only Graham's ability to laugh them off enabled him to cope. 'Anyway, what did you find out?'

Graham chewed his bottom lip. 'Nothing.'

'What? There must have been something, surely.'

'Nothing. Which is actually something in itself.'

Nathan shook his head. 'I'm sorry: you've lost me there. How can nothing be something?'

'Because,' explained Graham with the patience one would usually use with a five-year-old, 'there should have been something. You gave me the full name and address off his driver's licence, didn't you?'

'Yes — it's locked away in the skirting board safe upstairs.' Along with the rest of my files, he thought ruefully. Nothing like shutting the stable door after the horse has not only bolted, but been caught and boiled down into glue as well.

'So there should have been something: even if it was just a link into the DVLA computer. But there wasn't anything. As if—'

'As if he'd been deliberately erased,' Nathan completed. The whole investigation into the Elective had started with people disappearing; Nathan knew that he really shouldn't be surprised when it happened under his very nose.

He sighed deeply, a sigh of frustration and barely restrained anger. 'I should have guessed something like this would happen. I should have guessed.'

Six

Nathan shook his head, rattled by the fact that his usually logical, rational outlook had been so badly dented. 'Sorry, Graham – I'm being stupid. Of course the Elective can make people disappear: that's why I'm after them. I'm still a bit shaken up over John, I suppose.' He took a sip of his beer before whistling through his teeth. 'It's just so difficult to comprehend: the idea that everything about a person can just vanish.'

Graham leant forward on the sofa towards him and smiled reassuringly. 'Not quite everything, Nathan. I would have been here sooner, but I made a quick detour via my old offices.'

'Is that where you got changed?' said Nathan with a slight grin, his temper coming back to an even keel.

'Nah, no room to get changed there – the High Court judges were all putting their dresses and high heels on. Anyway,' he continued, his tone indicating that Nathan really shouldn't interrupt again, 'there are other records apart from computers: something which a lot of people in our technologically advanced age tend to forget.' He pulled out a sheet of paper from his back pocket. 'I'm guessing that the Elective purged as much as they could electronically – the police computers, the DVLA, the Inland Revenue – but neglected to look in certain dusty old box files hidden away in solicitors' offices.

'Five years ago, a certain Mr John Bury was arrested for soliciting: he'd been selling his arse down Piccadilly, got into a spot of bother with a punter who refused to pay, and ended up in the cells. Simple case of buggery. But then he was bailed out by a Mr Delancey who lived in Bayswater. Subsequently, all charges were mysteriously dropped.'

'Delancey, Delancey . . .' Nathan frowned. The name was familiar – very familiar. 'Of course!' He slapped his forehead. 'That name keeps cropping up in relation to the Elective. It's one of the pseudonyms of the Comptroller!'

Graham whistled through his teeth. 'As a solicitor, I should point out that this wouldn't stand up as evidence in a court of law, but it does suggest that your Mr Bury was somehow linked to the Elective.'

Nathan had to agree. 'And linked quite closely, if the Comptroller himself bailed him out. I don't suppose that the address in Bayswater checked out, did it?' Suddenly the chains of deceit and lies that had beset this case from the outset were beginning to unravel. For the first time since John's death, Nathan began to think clearly again.

Graham shook his head. 'What do you think? Nobody called Delancey had ever lived there. Then again, if he was the Comptroller, he could have given an address on the Moon and the police would have accepted it – the Elective's got more clout than the Freemasons, Nathan.'

'Oh well, worth a try.' Nathan sighed, and sank back into the sofa. 'Thanks for that, Graham – I really appreciate it.'

Graham winked. 'Any time. What are friends for?' He started stroking the long bulge which ran down his thigh. 'Fancy returning the favour?'

For a second, Nathan said nothing. Sex with Graham had always been magnificent, but that was before Scott had come on to the scene. Even though he had managed to just about bury his guilt over Brian at the baths, Graham was different: it would come across as being premeditated, especially since Nathan and Graham had a history together. But Nathan's body had different ideas: he could feel his erection growing, and any potential guilt began to rapidly subside, pushed to one side by his desire for Graham's fit skinhead body and thick skinhead dick.

Graham could tell that Nathan was dithering: he knew him well enough to read him like a book. He also knew him well enough to know all the techniques to persuade him to oblige. Standing up, Graham came over to Nathan and grabbed his head, grinding Nathan's face into his crotch and preventing him from moving away. But moving away was the last thing on Nathan's mind.

Nathan could smell Graham: the thick, musky smell of sweat and sex that he always had around him – the smell that Nathan associated with long weekends in hotel rooms, each of them exploring every inch of the other's body. As the memories came flooding back to him, any last doubts vanished: his mouth licked the rough, stained denim, brushing against the warm thickness that lay rigid against Graham's thigh. Then he pulled away slightly, and grabbed Graham's white polo shirt, forcing him down, forcing him to kneel in front of him, before kissing him roughly, pushing his tongue into his mouth and overcoming any resistance.

To ensure Graham's participation, Nathan put his hand on the back of Graham's head, stroking the bristles of his crew cut. But Graham didn't resist: his own tongue fought back, intertwining with Nathan's, while his hands stroked Nathan's back, roughly, brutally.

As one, they stood, Nathan's arms around Graham. They hugged, feeling the closeness and the intimacy that they both remembered so well, their hard-ons squeezed together, rubbing and exciting each other. Nathan pulled back and looked at Graham.

'We shouldn't be doing this, you know,' he said, knowing exactly how lame it sounded. It was blatantly obvious how much Nathan wanted to do it, how much he wanted Graham. *You've already done it once today,* came the little voice. *A second time won't make any difference.*

Graham nodded, but the mischievous grin on his face made it quite clear that he had no intention of stopping now. 'I know. But you and me go back to before Scott. And besides – you need someone now.'

Nathan had to agree. Brian had been fun, but Nathan needed the intimate history that Graham offered. Scott could have offered it, but it would have been coloured – tainted – by John's death. With Graham, he knew what he was getting, he knew what to expect. Reaching out, he stroked Graham's erection, his fingers running up from the tip, along the shaft, and finally arriving at the zip of his flies. His hands were trembling with anticipation as he pulled the zip down and squeezed his hand inside the white boxer shorts. Graham let out a small cry of pleasure as Nathan's fingers touched the warm flesh of his cock.

'It's been a long time since we've done this,' he said.

'Too long,' agreed Nathan, wondering how he could have stayed away from the skinhead solicitor for more than a day, let alone the three or four months it had been since they had last enjoyed each other. He took his hand from Graham's jeans and pulled on his braces, slipping them over his shoulders. Then he undid the single button and pulled the jeans down.

Unrestrained, Graham's thick, veined cock sprang free from his boxers, the foreskin fully withdrawn to show all of the glistening red helmet. Nathan started to kneel so that he could taste Graham's cock once again, but Graham stopped him.

'Let's go upstairs,' he said. 'I want to make this a bit more special.' Graham had a wicked look on his face, and Nathan knew that he couldn't resist. 'Game for it?'

Nathan raised an eyebrow. 'What do you think? Anyway, what did you have in mind?' He wanted to make it special too, but didn't know what Graham wanted. It didn't matter: at that moment, whatever it was was exactly what he wanted as well.

Pulling his trousers up, Graham walked over to his bomber jacket and reached into the pocket. When Nathan saw what he had retrieved, he couldn't help smiling. 'Where the hell did you get those from?' he asked. It was clear that he and Graham were on the same wavelength that afternoon.

Graham tapped his nose. 'Let's just say that I was helping the police with their enquiries.'

Holding the four sets of handcuffs, he gestured for them both to go upstairs.

Scott sat in the coffee bar, nursing his second cappuccino and wondering what to do. Until now, his regular afternoons with Adrian had been a bit of fun: sex with no strings attached and some beer money for his trouble. He managed to clear it with his conscience by saying that it was a business arrangement that he had entered into a long while before he and Nathan had ever met, but he knew deep down that that was a shallow excuse that he didn't really believe – but until now he had been able to live with it.

But now? Now he was being asked to take the deceit one stage further, to travel to New York with Adrian and not tell Nathan. Fair enough, Adrian seemed convinced that Nathan himself would be out of the country, but how much fun could a trip to the States be if he couldn't discuss it with his own boyfriend afterwards? It was clear that Adrian wouldn't take no for an answer.

Sighing, he sipped his cappuccino and lit another cigarette. Why did life have to be so complicated?

★ ★ ★

Graham and Nathan stood in the bedroom, their clothes removed. Both had taken especial care not to touch each other, even though that was exactly what they both wanted – no, longed – to do. But the whole point of the exercise was so that they could reach absolute arousal and excitement before the fun really started.

Completely naked, they stood about two feet apart, gazing at each other's body, thinking about everything they had done with one another, everything they *could* do with each other. Nathan's erection was harder, more insistent, than he could remember it being for a very long time; he felt so turned on that he wondered how long he would be able to hold out once Graham's hands started exploring his body.

He stared at Graham. He was of medium build, with a flat stomach and a smooth, reasonably muscled chest. His cock wasn't quite as big as Nathan's, about seven inches, but it was thicker, and his erection was hard enough to make it stand almost against his stomach. Just looking at it made Nathan want to come there and then.

'I want you to fuck me,' hissed Nathan. 'I want all of you inside me.'

Graham grasped his cock. 'You want all of this skinhead meat inside you?' he said roughly, assuming the vicious, violent persona that he knew Nathan found irresistible. 'You want this skinhead cock in your arse? You want this skinhead on your back, fucking you?'

It was all that Nathan could do to hold back his load. A weak 'yeah' was all he could manage. Being fucked by Graham was something he had wanked over for years, but it had never happened. Until now, it seemed.

'Get on the bed,' Graham ordered. 'On your back.'

Nathan obeyed, lying on the blue duvet, his arms spread outward, his legs apart. He knew what was about to happen, and he couldn't wait.

Graham picked up the handcuffs from the floor and attached

them in turn. Two sets were locked around Nathan's wrists, and then attached to the top bedposts. The other two were placed around his ankles before being locked on to the bottom posts.

Nathan lay there, unable to move, unable to touch either himself or Graham.

Graham got on to the bed and knelt over him, before forcing his tongue into Nathan's mouth. For a couple of seconds he kissed him roughly; then he drew his tongue down Nathan's chin, down his neck, through the thick black chest hairs and further, towards his stomach. Carefully, he avoided Nathan's engorged dick, apart from a teasing flick of the tongue that ran over Nathan's helmet and made him arch his back with the sensation.

Finally, his tongue slid between Nathan's thighs, before he ran it up and down the sensitive spot between his balls and his arse. All the while, Nathan writhed, unable to move far because of his restraints.

Finally, Graham pulled back. Unwrapping a condom, he rolled it on to his thick, veined cock; grabbing the tube of lubricant, he squeezed out a generous amount, which he divided between his cock and Nathan's hot, eager hole. Nathan winced at the cold of the lube as Graham rubbed it up and around his arse.

'Are you ready for this?' asked Graham in a low, urgent voice. 'Are you ready for this skinhead dick inside you?'

Nathan couldn't reply: his eyes were fixed on Graham's huge cock. Anal sex was one thing that they had never tried, but Nathan had always fantasised about having Graham inside him, and had wondered what it would feel like to have a cock that thick entering him. He was about to find out, and all he could do was nod.

Graham moved Nathan so that his legs were apart and his arse was more accessible. Then he manoeuvred himself so that his helmet was just touching Nathan's ring.

'Ready for this skinhead dick?' he growled.

'I want you to fuck me,' said Nathan. 'I want that skinhead dick inside me.' He looked up at the cropped hair and the violent expression and knew that he wanted it more than anything. He could almost imagine that Graham was a bit of rough that he had picked up, a dirty little bastard who was going to fuck him like he was just a piece of meat.

'Right – you're going to get it.'

Nathan felt the tip of Graham's hard-on enter him, and relaxed himself as much as he could. Even so, he had to grit his teeth as more and more of Graham's dick slid inside. The pain began to increase as Graham's thickness penetrated him, forcing his muscles apart, and it was all that Nathan could do not to cry out.

Suddenly the hurt stopped, giving way to an amazing feeling of fullness and contentment. He could feel Graham's cock inside him, filling him up, and the sensation was wonderful. His own erection, which had slightly subsided as Graham had entered him, returned almost immediately.

'Now I'm going to fuck you like the dirty little bastard you really are,' Graham spat, mirroring Nathan's own thoughts. 'You want that, don't you? You deserve to be fucked.'

'Oh yes,' said Nathan. 'I deserve it. I'm a dirty little bastard and I deserve it.'

Graham started to pull his cock out, and Nathan felt a slight twinge of pain. He guessed that Graham had withdrawn about half of his seven inches before he slid it back inside, even further than he had before. Even that slight discomfort vanished, replaced by a warmth and a pleasure that almost overwhelmed him.

Graham's cock continued to slide in and out, touching Nathan deep inside and bringing him closer and closer to orgasm. From the enraptured look on Graham's face, it was clear that Graham was in a similar situation: even if they had wanted to hold off, it wasn't an option. Graham's breathing grew heavier, and a thin sheen of sweat broke out over his chest and shoulders.

Then Nathan felt it: the stirrings of his orgasm, but magnified into a sensation that he had never experienced before. Almost before he realised what was happening, something he could only describe as an explosion of ecstasy burst within him: gouts of come spurted from his engorged cock, splashing on to his chest as white droplets against the thatch of black hair. He was desperate to touch his cock, but that desperation seemed to intensify his orgasm even further.

As he stared at his twitching hard-on, he was aware of a deep growl: suddenly he realised it was his own voice, crying out with the pleasure. Then it was joined by another scream of pleasure: Graham came inside him, and Nathan could feel Graham's cock throbbing within him. Nathan pushed down on it, forcing it even further inside him and making Graham's cries even louder.

'That's it,' Nathan grunted. 'Keep coming inside me. Shoot inside me.'

Graham gave one final scream of enjoyment before roughly pulling his cock from Nathan's arse and collapsing on top of him, smearing Nathan's come on to his chest as he did so. His breathing was heavy as he placed his mouth on Nathan's and kissed him with a gentleness that belied the urgency and brutality of earlier.

Nathan grinned. 'I'm not going to ask you what you had to do to get these handcuffs, but whatever it was, it was worth it.'

Scott didn't know what the time was, and cared even less: he found himself wandering through Piccadilly Circus, virtually oblivious to the bright neon signs and the bustle and noise of tourists all around him. Hands in pockets and head bowed, his mind was far away from the busy heart of the West End, full of people heading off to clubs or shows on a winter's Saturday night. Happy people, people free of the guilt that was threatening to crush him.

Nathan. What was he going to tell Nathan?

All he could think about was his boyfriend, and the way he was planning to deceive him. Nathan had always been honest with him, Scott felt sure; how would he react if he ever found out about Adrian? Because, if the truth about the States came out, the rest of it would come tumbling after: the whole story about the Saturday afternoons, the Wednesday nights, the 'business transactions' ... What had seemed like fun, an enjoyable way of supplementing his grant, was suddenly something sordid and unclean, something to be ashamed of. He felt sure that that was how Nathan would see it: that he was nothing more than a high-class rent boy. He'd be horrified and disgusted, and, when it was put that way, Scott couldn't blame him.

'Scott?'

Scott looked around in confusion at the mention of his name, and realised that Neil and Paul were standing a few feet away, just in front of the statue of Eros. He instinctively glanced at his watch and was shocked to see that it was almost eight o'clock: it was time to meet Nathan.

Time to face the music.

'We're all running a bit late tonight, I see,' said Neil, who was wearing his usual green bomber jacket over a white T-shirt and faded blue jeans. 'Nathan'll be furious if we don't get a move on.'

Matching step, the three of them headed towards Leicester Square.

'So,' began Paul, 'What have you been up to today?' Scott knew that it was an innocuous comment, a friendly enquiry intended to break the ice, but, to his guilty conscience, it sounded like the beginnings of the Spanish Inquisition. He tried to keep his voice calm and level as he replied.

'Saw a friend for lunch, then just mooched around for the rest of the afternoon. Nothing, really.'

'Where did you go for lunch?'

'Mezzo's,' he replied instinctively: one of his better-rehearsed lies, one that he had used to Nathan on the few occasions when he had asked about Scott's lunches with Adrian. Thankfully, he had been to Mezzo's – both Adrian and Nathan had taken him there – so he was able to elaborate on the meal without slipping up. The rest of the walk to the Crossed Swords was spent with a discussion of the menu, which soon spilt over into a discussion of Soho cuisine in general, with all three of them proposing their favourite restaurants, only to have their choices shot down by one of the others, who could give at least three good reasons why his favoured haunt was better.

By the time they reached the black smoked glass of the Crossed Swords, Scott had managed to relax sufficiently in Paul and Neil's company that his self-control had almost returned, and he wasn't afraid of blurting everything out the moment he saw Nathan. As they entered the bar, he made his mind up: he would have a few drinks, they would go for the meal, and he would explain everything when they got back to Nathan's. It was the only way that he could assuage his conscience. He just hoped that Nathan would understand the situation – the mess – into which Scott had managed to get himself.

The Crossed Swords was busy – as busy as it always was on a Saturday night, with a queue three deep at the bar and people pressed close to one another. Even so, Scott caught sight of Nathan the moment they walked in: he was standing in his usual position by the DJ's box. *The same position he was when you first met him. Before you started to betray him*, came the spiteful inner voice. Ignoring it, he realised that Neil was talking to him.

'Your usual, Scott?'

Scott nodded, and left Paul and Neil at the bar while he walked over to Nathan. As soon as he got within a couple of yards of him, he could see that something was wrong: Nathan's face was drawn into a heavy frown, as if he were carrying some terrible emotional burden.

You've been rumbled, came the voice. *He knows what you've been doing.* It was all that Scott could do not to shake as he approached him.

Feigning normality, he grinned and reached out for him.

'Hi!' Scott said affectionately, and gave Nathan a hug. But he could feel the tension in his boyfriend's back: the muscles were knotted. Without thinking, without preparing, he asked. 'What is it?'

Nathan sighed. 'We need to talk, Scott. A lot of things have happened today, and we really need to talk.' He nodded over towards the bar, where Neil and Paul were buying the round. 'I'm loath to spoil the meal, but I really don't feel like it tonight.'

Scott was confused: it didn't sound as if Nathan had found out about Adrian: if anything, it seemed as though Nathan was worried about something he'd done. Any further investigation would have to wait, though: Neil and Paul arrived with the drinks. Scott took his Hooch and sipped it thoughtfully. Something was going on, and he didn't like it. He didn't like the fact that he felt so guilty, and he didn't like the fact that Nathan seemed so disturbed. He could make a good guess at Nathan's problem: he'd slept with someone. But so had he . . .

How could he support Nathan, how could he forgive Nathan, when he had no right to the high moral ground himself? Those two wrongs were not making a right.

As Scott tried to work out what was going on in Nathan's head, he didn't notice the figure standing halfway up the open staircase, watching him intently.

It was Adrian. Smiling.

Nathan spent the whole of the taxi journey back to Docklands in silence, staring out of the window as they passed through

Holborn, along the banks of the Thames, over Tower Bridge and through Bermondsey. He knew that he was going to have to tell Scott what had happened: he had called off the meal, much to the consternation of both Neil and Paul, and that sort of disruption deserved an explanation. But he knew that he would have to explain it to Scott before he told the others: he owed him that. But not in the bar, and not in the taxi. Some things had to be discussed behind closed doors.

To his credit, Scott stayed silent as well. Nathan could tell that Scott wanted to talk, but he just sat there, keeping his own counsel, rather than badgering him for information that he wasn't ready to give.

It was the longest taxi journey Nathan had ever endured.

The house was dark and unwelcoming when they entered: with all of the chaos of the previous night, Nathan had forgotten to set the central heating, and the living room was cold and uncomfortable. Like the grave, he thought, before instantly chiding himself for being so daft.

That's it, Nate, he thought. As if things aren't bad enough, without you overdramatising everything.

He indicated for Scott to sit down, before going into the kitchen to get a couple of cans of beer and switch on the heating.

Back in the living room, he handed a can to Scott and sat opposite him. 'It should warm up in a minute,' he said. *In more ways than one.*

Scott swigged from the can. 'OK, OK, what's the matter?' he asked. 'It's obviously something serious. Neil and Paul are really worried about you.'

And so they might be, he thought. 'All right – but this isn't going to be easy.' He gave a worried smile that clearly did nothing to reassure Scott.

'Firstly . . . John's died. It looks like the Elective murdered him when he failed to get the evidence they wanted.'

'Dead?' Scott's face was a mask of disbelief. 'As in "murdered"?' He shook his head. 'I can't believe that they'd kill him for that.'

'I've been warning everyone about the Elective,' Nathan said angrily, as all his feelings of outrage and guilt began to bubble up once more. 'But no one would listen, would they? Perhaps now they'll take me seriously.' He realised he was shaking.

Scott went over to him and put his arm round him, but Nathan found himself pulling away, unable to accept Scott's support after what he had done.

'Scott, listen to me. It's . . . worse than that. For us that is,' he added, doubting that John Bury would consider a couple of illicit shags worse than murder. 'I . . . I . . .' He sighed. The only way to do this was to let it all out in one go and fall on Scott's judgment.

'I've been unfaithful to you,' he whispered. There: he'd said it. Now he was going to have to live with the consequences.

'When?' Scott's voice was quiet and unemotional.

'Today . . . with someone in the swimming baths. Some Irish bloke that was interested in me. It just happened.' He fell silent, but continued before Scott could respond. 'And then with Graham . . .'

'Graham?' Scott was shocked. 'Your skinhead solicitor friend?' He shook his head. 'I can't believe I'm hearing this.'

'That's right,' he confirmed flatly. 'He came over with some information about John and –'

'Let me guess,' said Scott cruelly. 'It just happened. You bastard.' But it wasn't anger in his voice: just a thin seam of hurt.

Scott closed his eyes, and Nathan tried to sense what the boy was really feeling. Was he angry, upset, disappointed? Or had it left him cold and empty, unable to register what had happened? In a way, it would have been better if Scott had just exploded, releasing all of his emotions in one go. Nathan was sure he could have handled that better than the cold, unforgiving silence that almost formed a barrier around Scott.

'I can't expect you to believe this, but it didn't mean anything to me. Either of them. I was confused . . . upset. That business with John . . .' He shrugged, knowing that these were nothing more than feeble excuses which offered no defence for his actions. Scott said nothing, simply staring in front of him.

'Say something,' Nathan begged. 'Please.'

Suddenly Scott stood up. 'I'm going home,' he said quietly. 'I need time to think about this.'

'I'll get you a taxi,' said Nathan, but Scott shook his head.

'I'll pick one up on the main road. I need to clear my thoughts, and the fresh air will do me good.'

He grabbed his jacket and headed towards the front door. 'I'll call you,' he said over his shoulder. 'When I've sorted this out. But we're finished, Nathan: I can't handle what you've done.'

With that he was through the door and out into the night, leaving Nathan alone on the sofa with a half-empty beer can and tormenting, bitter emotions.

You've only yourself to blame, said that bitter, twisted inner voice. *Your last best hope for happiness, and you've destroyed it.*

Then it hit him. It hit him hard. John's death. His infidelity. The ruins that remained of his relationship with Scott.

He wandered over to the back of the house and opened the curtains, staring out into the night, thinking about what had happened.

He stayed like that for a long time.

Seven

———

Scott lay on his bed, the lights off, staring at the dancing shadows on the ceiling of his room. According to the luminous clock face next to him, it was three o'clock in the morning: a cold, dark time which was unsettling at best. And this was definitely not the best of times.

Scott's mind was a mixture of emotions, which battled each other relentlessly, forcing him to replay the events of the last couple of days over and over again. His own guilt over his . . . his business agreement with Adrian, clashing violently against his feelings of betrayal over Nathan's infidelity and the total shock that he felt over the death of John Bury. Together, they caused a sickness in his stomach that he had never experienced before. And if he had never experienced it before, how the hell was he supposed to cope with it?

He shut his eyes, but that only made it worse. Instead of the featureless shadows, the darkness of his own mind formed itself into painful images of Nathan, Adrian and John.

How could Nathan have done it? After the month they had spent together, after all that Nathan had said to him, how could he just go off with someone else like that? Scott didn't know what was worse: the anonymous encounter in the swimming baths, or the session with Graham. Nathan had told him a little about Graham: enough for Scott to know that any sexual situation between them would be charged with emotion. Emotions that Scott had felt sure were sacrosanct to his relationship with Nathan.

All the promises, all the times when Nathan had told him that he loved him, and then he shattered the trust between them, not just once but twice in the same day, as easily as smashing a mug.

Then he thought about Adrian. He and Adrian had been having regular sex for the last three months, but there wasn't any emotion involved: it was a business transaction, pure and simple. He didn't love Adrian; he wasn't even that fond of him. It was just a service, a contract between two consenting adults which fulfilled a need in Adrian and gave Scott a helping hand with his student loan. Because of that, Scott could just about forgive Nathan's indiscretion in the swimming baths: sex without feeling posed no threat to their relationship. But as for Graham . . . Graham was an ex, pure and simple. Nathan had feelings for Graham: that was clear from the few times Nathan had mentioned him. And those were feelings that he should have kept between himself and Scott.

Even his excuse that he was screwed up over what had happened to John didn't hold water; yes, it was horrible, and yes, Scott himself was upset that he was dead, even if the bloke had been trying to burgle Nathan's house. But Nathan should have turned to Scott for support, not to some skinhead solicitor. His conscience made a last, desperate attempt to remind him that, even if Nathan had wanted to turn to Scott, Scott had been with Adrian. But that doubt was drowned in the conflicting emotions.

Scott opened his eyes and knew that he had made his choice.

The decision was made. Nathan was history. And Scott was

going to the States with Adrian. He deserved to be happy, and perhaps Adrian could offer him that.

The taxi dropped Nathan off outside the Harness at about three o'clock in the morning, the dark streets of Vauxhall virtually deserted apart from a couple of drunken football supporters singing loudly and discordantly under one of the arches. The cold and loneliness didn't depress Nathan; he welcomed the way it mirrored his own emotional state.

Nathan had known that he had to go to the Harness, but he wasn't exactly sure why. It may have been the simple fact that he couldn't stay at home on his own, knowing that everything he saw in the house would remind him of what he had destroyed. Or it might have been the vain hope that Scott would be there, and they could talk and try to sort out the mess. Maybe he just wanted to get drunk and blot the whole sorry mess out.

But deep inside, he did know the real reason. He wanted sex. He needed to be reassured that he could still attract men. He had to rebuild his shattered self-confidence, and sex was the easiest, least painful way to do that.

He knocked on the solid black door, and waited for about a minute before the small metal flap opened and Oz, the man-mountain of an Australian bouncer, peered through.

'A bit late, Nate,' he had said, before grinning at his little rhyme. 'Still, plenty of life left in the club.'

'Just needed to get out of the house,' Nathan replied as Oz let him in.

'Full works, I see.' Oz was admiring Nathan's outfit, and Nathan had to admit that he had made an effort. He was dressed from head to foot in leather, from his polished biker's boots to his faithful leather jacket, with his leather trousers and leather shirt completing the outfit. Part of it had been an attempt to impress, but it also made him feel safe, protected. Like battle armour.

Even at three in the morning, the Harness was busy. No one was completely sure how, but the place stayed open until the last customer had left. Nathan suspected the influence of the Elective – when didn't he? he thought wryly – but even he had often had reason to be grateful to the place.

Especially tonight.

Making his way to the bar, he looked around to see if there was anyone there that he knew. There were a few faces that he recognised, but no one he knew well enough to talk over what had happened. He was slightly disappointed, but at the same time, he was relieved: he wasn't sure that he could have held himself together long enough to explain it. Better that what he was about to do was carried out in a crowd of uncaring anonymity.

Buying himself a can of Breaker, he considered his options. There wasn't anyone that he could see who he fancied bringing back to Docklands; actually, he just didn't want to spend the night with anyone. Sex tonight would be cold and clinical, the faceless pleasure of the darkroom rather than the warm intimacy of the bedroom.

Besides, the last person he had picked up in the Harness had been John Bury, and he couldn't take the chance that anything similar would happen again. Not tonight.

He pushed his way through the throng of people hovering in front of the bar, and started to make a beeline for the darkrooms on the other side of the room. Suddenly, a hand clasped his shoulder.

'Hi, Nate! Haven't seen you for ages.' The six-foot-six figure of Joe loomed over him, wearing even more leather than Nathan. Joe grinned, an expression of genuine pleasure coming over his bearded face. Joe was a grade-A hunk: Nathan had to admit that. His huge frame was almost solid muscle, the result of years of determination at the gym, with big, muscular arms and legs and a broad, well-defined chest. A short, full, brown beard covered his square jaw. He wasn't the brightest of people, but he was one of the most loyal. And sex with him was always quite an experience: what Joe lacked in intelligence, he more than made up for with sheer enthusiasm and staying power, and one of the biggest dicks Nathan had ever seen.

Nathan had had sex with Joe on quite a few occasions before he had met Scott, but hadn't actually seen him for a couple of months: Joe tended to visit the Harness in phases, and then vanish for months on end while he tried out some other bar.

Nathan put his arm around Joe's solid waist and gave him a brief hug.

'How's it going?' he asked warmly.

Jo shrugged in a noncommittal way. 'Same as ever. Someone said you'd got yourself a new bloke.'

That hurt. Nathan would never have believed that such an innocent enquiry could cut him to the core. He swallowed before replying. 'Sore point, Joe.'

Even Joe could pick up on the pain in Nathan's voice. 'Sorry, mate. Anyway, if you're free later . . .' The invitation was clear, but Nathan just wished the circumstances were better: he always enjoyed Joe's company, and the thought of that big muscular body and huge cock was tempting, Nathan had to admit. But Joe lacked the one thing Nathan was looking for.

Anonymity.

'Another time, Joe: I'm still a bit cut up over my boyfriend –' He stopped and made one of the most painful corrections in his life. '*Ex*-boyfriend. See you later.'

Leaving Joe virtually in shock – no one ever turned down a chance to have sex with him – Nathan pushed through a group of skinheads and reached the three doors. The three darkrooms.

Nathan paused for a moment. Did he want the darkened anonymity of the back room, or the more adventurous play-room. The third darkroom was, as ever, out of bounds.

'Which one do you fancy?' came a rough East End accent. Nathan turned to see a man standing close to him. Very close.

'Haven't decided yet,' he admitted, sizing up the stranger.

He was about Nathan's height, but much heavier. He was wearing a white singlet, which clearly showed pierced nipples, and swirling black tattoos over his upper arms. His chest was hairless but well muscled.

He had a round face with a full but short black beard: in many ways, he looked like a cut-down version of Joe. And Nathan knew immediately that he fancied him.

'I'm Nick,' he said, and held out his hand.

'Nate,' Nathan replied, and was aware that he was roughening up his own accent to make himself more appealing. He took Nick's hand, and was shocked by the strength of the grip. 'Haven't seen you around before,' he said.

'I'm here most nights,' said Nick, 'but I'm usually in the other bar.'

'Other bar?' As far as Nathan was aware, this was the only bar in the club.

'That bar,' explained Nick, gesturing towards the third door. The secret door. 'Members only.' Then he smiled. 'Well, members and guests. Fancy a drink in there?'

Nathan was momentarily speechless. After all these years of coming to the Harness, he had never even met someone who had been through the third door. And now he was being invited in for a drink!

'I'd . . . I'd love to,' he replied. This was unbelievable.

'Fine.' Nick walked over to the door and knocked. After a second it opened, to reveal a bouncer who made even Joe look small, with a shaved head and a brutal expression.

'Bringing a guest in, Pete.' The bouncer nodded and stepped aside to allow Nick and Nathan to enter.

Over the years, Nathan had often wondered what lay behind the third door. But even his wildest imaginings hadn't prepared him for what he saw.

It was another bar, just as big as the one with which he was familiar. Nathan assumed that he must be inside the archway next to the Harness, the one that was boarded up and looked derelict.

Like the other bar, it was dark, but not dark enough to prevent Nathan from seeing the main difference between the public and private faces of the Harness: sex wasn't confined to the back rooms here. All around him, some of the best-looking blokes he had ever seen were having sex in couples and threesomes, taking full advantage of the equipment that was dotted around. Bears, skinheads and leathermen were in harnesses suspended from the ceiling, or chained to the walls, all pleasuring one another.

Nathan felt his hard-on forming: this couldn't be real. It was as if he had wandered on to the set of the best porn movie he had ever seen, and he could feel the excitement growing within him: everywhere he looked was sex, and there was a familiar, heady smell in the air. Men and sex. He realised that Nick was talking to him.

'Come over and meet my mate.'

Nathan followed Nick across the floor, past two gorgeous skinheads who were taking it in turns to fuck a third one who was bent over a metal chest. Nathan couldn't help but be envious: he wished it was him over the chest.

'This is Mike.' Nick introduced him to a stocky guy wearing a green flight suit. Mike had slightly longer hair than Nick, but a similar beard. He smiled a toothy grin, and Nathan virtually melted. He began to imagine the two of them, one of them fucking his arse, the other one fucking his face. The image was almost more than he could bear, and he could see Mike surreptitiously glancing at his erection, plainly visible under his leather jeans.

'First time in here, is it?' asked Mike in a rough London accent.

Nathan nodded. 'I had no idea . . .' he whispered.

Nick laughed. 'Gets everyone like that the first couple of times. Even then, you never really get used to it.'

Nathan looked to his left, where a tall, moustached man wearing only a full body harness and a cockring was sucking off a tattooed skinhead in twelve-hole Docs and little else. 'I can imagine.'

'Well, fancy a bit of fun with us?' asked Mike, moving closer and stroking Nathan's hard-on through the black leather. 'Nick spotted you the moment you walked in.'

Nick grinned. 'I've seen you a few times, but we don't often venture into the public bar.' He made *public bar* sound like something distasteful. He put his arm round his boyfriend's broad, muscular shoulders and ran the other hand up and down Nathan's chest. 'You're a bit of a hunk, aren't you?'

Nathan gave an embarrassed smile. A twinge of guilt assaulted him over Scott, but he had to admit, this was the reason he had come here. And what was behind the third door of the Harness was beyond his wildest fantasies.

'The thought of you two screwing me . . . I can't think of anything else I'd rather do.'

Without saying a word, Nick and Mike led Nathan across the darkened room. They stopped when they reached a doorway.

'This bit's more private,' said Nick, walking through.

Nathan found himself in an empty, dimly lit room about the size of an average living room. Like the rest of the Harness, the walls were black, and dotted with manacles and chains.

'Now, let's see what you've got.' Nick removed Nathan's leather jacket and threw it on to the floor. Then he slowly unbuttoned Nathan's leather shirt. Meanwhile, Mike pulled off Nick's singlet, revealing even more of his stocky body and dark tattoos.

'Nice chest,' said Mike, as Nathan's own muscular torso was revealed. He reached out and squeezed Nathan's nipples, eliciting a cry of pleasure at the sharp but exquisite pain.

Nick continued to undress him, pulling the leather jeans down to his ankles, making sure that he ran his hands down

126

Nathan's legs as he did so. As this happened, Mike unbuttoned Nick's denim jeans and let them fall. Nick wasn't wearing any pants: his cock, thick, veined and about six inches long, sprang free. A silver Prince Albert glittered in the dim lighting. All Nathan wanted to do was fall to his knees and try to take it in his mouth.

By now, Nathan was wearing only his boots and his white silk boxers; his hard-on was stiff against his stomach, his moist red helmet poking out from the elasticated waistband. Mike had unzipped his flight suit to his waist to reveal a solid chest with a light covering of brown hair. Like his boyfriend's, both of his nipples were pierced; Nick had silver rings through his, while Mike's were pierced with little silver bars. A tattoo of a dragon decorated his left shoulder, and Nathan suddenly thought of Leigh – where was he? It had been weeks since they had last spoken.

But thoughts of Leigh vanished when Nick fell to his knees and began to lick Nathan's cock through the thin silk. Nathan could feel the roughness of Nick's beard teasing at his groin, and he longed to pull down his boxers and let Nick grab his cock in his mouth.

As Nathan's dick vanished into Nick's mouth, Mike unzipped his flight suit down to his groin and displayed his proud, thick cock. Although it wasn't as thick as his boyfriend's, it was just as long. He too had a Prince Albert, and Nathan couldn't wait to flick the little silver ring with his tongue.

Nick suddenly moved back and released Nathan's cock, allowing Mike to kneel down and take it in his mouth. Nick moved behind his boyfriend and put both hands on his nipples and began to tweak them. The pleasure that Mike gained from this was obvious: with each squeeze, he closed his eyes and would have gasped, if Nathan's hard-on hadn't been filling his mouth.

Then Mike stopped and stood up. Placing both hands on Nathan's bare shoulders, he forced him on to his knees.

'Now you're going to have both these cocks,' he said roughly.

Nathan almost choked as the two dicks forced their way into his mouth. Mike's was thick but would have been manageable on its own; but the width of Nick's as well meant that he could get only their helmets in his mouth. He took turns in flicking his tongue across each of their Prince Alberts, relishing the groans that came from them as he did so. Salty pre-come leaked from both of them, and Nathan lapped it up as if it was the most important thing on Earth. Which it was: all thoughts of Scott were temporarily banished; all he wanted to focus on was the here and now, and he intended to make Mike and Nick the centre of his world at that moment.

Simultaneously, the two of them pulled back.

'Good boy,' grunted Nick. 'You've been a good boy and now you deserve a good fucking.'

Rough hands pulled him to his feet and directed him to one of the metal chests in the corner of the room. Nathan was also aware that someone else was in the room: a stocky man with a moustache, dressed in denim. Nathan hoped that he would join in; at the very least, he hoped that the bloke would be sufficiently impressed by his appearance and performance to come home with him.

Nathan wasn't sure whether it was Nick or Mike who forced him over the chest – and, to be honest, he didn't actually care. The trepidation he felt over having Nick's huge dick inside him was outweighed by the desire for it: he wanted to feel that manhood inside him, and if it hurt, well, he deserved it. He'd been a bad boy, and he needed to be punished. Somebody put his hands on his shoulders – whether it was Mike or Nick, Nathan didn't know. He wanted them both, so the order didn't matter.

Seconds after the shock of the cold lubricant, Nathan felt the pressure forcing his ring open. As he relaxed, he guessed that it was Mike who was entering him: after penetration by Graham,

Mike's cock – although sizeable – was a relief, and no effort at all. Indeed, Nathan was looking forward to the challenge of taking Nick.

Once Nathan sensed that Mike was totally inside him, he clenched his arse around Mike's cock, squeezing it rhythmically and enjoying the gasps of pleasure that resulted. As he did that, he felt a hand – Nick's? – grab his engorged cock and start wanking it.

Mike started to pull out, until his helmet was just inside Nathan's ring; then he plunged back inside. It was Nathan's turn to gasp, as the force of Mike's cock inside him began to bring him close to orgasm. After about five long, deep penetrations, Mike pulled out completely.

'My turn,' said Nick, and Nathan braced himself for that huge dick inside him.

As Nick's helmet touched his ring, Nathan relaxed as much as he could, but even that wasn't enough. The three-inch-thick cock bullied and bruised its way inside him, and Nathan felt as if his arse was on fire. For long, agonising seconds, the pain was worse than he had ever imagined; but then his arse learnt to accommodate Nick's massive dick, and pleasure took over.

As Nick started to slowly pull and push his cock inside him, Nathan was aware that Mike was standing on the other side of the metal box, his cock inches away from Nathan's mouth. Nathan leant forward and hungrily took it all, his tongue playing with the metal ring and making Mike groan.

More groans came from behind him: Nick was obviously very close, and the trembling in Mike's cock indicated that so was he. After holding himself back, Nathan allowed himself to embrace the pleasure of Nick's thick cock inside him, and sensed the tingling feeling that was growing around his own dick.

When they came, it all happened at once. With one last thrust, Nick forced himself into Nathan and yelled in ecstasy;

Mike in turn forced his cock into Nathan's mouth and shot load after load of hot come against the back of his throat.

At the first taste of Mike's spunk, Nathan abandoned himself, reaching down to administer the last few strokes to his desperate cock. Still swallowing Mike's load, he shot his own over the metal of the chest, white gouts of come against the black of the metal.

Finally, he released Mike's cock from his mouth and virtually collapsed on the chest. Nick gently pulled himself out of Nathan and lay down over him, giving him a big strong hug as he did so.

'How was that?' he whispered.

Nathan sighed. He felt satisfied and sated, but there was still a nagging worry: he'd just had some of the best sex in his life, but how was Scott managing? Was he OK?

'It's a bit late, isn't it?' came the voice over the intercom. The voice sounded tired, but then again, it was half-four in the morning. Scott had just had to get out of the halls of residence, and his options were limited at that time of the morning. He could always have gone to the Harness, but there was a very good chance that he would have bumped into one of Nathan's friends, and he didn't want to have to explain why he was there on his own. Although he was a member, he had always confined himself to the back room, not really building up a circle of friends himself.

Actually, he thought, there was just as good a chance that he would have bumped into Nathan himself, and he just couldn't face that. Not tonight.

'I'm sorry, Adrian,' he muttered into the speaker grille, 'but I didn't know what else to do. Something's happened.'

'You'd better come up.' The buzzer rang, and Scott let himself through the outer door and mounted the steps to Adrian's first-floor flat two at a time.

Adrian was waiting at the door when he got there. He was

dressed in a blue towelling bathrobe, and the expression on his darkly stubbled face made it clear that Scott had woken him up.

'I'm really sorry about this, Adrian,' he repeated.

Adrian shrugged. 'What are friends for? Would you like a drink?'

Scott nodded, and sat down on the comfortable white leather sofa, the scene of so many of their sexual encounters. It felt strange being there for something else rather than sex; when he and Adrian were acting our their fantasies, the room was almost like a film set. It seemed odd to realise that Adrian actually lived there.

Adrian came back over from the drinks cabinet with two glasses of what looked like whisky, and sat down next to Scott on the sofa. In a display of affection that was at odds with their normal master-slave relationship, he put his hand on Scott's knee.

'What's up, then?'

Scott took a sip of the whisky and then told Adrian everything. The threesome; the burglary; John's murder. And Nathan's infidelities.

Adrian listened attentively, interrupting only when he wanted clarification or to offer Scott another drink. After about half an hour and two more Scotches, Scott was finished.

'So, you don't feel that you can forgive him?' said Adrian. 'Has he really hurt you that badly?'

Scott frowned. 'I just can't understand him. It's as if I don't know him any more. This business with the Elective has become an obsession: every part of his life seems to take second place to this case. And now it's even got involved in our relationship.'

'How do you know that this was the first time?' asked Adrian quietly. 'How do you know that the only reason he told you about the two yesterday was because of his shock over this John Bury's death?'

Scott fell silent. Adrian had a point there. Scott's initial reaction had been that Nathan's actions had destroyed the trust between them. But what if that trust had never existed? What if Nathan had been screwing around since day one? It wouldn't have been difficult for Nathan to cover it up: there were a lot of places on the gay scene, and most of the ones that Nathan frequented – or had frequented, before he and Scott had started seeing each other – were members-only clubs that Scott wouldn't have stood a hope in hell of getting into, anyway.

What if he'd never given up going to places like Black Fist, or the Shaft, or Cockring? What if those nights when he had claimed to have been out investigating his sources or chasing another contact in his endless quest for the Elective, he'd actually been having sex? It wasn't as if Nathan's friends would have told him anything; they were a nice bunch, but it was obvious with whom their loyalties lay.

'Do you think he was?'

Adrian sighed, and squeezed Scott's knee once more. 'It probably won't surprise you to know that Nathan Dexter and I are members of a number of the same clubs? I've actually seen him in Black Fist on a number of occasions.'

A nasty, sick feeling overtook the warmth that the Scotch had temporarily provided. 'Recently?' Scott asked quietly.

'I'm sorry to say that I saw him in there last week. Chained up to the wall and being fucked by two people taking turns.' Adrian's words were straightforward and matter-of-fact, but they hit Scott like a fist in the stomach.

'Are you sure?' But Scott was sure. It all started to make sense now: nobody had so many night-time rendezvous. Nathan had never been satisfied with Scott, but Scott had been too naive, too trusting to realise. He closed his eyes tightly, trying to stop the pain from overwhelming him.

Adrian put his arm around his shoulders. 'It'll be all right,' he said softly. 'Why don't you stay here tonight? Things might make a little more sense in the morning.' He stood up. 'The spare room's all made up.'

But Scott knew that he couldn't be on his own that evening. Despite all of his protestations to himself that what existed between him and Adrian was strictly business, he realised that he had simply been trying to justify his own behaviour.

Now that he knew that Nathan had never been worth the feelings that Scott had wasted on him, he also knew that the relationship that existed between himself and Adrian was a lot stronger, a lot more intimate, than he had ever dared to admit to himself.

'I'd rather stay with you, Adrian,' he said quietly. 'Unless you've got someone else here.'

Adrian shook his head. 'My little slave needs his master tonight, doesn't he?'

Willingly, longingly, Scott allowed himself to be led into the bedroom. The master bedroom.

By seven o'clock, only a handful of people were left in the private room of the Harness, but the majority of them were still having sex. Nathan was leaning against the bar nursing a large vodka and Coke, chatting away to Nick, Mike and an Australian bloke called Marco. Marco had been the keen spectator when Nick and Mike had been fucking Nathan, and afterwards had made it clear that he fancied a solo session with Nathan himself.

The conversation was warm and witty, with an underlying friendliness that was just what Nathan needed. His pain over Scott was dulled, and although Nathan knew that he would still have to deal with it, this respite was definitely welcome. After covering topics ranging from the leather scene to their respective careers, Nathan decided to broach the subject that had been needling him since he had first learnt about the third bar years ago.

'So,' Nathan began, his tongue loosened by the vodka, 'how do you get to be a member of this bar?'

The atmosphere suddenly became noticeably less friendly – chilly, even. The smiles on Nick's and Mike's faces vanished, and Marco looked very uncomfortable.

'That's not something you ask, Nate,' said Mike quietly. 'Members are occasionally allowed to bring guests in, but the policy's quite clear: those guests had better not say anything about this place, or they're liable to get barred from every gay club and pub in London. Or worse.'

In that moment, Nathan realised what he had stumbled into. Preoccupied by the events of the last couple of days, he had totally failed to notice the most obvious thing about the private bar: it could exist only if it was under the protection of an organisation of unimaginable power and influence, an organisation cloaked in secrecy but with the muscle to make people disappear.

The Elective.

He had to recover his ground, and he had to do it quickly. Accidentally, he had given himself an advantage. And it was an advantage that he had to play quickly or not at all.

Adrenaline sobering him up, he assumed a contrite expression. 'I'm sorry – must have been the drink talking. Anyway, you can rely on me to keep my mouth shut.'

'Of course we can,' came an unfamiliar voice. 'We can rely on anything we want, Mr Dexter.'

Nathan turned to see a well-built man in his late thirties, with short blond hair and a beard, standing behind him. Incongruously for a club full of men in leather, rubber and uniforms, he was wearing a tuxedo.

'You have me at a disadvantage,' Nathan replied. He suspected who the man was – or, rather, who he represented – but couldn't be sure. He decided that the best course of action was to listen to what the man had to say.

'I know,' said the other without a trace of humour. Nathan

was aware that Mike, Nick and Marco had discreetly distanced themselves and were making a deliberate attempt to ignore what was going on.

'Mr Dexter, this is one of the most exclusive bars in London, if not Britain. Under normal circumstances, Nick and Mike wouldn't have been allowed to bring you in here.

'But I wanted to meet you. You've been quite a nuisance to the people I represent, and I wanted to meet the person responsible.'

'The Elective, I presume.' Nathan steeled himself: how could he have been so stupid to think that they wouldn't have realised who he was? If they could arrange to have John Bury invade his home, they must have been watching him for a long time. For a moment, he was overcome with worry about Scott: despite what had happened, he still loved him, and the idea that the Elective could hurt him filled him with dread.

But there was nothing he could do now: he was stuck at the centre of the Elective's operations, in a direct confrontation with someone who could very well have been the Comptroller himself, for all Nathan knew.

The man continued. 'Yes, Mr Dexter. Your prying into our affairs must cease, you know. Stop, or you will be crushed underfoot.'

Nathan almost burst out laughing: he was having a conversation with a spokesman from the Elective, and the man sounded like a second-rate James Bond villain. But he knew better than to cause trouble here. However clichéd it sounded, Nathan knew that the Elective had the power to make him simply . . . disappear. That didn't stop him from making an attempt to protest.

'What are you going to do?' he said sharply. 'Kill me, like you killed John Bury?'

'Not at all, Mr Dexter.' Then the other's voice grew ominous. 'Not *you*, at any rate. I understand that you were once close to a young man called Scott James.' It wasn't a question – it was a statement.

Nathan was gripped with terror. His worst nightmares seemed to be coming true, one by one, like dominoes toppling over. 'What have you done with him?' he asked quietly.

'Nothing – yet. But he's no longer in the country, Mr Dexter.'

'What have you done with him?' Nathan repeated. 'If you've hurt him . . .' And he knew they could: the Elective had been fatally real to John Bury, and the truth was that they could hurt Scott badly.

'Scott is safe, Nathan,' said the spokesman in a worryingly friendly tone. 'And he'll remain so if you drop your investigation. For God's sake, the Elective's made up of people like you: good-looking, well-off professionals. Drop the case, and Scott will be safe, and the resources of the Elective will be at your disposal.' He smiled. 'What do you say?'

Nathan swallowed. Abandon his principles, or lose Scott for ever. It was a no-win scenario now, and Nathan knew that the spokesman wasn't joking. The Elective never joked.

He simply didn't have a choice. 'You win,' he said quietly.

The spokesman raised an eyebrow. 'We always do, Mr Dexter.' He looked over at Marco. 'Mr Cappiello, will you take Mr Dexter back to his house in Docklands and see that he . . . relaxes.' He held out his hand, but Nathan couldn't bring himself to shake it.

'You're a bastard,' Nathan spat. 'Do you know that?'

The spokesman gave an oily smile. 'We win, Mr Dexter. We always win. That's all that counts.' With that, he walked away.

Nathan leant against the bar. So, that was it. All over. His investigation was finished, and Scott was gone. What had begun as an evening designed to divert him had ended in the loss of the two things that he cared about most in his life. What was he going to do now?

'OK, mate?' Marco put his arm round Nathan's shoulders. 'Don't feel too bad: a similar thing happened to me a couple of years ago. I trod on the Elective's toes, and they made me an offer I couldn't refuse. They can't be beaten, you know.'

Something inside Nathan broke. Or, rather, hardened, like steel being quickened or ice freezing. They could take Scott from him, but they couldn't take his career from him. He was a journalist – that defined the whole of Nathan's life. If he backed down now, he would never be able to look at himself in the mirror again. He wouldn't let the Elective win. He would show them that some people couldn't be beaten, crushed underfoot.

There was an innate fairness in the world – Nathan believed that with a passion. There had to be, or else what was the point? The Elective wasn't fair: it stood for everything that was unfair in the world. And the Elective was going to learn that it couldn't play people like puppets and manipulate lives like so many chess pieces on a world-sized board.

Despite the threat – no, *because* of the threat – Nathan would continue to pursue the Elective until it was broken. He owed it to himself to carry on until the end – whatever the consequences.

'I don't have to come home with you if you don't want,' said Marco, shrugging. 'If you want to be on your own . . .'

Nathan made a decision. The pain and hurt that his break-up with Scott had caused would take a long time to go away, but it would be the fuel that drove him on until this whole sorry business was over. He would find Scott, he would keep Scott safe, and then he would destroy the Elective, tearing it apart bit by bit until he was finally face to face with the Comptroller himself.

And then *he* would win.

But now, in the cold twilight of a December morning, he wanted comfort, he wanted the reassurance that everything was going to be all right. He wanted Marco.

He smiled at the Australian, realising for the first time that he was quite a hunk, with his solid frame and big, hairy arms. 'Come home with me, Marco. I'd like that. I need some company this morning.'

Because afterwards, Nathan was going to fight the biggest battle of his life.

Eight

———

Scott woke up with a start, and was momentarily confused as to where he was. The white walls hung with expensive-looking paintings and the huge soft bed and white duvet definitely meant that he wasn't in his rooms in the halls of residence – and nor was he in Nathan's house. What the hell was going on? he wondered, his thoughts befuddled and unclear.

Then he remembered, and the pain hit him like a fist in the stomach. He and Nathan were history – and he was in Adrian's flat in Bayswater. Scott sat up in bed and sighed, trying to fight off the almost physical pain that he was feeling. How could things have gone wrong so quickly? Then he got a grip: OK, so everything was a mess, but he had to keep going – there simply wasn't an alternative. And Adrian was offering him a chance to do just that. But where *was* Adrian?

They hadn't had sex when they had gone to bed: all Scott had wanted was for Adrian to hold him and keep the nightmares away, make it all somehow be all right. Adrian was probably frustrated, but he had understood: even though Scott had been able to feel Adrian's hard-on pressing against his leg, they had just lain there and talked, until finally Scott must have fallen asleep in his arms.

But Adrian wasn't there any more, and, from the coolness of the sheets, he hadn't been there for some time.

Scott got out of bed and grabbed Adrian's dressing gown. As he did so, he heard the front door shut: was that Adrian leaving, or coming in? There was so much about Adrian that he didn't know. Somewhere, at the back of his mind, an alarm bell went off: *perhaps you'd better find out more – what you don't know can hurt you.*

Brushing this aside, he walked into the living room, and saw Adrian at the drinks cabinet, pouring himself a scotch. For some strange reason, he was wearing a dinner suit.

'Where have you been?' Scott asked mildly: he didn't want Adrian to think that he was keeping tabs on him – that wasn't the sort of relationship that they had. But it was definitely a bit odd, wandering around in a dinner suit in the early hours of the morning. The subconscious alarm bell rang once more.

Adrian came over to him and put his arm around his waist. 'Sorry if I worried you.' He gave Scott a kiss on the cheek. 'I got a phone call after you fell asleep. There was some trouble in one of the clubs – they needed me to sort it out.' He shrugged. 'The responsibilities of command, I'm afraid.'

Scott didn't know much about Adrian, apart from the fact that he was involved in a vast range of business interests, including a string of private clubs – undoubtedly the sorts of club where you had to wear dinner suits. Deciding that that was the answer to this particular little mystery, he smiled. 'I was worried about you.' But was he? Did he have the same compassion for Adrian as he had felt for Nathan?

It isn't important, said the voice. *Adrian has shown he cares about you. The sex is brilliant. And he's absolutely loaded.*

His doubts quelled, Scott allowed Adrian to lead him to the sofa and sat down. Scott couldn't be sure, but there was an air of smug satisfaction around Adrian: as if he was secretly delighted about something. Obviously he had sorted out the problem at the club and done himself some good into the bargain.

'I didn't leave a note because I didn't think you'd wake up before I got back.' He pouted: an unfamiliar expression on his bearded face. Somehow, it really endeared Adrian to Scott, showing a more vulnerable side to him. 'Sorry if you were concerned. Anyway, it's all sorted out now.' Then he broke into a grin. 'By the way, you've got about two hours to get ready.'

Scott frowned. 'Get ready for what?'

'Your holiday, of course,' Adrian replied, still smiling. 'Our flight to the States leaves in about four hours.'

Scott couldn't help grinning in return. Even though he still couldn't believe what was happening, he wasn't going to look a gift horse in the mouth. He gave Adrian an affectionate squeeze.

'New York, here we come.' Despite all that had happened, he found that he was beginning to get really excited about the trip.

'Still, since I'll be buying both of us a complete new wardrobe when we get there, that gives us two hours to kill before the taxi arrives, doesn't it?' Adrian's hand, which had been sitting on Scott's knee, moved further up his thigh until it was resting against his cock. Then Adrian moved his hand underneath the dressing gown and ran a finger up and down Scott's dick; automatically, Scott's hard-on began to develop.

'That's my boy,' whispered Adrian. 'Daddy wants to play, and Scott wants to please his daddy, doesn't he?'

Even if he didn't feel grateful to Adrian for all that he had done, Scott realised that he felt incredibly randy. And two hours was a long time . . .

Scott pulled open his dressing gown to reveal his muscular, hairy body and swollen, willing cock. Adrian bent down and took it in his mouth, his tongue licking the red helmet, while his hand sought out Scott's balls and gently squeezed them.

PAUL C. ALEXANDER

Scott was pleasantly surprised: it was very different from the usual master-and-servant games that they played. This time, he felt like an equal, rather than a paid-for slave. He gasped as Adrian's finger reached round and penetrated his arse, pushing roughly into the warm hole and stroking the hot flesh within.

Adrian continued to suck Scott's cock, taking all of it into his mouth right down to the thick, hairy base. Scott's erection was now rock-hard, and he could feel his helmet touching the back of Adrian's throat.

Suddenly Adrian stopped, and took his mouth away from Scott's cock. He looked up at him. 'I want you to fuck me.'

Scott was shocked: he had never known Adrian to be submissive. But the idea of forcing his cock into Adrian's arse was irresistible. 'Are you sure?' he asked.

'Fuck me, boy,' Adrian ordered. 'I don't want to have to repeat it.'

At the familiar sound of Adrian in his role as master, Scott had no option but to comply. Condoms and lubricant were lying by the side of the sofa, presumably since the last time that they had had sex. But that time, it had been Adrian's impressive, thick cock deep within Scott; this time, it would be all of Scott's manhood, forced into the man who had been his master.

Rolling on the condom and liberally applying lubricant to himself and Adrian's blond-furred ring, Scott moved himself round so that he could slide his cock into him. Adrian was lying on his back, obviously wanting Scott to penetrate him that way. Scott placed his hands on Adrian's legs, and pushed them upward, forcing Adrian's arse towards him in the process.

'Fuck me hard, boy,' Adrian insisted. 'I want you to show your gratitude towards me.'

Scott didn't need to be told twice. Moving forward on his knees, he touched his helmet to Adrian's lubricated arse. And then he pushed himself forward, hard as he'd been asked – told.

His cock slipped into Adrian without difficulty, all nine inches inside Adrian's willing arse. Scott's big balls slapped

142

against Adrian's cheeks as the last inch penetrated. Scott looked at Adrian, and was pleased to see an expression of immense joy on his face. This was obviously something that Adrian got a real kick out of.

'Rougher, boy,' came the order, and Scott complied. Without a trace of gentleness, he pulled his cock halfway out, before plunging it back inside. As Adrian groaned, Scott continued, pulling it out until his helmet was just inside Adrian's ring, and then forcing it back inside. As he built up his rhythm, Scott took his hands from Adrian's thighs and laid them on his smooth, muscular chest. His fingers squeezed both nipples, playing with the silver rings that pierced them, and Adrian grunted with the pain. Scott suddenly realised that he was enjoying being in this position: he liked the fact that he had power over his master.

That knowledge excited him, and he started fucking Adrian even harder, ramming his big cock into his master's arse. As the speed of his strokes increased, so did the intensity of the pain he was inflicting on Adrian: he pinched and squeezed and tugged on his nipples, trying to hurt him, trying to humiliate him.

Then he realised that he was getting very close. But somehow, he didn't want to come inside Adrian; he pulled out and took the condom off, and leant forward so that his cock was over Adrian's chest.

'That's it, boy: shoot that load all over me,' urged Adrian.

Adrian's insistence didn't make any difference: Scott was so close that it took only a couple of strokes of his own cock before he came. With his whole body tensing, Scott felt the burning, overwhelming sensation overcome him: his thick cock twitched as gout after gout of warm white come shot from the end, landing on Adrian's chest, his beard, and round his mouth.

Adrian grinned and then licked the drops from around his mouth, his hand seeking out his own cock.

'Suck my cock,' he gasped, forcing Scott's head downward.

Scott needed no encouragement: he went down on Adrian's swollen cock and sucked it gratefully. It had a hot, sweaty, salty taste, and despite his recent orgasm, he could feel his erection returning. He licked the damp helmet, drinking the pre-come leaking from the slit; then he took all of Adrian's cock in his mouth, allowing the thick hot meat inside. He slid his lips up and down the shaft, while his hands continued to play with Adrian's nipples.

As Adrian's breathing became faster and deeper, Scott prepared himself for Adrian's orgasm; when it finally happened, however, even Scott was surprised. The hot spurts of come filled his mouth, so much come that he couldn't swallow it all. As Adrian's cock continued to shoot its load into Scott's mouth, come dribbled from Scott's lips and dripped on to the thick bush of dark blond hair around the base of Adrian's cock.

Finally, Adrian was finished. He gently pulled his cock from Scott's mouth and sank back on the sofa.

'Was that all right, master?' Scott whispered.

Adrian ran his hand through Scott's short, wavy hair. 'Good boy,' he said, the pleasure clear in his voice. 'This is something we're going to have to practise in New York.'

Suddenly, Scott realised that he really was looking forward to his trip to the States.

Marco was snoring gently on Nathan's lap. Both of them were still fully clothed, with Nathan in leather and Marco in denim. Once they had reached Docklands, sex had somehow seemed unnecessary: the comfort of knowing that they were there for each other was enough. Sometimes, having someone to look after you was all that was needed.

Gently moving Marco's head, Nathan got up and went into the kitchen. Pouring himself a glass of water, he stared out of the window into the cold dawn of December London and tried to marshal his thoughts into some kind of a coherent pattern.

According to the mysterious spokesman from the Elective,

Scott was missing. Was that true, or was it an empty threat? But from Nathan's investigation, the Elective never made empty threats, because they didn't need to: they had the power to back up every threat and make good every promise. So where was Scott? Nathan had tried to ring him when he got in, but his mobile phone was switched off. Nathan groaned. Think logically, Nate, he reasoned. Assume that he *is* missing. Assume that the Elective *are* holding him hostage to buy your silence. Where would he be?

Nathan's investigations had shown that the Elective's power base was distributed across the world, split into semi-autonomous regions. Each of the regions was run by one of their Comptrollers, such as the mysterious Delancey in Britain, and coordinated by the Director, a figure whose shadowy presence made the Comptrollers look like public figures. Their influence was absolute: they could have spirited Scott away and put him anywhere without any trouble.

'OK, mate?' Marco was standing behind him, squinting at the dim sunlight through the window.

'Morning,' said Nathan, giving him a brief peck on the lips. 'I was just thinking about Scott. Do you think they'd hurt him?'

Marco sighed. 'Yes, Nate, they would. Do you remember the once-a-week leather night in Bermondsey?'

Nathan had to think about that for a moment. Then he remembered a dingy little club off the Jamaica Road – he'd had quite a few good nights in there.

'The Bronx Club?'

'That's right,' said Marco. 'The Elective wanted to take it over. They told me that unless I gave up running the club that I was running, they would break my boyfriend's legs.' The pain of the memory was clear in his voice. Nathan moved over to him and held his hand. 'I told them to fuck off.'

Although he could guess the answer, Nathan still had to ask. 'So, what happened?'

'I refused, my *ex*-boyfriend is now paralysed from the waist down – and I don't run the club any more. They mean what they say, Nate.' He shook his head. 'You just can't fight them.'

Nathan refused to be frightened off. 'I won't let them win. There has to be a way to save Scott, *and* bring them down.'

Marco sighed. 'If there is, tell me. I'm just numb to it all now. Any chance of coffee?' he asked.

As Nathan put the kettle on, he tried to think what to do. He was cornered, on the run, and the Elective's number-one target. But there was a question to which he needed an answer. 'So if the Elective did that to you, why do you go to the private bar at the Harness? Aren't they just rubbing your nose in it?'

Marco shrugged. 'Sometimes it's easier to go with the flow. Sometimes you just get tired of fighting.'

Although he could see that Marco had a point, giving up was the last thing on Nathan's mind. Sometimes it was better to fight for what you believed in, however stupid or suicidal that was. He looked through the kitchen door at his computer, wondering whether he could use that to track Scott down. Then he saw it, an innocuous but incongruous addition to his desk.

'What's that?' There was an envelope – a white, padded envelope – on his desk.

'Search me,' said Marco, 'It's your house.'

Nathan picked it up and looked for some identification, but there were no markings – no name, no address. For a second, he wondered whether it was a letter bomb – and then decided that there was healthy suspicion, and then there was paranoia and pure stupidity. If the Elective wanted to do *that*, they had far more subtle ways.

Opening it, he saw that it contained two plane tickets and a guidebook. He peered at the tickets, momentarily unable to believe what he was reading. The tickets were in the names of Marco Cappiello and Nathan Dexter. And they were for Amsterdam.

'Amsterdam?' muttered Nathan. 'Who would send me –' He stopped. It was obvious. Who else had the resources to just walk into his house and leave the envelope there?

Suddenly the phone rang. Hoping it was Scott, Nathan ran over and picked it up.

The voice at the other end was bland and forgettable and totally unfamiliar. 'Take yourself away from all of this, Mr Dexter,' the voice said. 'You're booked into the Royal Amsterdam Hotel for a week, all expenses paid. Consider this a reward for your . . . cooperation. You'll be picked up from the airport when you arrive.' Then the line went dead.

Nathan shook his head: this, hot on the heels of last night's confrontation with the nameless representative of the Elective, just didn't make sense. For a moment he considered refusing the offer, but realised that that would be futile: the Elective was an organisation capable of making people simply disappear, and Nathan knew that he simply couldn't fight it. Yet. He needed a bit more time for what he had in mind.

Five minutes later, he and Marco were sitting on the sofa puzzling over their dubious good luck.

'I just don't understand, Marco. One minute they're trying to kill me, the next they're sending me on holiday. It doesn't make sense.'

'That's how the Elective works, Nate. Cross them and you're dead meat. Do what they ask and the rewards are unbelievable.' To Nathan, it sounded as though the Elective had taken all of the fight out of the Australian. But he was determined that they wouldn't do the same to him.

'Bribery. Pure and simple,' Nathan spat. 'First threats, then bribery. I'm not going to stand for it.'

Marco put a calming arm around him. 'Come on, Nate, what harm can it do? I don't know about you, but I could do with a holiday.'

Nathan was about to launch into an attack on faceless organisations and why ordinary people shouldn't be manipulated when he realised that a holiday was probably the best thing for him. It wasn't as if he had anything to fear from walking into a trap: the events at the club had proved that the Elective could get him anywhere. If they were going to kill him, Amsterdam was no worse than London. At the very least, its leather scene was better.

Nathan sighed. 'What the hell,' he muttered. 'I've never been to Amsterdam. Always fancied it.' At that moment, his life was being dictated for him, and he had no choice but to take Marco's advice: 'Go with the flow.'

The tickets said that the flight left Heathrow at three o'clock that afternoon, so that gave him enough time to make sure that Scott really was missing. If Scott wasn't, then matters would be different. But something told him that the Elective was too powerful to make empty threats: a holiday with Marco was probably inevitable – and, on reflection, was it that bad an idea?

Then suspicion took over, and he looked at Marco and wondered whether the hunky Australian really was what he appeared to be. Deceit and betrayal seemed to be watchwords for his investigation into the Elective, and there was a very good chance that Marco was nothing more than a spy, bought and paid for. But what the hell: at this point in his life, Nathan really didn't have anything to lose. And everything to win.

He gave Marco an affectionate punch on the shoulder. 'If we're off to Amsterdam in a few hours, you'd better go home and pack.'

'That can wait for a while,' said Marco, stroking the back of Nathan's neck. 'Since we're going to be spending the week together, perhaps we should get to know one another a bit better.' His other hand wandered to the buttons of Nathan's leather shirt.

For a moment, Nathan thought about protesting, before realising how futile it all was. Scott was gone, the Elective had the upper hand, and there was an Australian hunk sitting next to him on the sofa. Leaning over, he kissed Marco on the lips, his tongue entering his willing mouth. As Marco's fingers undid Nathan's buttons, Nathan did the same with the buttons on Marco's denim shirt, and slid his hand inside.

His hand found a solid chest, thick with soft brown hair. Moving downward, he located Marco's nipple and stroked it softly. Pain was all well and good, but sometimes sex was more about tenderness and affection than the more brutal pleasures that Nathan usually enjoyed.

Marco obviously had the same idea: his hand softly stroked Nathan's chest while his kissing became more passionate. Then he pulled away and smiled at him. 'You're a good man, Nate. I'm sorry that the Elective got to you, but I'm glad we met.' He winked at him. 'I can tell you're something special, and I'm looking forward to spending some time with you.'

Nathan had to agree: he knew he was on the rebound – it would be a long time before he felt ready to commit himself to somebody as totally as he had with Scott. But what was wrong with a holiday romance, even if it did begin before they even got on the plane? Especially if it was at the Elective's expense, he thought with a trace of deserved cynicism.

'You're not so bad yourself, Marco. I have to admit, I've always had a soft spot for Australians. Especially ones built like you.' Nathan's hand was rubbing Marco's crotch, and he could feel the thick stiffening beneath the denim. Marco's dick was certainly impressive.

'They grow us big in Melbourne,' he said. 'Anyway, there'll be enough time for talking when we get on the plane.' He moved his head downward until it was over Nathan's groin: then, like an affectionate puppy dog, he nuzzled the leather.

Nathan ruffled Marco's hair, both to arouse him and to gently force his face into his groin. For a few seconds, Marco continued, before stopping. He looked up at Nathan with a cheeky grin on his face.

'I think it's about time I examined the real thing.' He unzipped the flies and reached inside, pulling out Nathan's rigid cock with some difficulty: his hard-on made it difficult to manoeuvre it out of its leather enclosure.

Once it was freed, Marco looked up and grinned. 'It's as good as I remember it from last night. I was really jealous, Nate, watching those two hunks fucking you. I'm glad I've got the chance to try it first-hand.' He leant down and took the waiting helmet between his lips. 'Tastes good as well.' For a few long, wonderful moments, his tongue flicked over the red helmet, and Nathan almost whimpered with pleasure: this man certainly knew what he was doing.

Then Marco stopped and pulled away. 'Want to go upstairs?' he asked.

For a second, Nathan hesitated: going to the bedroom reminded him of Scott too much. *But Scott's gone*, the voice said, *Scott left you. Start getting on with your life.* Nathan stroked Marco's head again and smiled.

'I'd love to.'

Scott sat on the sofa while Adrian busied himself in the bedroom. Adrian had told him not to bother about clothes - they could get them in the States – so Scott didn't really have much to do while they waited for the taxi that would take them to Heathrow.

'Anything I can do to help?' he called out.

Adrian appeared in the doorway. 'All done, Scott. Just got to wait for the taxi.' He sat down next to Scott and put his arm round him.

'Should I phone Nathan?' asked Scott. 'He must be worried.'

Adrian shrugged. 'It's up to you. But from what I know of him, he's probably already shacked up with someone else.'

Scott frowned. Although that didn't sound like Nathan, how could he be sure? What did he really know about Nathan Dexter? A sudden moment of doubt overcame him: how come Adrian knew so much about him?

'No, I'd like to phone him: I just want to make sure that he's OK.'

Adrian sighed. 'You've got to face it, Scott: Nathan isn't the person you thought he was.' Then he frowned, as if he wasn't sure whether he should continue.

'What is it?' Adrian obviously knew something.

Adrian sighed. 'I suppose you've got a right to know. Remember I said that I doubted that Nathan would be in the country when we went to the States?'

Scott nodded, although he had actually forgotten all about it.

'Then you'd better look at this.' Adrian reached into the pocket of his brown leather jacket and pulled out a folded piece of paper.

Scott unfolded it and read the contents with mounting disbelief. It was a printout from one of the airline computer systems – a printout detailing the flight times for a certain Mr Nathan Dexter and a Mr Marco Cappiello from Heathrow to Amsterdam.

That afternoon.

'He's going on holiday?' Scott asked incredulously. 'With this Cappiello bloke?'

'It was booked and paid for weeks ago, Scott. And Marco and Nathan were certainly very friendly last night.'

'Last night?' How did Adrian know what Nathan was doing last night? 'Who's this Marco?' The pain he had felt earlier was coming back, a twisting, tightening feeling in his stomach.

'That business I had to attend to last night – well, it was your heartbroken ex-boyfriend causing trouble in the Harness, Scott. I was called in because somebody recognised him, and knew he was a journalist. When I got there, he was having a drunken argument with this Marco person – an Australian, I might add.' He made it sound as if Australians were something to be avoided.

Scott couldn't register it. 'Are you saying that he's already met someone else?' Surely Nathan wasn't like that? Surely he would have waited more than one day before starting another relationship?

Adrian gave Scott a hug of reassurance. 'Scott, Nathan and this Marco have been going to the Harness together for months. Before you ever met him. They were there the night that *we* first met, if you must know.'

Scott closed his eyes and tried to fight off the pain that he was feeling inside him. There had always been someone else: Nathan had never been his to begin with. Why should he feel any regret or guilt towards someone who had lied to him since the beginning?

A buzzer rang: the door. Adrian stood up and gestured for Scott to do the same.

'The taxi's here. It's time to put all of this behind you and start again, Scott. What do you say?'

The last month had been a lie, he realised. His relationship with Nathan had been a fake, a shallow copy of what he had thought it was. Perhaps the truth lay with Adrian after all.

Filing his relationship with Nathan away in the mental drawer marked 'closed', Scott picked up Adrian's suitcase – Scott himself was travelling light, knowing that a whole wardrobe of clothes awaited him in New York – and followed him out of the flat.

To the future.

Marco lay on the bed, naked, looking up at Nathan with a friendliness and warmth that made Nathan feel guilty about ever suspecting him of being in the pay of the Elective. There was something about Marco that made Nathan want to trust him, to open up to him. He knew that it would be a long time before he felt ready to trust someone again, but at that moment, all he wanted was to be close to the big Australian.

Marco was slightly tubbier than Nathan, but with the same thick covering of body hair: an Australian bear by any standards. His cock was equally as impressive: seven inches of thick

Australian meat, surrounded by a bush of dark brown hair which grew into the fur over his stomach and chest.

Nathan removed his boxer shorts and climbed on to the bed – and on to Marco. He enfolded him in his arms, feeling the warmth of having another person that close to him. Scott was gone, and Nathan's regular, ordered life was upset, but the fact that there was another person on the planet who cared for him, who wanted him, gave him a reason to keep going. Whether Marco really felt for him, or was simply in the pay of the Elective, was irrelevant: he was a living, breathing human being and he wanted Nathan.

Nathan started at Marco's neck, nibbling the stubbled chin from one ear to the other, before moving up to the face. He licked Marco's ears, nibbling the lobes, and then lingered around Marco's waiting mouth, where the Australian's tongue reached out to entwine with his own.

As he continued to work on Marco's mouth, Nathan's hand moved down, through the brown fur of the chest and stomach to Marco's waiting cock. Grasping the thick erection, he started to wank it with slow strokes which caused Marco to groan with pleasure.

'Enjoying it?' he whispered into the Australian's ear as he bit the lobe teasingly.

'You bet!' said Marco. 'I wanted you so much last night: it's been worth the wait to get you on my own.'

Nathan grinned. 'I haven't started yet.' With that, he moved further down Marco's body, drawing his tongue through the brown hair, biting on both of the erect nipples before he reached Marco's stomach. His tongue lingered around Marco's navel – and, by the sounds that Marco was making, he had found one of his soft spots. But that wasn't Nathan's target. Moving down again, his tongue found the damp red helmet of Marco's dick. He took the salty warmth in his mouth, returning the favour of earlier with interest.

Marco shuddered as Nathan's mouth took all of his cock,

swallowing the thick length before teasing the hot, damp slit with his tongue. Nathan was enraptured: somehow, pleasing this Australian guy had become the most important thing in his life. He wanted Marco, and he wanted Marco to want him.

As his tongue played with Marco's cock, his hand moved to Marco's arse. One finger caressed his ring, driving it open with more and more pressure. Gentle at first, Nathan pushed harder and harder, aware that he didn't want to hurt Marco, but equally aware that he wanted to prepare the way for what he ultimately wanted to do to him. Marco didn't resist: if anything, he forced his arse on to Nathan's finger.

Nathan pulled his finger out and put it into his mouth. The taste of Marco was strong: he tasted of sex, of raw, uninhibited manhood. As he licked on his finger, he became aware of Marco's finger, probing, searching for his own arse. Moments later, Marco's finger was inside him, pushing deep. Nathan gasped with the violation: he wanted the Australian inside him so badly that the pain just didn't matter.

It didn't last: Marco withdrew his finger and put it to his own lips and sucked it.

'You taste great,' he said. 'Can't wait to put my tongue up there.'

The thought of Marco rimming him drove Nathan on. He moved his mouth from Marco's cock to further down, to his big, hairy balls. He started off by licking them, before taking each one in his mouth. As he did so, he put both hands on Marco's chest and sought out his nipples. Squeezing them tightly, he released Marco's balls and sent his tongue probing the Australian's arse.

The musky smell of Marco's ring was overwhelming: it personified sex, and made Nathan realise how much he wanted to take this big, hairy man.

'Can I screw you?' he asked, looking up at Marco.

Marco sighed. 'I thought you'd never ask. I just want you inside me.'

Nathan reached down and grabbed the condoms and the lubricant from the side of the bed. He realised from his trembling fingers that he was nervous – but why? Was it the aftershock of his break-up from Scott, or was it something more: the knowledge that Marco represented life *after* Scott, the realisation that he could carry on after Scott had left his life?

Whatever the reason, he still managed to roll the condom over his stiff hard-on and smear the latex with white lubricant. As he went to lubricate Marco, the Australian grabbed his hand.

'Be rough, Nate.'

Nathan squeezed some lubricant on Marco's fingers, and then rubbed it over his ring and pushed it up his arse. Marco forced Nathan's fingers to penetrate him further, and the way he was writhing made it obvious that he was waiting for Nathan to put his cock there. And Nathan didn't want to disappoint him.

With Marco still face up on the bed, Nathan knelt over him. 'I want to screw you, Marco,' he whispered. 'I want to feel my cock inside you.'

Marco put his hands on Nathan's solid shoulders. 'Not as much as I want you inside me.' He moved his legs, opening them to make himself available to Nathan. Nathan didn't hesitate: he manoeuvred himself so that his helmet was touching Marco's ring.

'You want me inside you?' he demanded. 'You want this thick cock inside you?'

'Fuck me, Nate!' Marco growled. 'I want you to fuck me!'

Nathan pushed his cock into Marco, pushing it as far as he could until he felt resistance. He leant down and kissed Marco on the lips, sinking his tongue deeply into his mouth. As he did so, he forced his cock further into him, his tongue stifling any protests.

Once he was as far into Marco as he could be, he gently, slowly withdrew, until his dick was almost out. Then he plunged in once more, and stopped kissing Marco long enough to appreciate his groans of pleasure.

'Like that? D'you like me inside you?' Nathan suddenly felt brutal: it wasn't that he wanted to hurt Marco – at this moment, Marco meant everything to him. He just felt this desperate need to show his power over another person.

Marco nodded furiously. 'Don't stop. Keep fucking me.'

Nathan resumed what he'd been doing, thrusting his cock into Marco and then drawing it almost all of the way out. He continued this as he leant down over the hairy Australian and forced his way into his mouth, penetrating him with both his tongue and his cock.

Marco began to writhe beneath him, and his big hand reached down and found his own cock. As Nathan continued to fuck him, well aware that he was drawing close to his orgasm, Marco started to wank himself off.

Nathan pulled away from Marco's mouth and stared into his dark brown eyes: 'I'm coming.'

Marco nodded. 'I want you to shoot inside me, Nate. I want your load inside me,' he gasped, and Nathan could tell that Marco was only seconds away.

Suddenly, Marco screamed out in pleasure, pulling desperately on his thick cock and letting streams of hot white come shoot on to the dark hairs of his stomach and chest. Seeing this, Nathan couldn't hold back: with one last thrust into Marco, he felt himself coming, and yelled out as the orgasm spread from his cock and across his body, tingling down his arms and legs. He collapsed on Marco and grasped him, desperately hugging him for all that it was worth, his cock still inside the grunting Australian.

'All right?' Nathan gasped. He just felt that all of the strength had been drained from him, and found it difficult to move.

'Wow – I can't wait for the holiday,' Marco replied breathlessly. He responded to Nathan's hug by putting two hairy arms around him and drawing him closer. 'But how are you feeling?' he asked, genuine concern in his voice.

Nathan rolled off him and sat up on the bed. How did he feel? He looked round at Marco and grinned.

Rebound or not, Marco was hot stuff. Nathan had thoroughly enjoyed screwing him, and couldn't wait to let him return the favour. He still missed Scott – how couldn't he? – but fate, and the Elective, had brought him and Marco together. Despite it all, he wasn't going to look a gift horse in the mouth. He leant over and gave Marco an affectionate kiss.

'You'd better pack.'

Marco nodded. 'Once we've finished our coffee.'

Nathan laughed. 'That's what I like: a man who knows his priorities.'

With that, he jumped from the bed and pulled on his bathrobe. Marco wasn't Scott, but he appeared to be someone who cared about him.

And, at the moment, that was the best that Nathan could hope for.

The taxi pulled up outside the terminal at Heathrow. Scott got out and waited while the taxi driver unloaded Adrian's suitcase from the boot.

'I still feel –' he began, but Adrian grabbed his arm.

'Please, Scott – promise me one thing. You won't mention Nathan when we're away.'

Scott was about to protest, but suddenly realised how ungrateful he was being. Adrian was paying for his holiday, Adrian was paying for his clothes when they got there – and it wasn't as if he owed Nathan anything. He'd been taken in by Nathan's charm, by the fact that Nathan apparently offered him a better life, but none of it had been true. Nathan had lied to him from day one, and Scott didn't deserve to suffer any guilt or regret.

OK, so he didn't entirely trust Adrian – how could he,

knowing so little about him? But he had trusted Nathan, and look what had happened.

It was time to enjoy himself, and to hell with the consequences.

He put his finger to his lips. 'Not another word, Adrian. I promise.'

Adrian put his wallet in his pocket after paying the taxi driver, and gently tapped Scott on the shoulder. 'That's my boy. Anyway, we've got a couple of hours, so why don't we try out the Upper Class Lounge? I don't know about you, but I could do with lunch.'

Nathan locked the door of his house and hefted his two bags off the ground. The taxi was waiting for him: waiting to take him to Heathrow where Marco would – hopefully – be waiting for him. As he heard the key click in the door, Nathan was aware that he was closing more than one door: he was closing the door on Scott, on the life that he had hoped to forge with the boy. But it was over: his own behaviour and the intervention of the Elective had made sure that that was not to be. He had tried to phone Scott again, but there hadn't been any answer. Determined to find out what had happened to Scott, one way or another, Nathan had even gone to his halls of residence – and that had given him the answer that he needed. Even if it was an answer that he didn't really want.

According to one of Scott's friends, he had gone on holiday for a week; gone to the States or somewhere 'nice like that'. Gone where the Elective could keep an eye on him, and Nathan couldn't reach him. Wherever it was, he was out of Nathan's life. And it was time that Nathan accepted that.

Walking down the front path, Nathan knew it was over. It was time to break through the pain that was tearing him apart, time to get on with things. He deserved that. Nathan opened the taxi door and got inside.

His trip to Amsterdam offered some downtime, and the

possibility of loads of wonderful sex with Marco – and others, depending on what sort of ground rules he and Marco set down. One of his travel guides had furnished him with a list of bear and leather bars in Amsterdam, and he felt sure that Marco would enjoy checking them out with him. The last thing that Nathan wanted was another relationship, but he felt a closeness to Marco that he needed. Even after the short time they had known each other, Nathan knew that he enjoyed having the big Australian around. Whether it was because of growing feelings for him, or simply that he took his mind off everything else, Nathan didn't know. But a week of Marco in a top-class hotel in Amsterdam, well . . . who knew what might happen?

As the taxi pulled away, Nathan took one last look at his house. Who knew what awaited him when he next saw it again? Would he be over Scott? Would something have formed between him and Marco? Or would he have finally fallen prey to the machinations of the Elective?

With that thought in his mind, Nathan sat back as the taxi set off for Heathrow.

Nine

'I've got a bit of a surprise for you,' said Adrian as he sipped a well-made Bloody Mary in the luxury of the Upper Class Lounge. He reached into his hand luggage and pulled out a stylish padded jacket. 'Hope it fits.'

Scott didn't know what to say: the jacket was exactly the same as the one he had been looking at the other week. Up till now, his relationship with Adrian had simply been financial. But since he had turned to him after his split with Nathan, it was almost as if the older man was treating him like his boyfriend.

And Scott found that he actually quite enjoyed the idea.

Nathan checked his watch for the umpteenth time, looking around the packed terminal building for some sign of Marco. They had agreed to meet at six o'clock in front of the airline check-in desks, but it was now six thirty and he wasn't there.

You've been set up Nate, said the little voice. *Another of the Elective's games.*

'Hi! Sorry I'm late!' The cheery voice came from behind him; Nathan turned to see Marco a few yards away, struggling

161

with a heavy suitcase and a holdall. 'I had trouble getting a taxi.'

Nathan laughed. It had never occurred to him that the answer could be something so mundane as a taxi. *Send your paranoia on holiday, Nate. Preferably somewhere a long way away from Amsterdam.*

With that thought in mind, he picked up his suitcase and made his way to the check-in desk.

Scott reclined in the soft luxury of his seat and looked out of the window of the 747. They had taken off about an hour ago, and the steward had just finished plying them with the latest of many complimentary drinks. Scott watched the steward with interest: he was short and lithely built, with a short brown flat-top; Scott guessed that he was in his mid-twenties.

The steward must have sensed this attention: he turned round from serving some rich-looking woman and looked straight at Scott. And smiled.

Scott glanced round at Adrian, but he was fast asleep: hardly surprising, given the small amount of sleep he had had the night before. Scott returned the smile, and got up to stretch his legs.

The steward joined him at the bar. 'Enjoying the flight?' he asked.

Scott nodded. 'I've never been to the States before,' he added, more for something to say than anything else.

The steward grinned. 'Wish I could say that. I've been flying back and forth to New York for the last three years. My name's Jim, by the way.' He held his hand out and Scott shook it. As he did so, Jim squeezed his hand and looked deep into his eyes. 'Do you fancy a look around?'

Scott knew exactly what the steward meant. He glanced at Adrian, and found that he was relieved to see that he was still asleep. He knew what Jim had in mind, and part of him said that he shouldn't: Adrian was taking him to the States, and he was considering having sex with one of the stewards. However,

Adrian wasn't his boyfriend, and Scott did feel incredibly horny. The idea of having sex in a jumbo jet, somewhere over the Atlantic . . .

'OK,' he said to Jim. 'Where did you have in mind?'

Jim gestured for Scott to follow him. He walked over to a curtained area at the end of the first-class section of the plane, and pulled the curtain open to reveal a door. The executive washroom.

Scott would have preferred somewhere better, but where else could he have sex on a 747? Looking around, he was relieved to see that no one else in the first-class section was paying them the slightest bit of attention. Jim had opened the door of the washroom and was beckoning for him to come inside.

Scott had expected it to be a bit of a tight squeeze: his experience of flying was limited to a package flight to Spain, and he was used to cramped and unpleasant toilets. But this washroom was much bigger, and white-tiled rather than coldly metallic. It reminded Scott of the toilet of some high-class hotel, rather than a plane.

Jim grinned. 'This isn't something I do all the time,' he said. 'I know airline stewards have a bit of a reputation . . .'

Scott laughed. 'Don't worry about it.' He reached out and slowly undid Jim's dark tie and slipped it from around his neck. Then he undid the first few buttons of his crisp white shirt. Jim's chest was solid and hairless, with stiff nipples brown against the tanned skin. Scott leant forward and buried his face against Jim's neck, smelling the expensive aftershave mixed with Jim's natural musk. Jim put his arm around Scott and pulled his white denim shirt from the waistband of his jeans. Scott pulled away from Jim's chest and moved upward, placing his lips against Jim's and forcing his tongue into the steward's mouth.

As he did so, Jim's fingers found all the buttons of Scott's shirt and undid them urgently, before taking off the shirt and allowing it to fall to the floor. Standing there in front of Jim, topless, his well-built frame reflected in the nearby mirror, Scott couldn't help a moment of vanity. You're quite a catch, he thought to himself.

Jim was undoing the rest of his buttons; Scott decided that he couldn't wait, and reached out to take the shirt off. Jim was thin but well built, obviously working out quite frequently. The definition of the muscles was clear and impressive. Lower down, a metal ring pierced his navel.

Having removed Jim's shirt, Scott didn't stop there. He tugged at Jim's belt to undo it, before unbuttoning his blue trousers and pulling them to the floor. Jim's legs were well muscled and lightly covered in dark brown hair. He was wearing a pair of black briefs, which barely covered the large bugle inside them. Scott fell to his knees and began to lick Jim's hard-on through the briefs, dampening the light cotton. He could taste the sticky pre-come through the material, and could tell that Jim was as desperate for sex as he was.

As he licked at Jim's cock, he undid his own trousers, and felt the relief as his hard-on escaped from the confines of the denim and sprang free. He grasped his dick with his left hand and gave it a couple of slow wanks, ensuring that it was as hard as it could be. Then he stood up, and forced Jim to get down on the floor.

Not that Jim needed much forcing: greedily, he took Scott's cock in his mouth, taking the whole length. Then he ran his lips back and forth along the shaft, his tongue rubbing against Scott's sensitive helmet.

Scott gasped with the pleasure, and reached out to the wall to steady himself. It was obvious that Jim was no novice where sex was concerned, and Scott wondered how many other passengers had experienced this sort of in-flight service. As Jim continued to suck on Scott's hard-on, Scott put his hands on the steward's shoulders: partly to feel the solid flesh, and partly to urge him to continue what he was doing. He moved his right hand to Jim's stomach and gently played with the metal ring. Since he had had his navel pierced, Jim was obviously drawing attention to it, and Scott wanted to see what the reaction would be.

Scott didn't have to wait another second: as his fingers tugged and played with the ring, Jim became even more frantic, his lips and tongue running over Scott's hard-on with unrestrained desire. Scott felt the familiar sensation starting to grow inside him, and knew that he wouldn't be able to last out very much longer. But he didn't stop Jim: Scott wanted him to bring him even nearer before he tried something else.

Suddenly Jim stopped and looked up at him with hungry eyes. 'Will you fuck me?' he said. 'I really want you to fuck me.'

Scott didn't need to think about it: the idea of being inside the trim airline steward was irresistible, and exactly what he had been hoping for. He reached into his back pocket and pulled out a packet of condoms and some lubricant.

'Bend over the toilet and spread your legs,' he said.

Jim quickly removed his shoes and trousers so that he could comply. Scott looked at the firm arse; he couldn't wait to pull the cheeks apart and shove his hard-on into Jim's waiting hole. He squeezed some lubricant on to his index finger and rubbed it into Jim's arse, feeling the ring tighten around his finger.

'Did you like that?' he said roughly.

'Oh yes,' said Jim. 'I can't wait to see how it feels with your cock inside me.'

'You're not going to have to wait,' Scott replied. Placing one hand on Jim's shoulder, he used his other hand to guide his cock inside Jim. He felt a little resistance, and pushed harder, eliciting a groan from the air steward. Inch by inch, his thick cock slid further inside Jim, until finally it was all inside, all of Scott's hard-on inside the steward's hot arse.

'That feels great,' gasped Jim. 'Come on, fuck me. And don't be gentle. I like it when people get rough.'

Scott needed no encouragement. He pulled his dick halfway out before plunging it back in. Jim groaned even more loudly in a mixture of pleasure and pain, and that made Scott even more excited. He pulled out again and forced his way back in, establishing a rhythm that satisfied him. As he continued to fuck Jim, the hand that wasn't supporting him moved round and sought out the steward's cock. It was still restrained by the briefs, so Scott wasted no time in releasing it. The moment that his hand touched the impressive erection, Jim shuddered; Scott guessed that keeping away from Jim's cock until now had made Jim all the more sensitive. He started to wank Jim off with the same rhythm with which his cock was sliding in and out of Jim's arse, tugging at the moist flesh and pulling the foreskin back and forward over the wet helmet. All the time, his other hand massaged Jim's firm, muscular back.

Within moments, Scott knew that he was going to come. His rhythm became even faster, more frantic, and his wanking became even more brutal. Something told him that Jim wasn't far off, and that drove him to fuck the steward even harder.

With a deep grunt, Scott felt the warm churning feeling at the base of his stomach explode, and he sensed his load shooting inside Jim. Jim let out a cry of pleasure, and Scott saw a jet of white hit the toilet lid as Jim shuddered with the force of his orgasm.

Slowly, Scott pulled his cock out of Jim's arse. 'Thanks,' he whispered, licking a few white drops of Jim's come from his hand. Having sex on the plane had been the last thing on his mind, but he now felt quite pleased with himself. This was something to tell his friends, when he finally got back to Britain.

The airline steward grinned. 'All part of the service, sir.'

The flight to Schipol Airport was short and uneventful; less than an hour after leaving Heathrow, Nathan and Marco were in Amsterdam, striding through customs.

'Have you ever been to Amsterdam before?' asked Marco.

Nathan nodded. 'Been three or four times, actually. Normally in the summer though: it gets a bit cold in the winter.'

Marco pointed to the barrier, where a small crowd of people were waiting to meet the new arrivals from Britain. A short, stocky man with dark cropped hair was holding up a handwritten sign which simply said 'Dexter'.

'I guess that's our lift,' said Marco.

A couple of minutes later, they were sitting in the back of a black BMW, as it negotiated its way out of the airport towards the city centre.

'Well, we're here for a week. Anywhere that you'd like to see?' Nathan asked.

Marco frowned for a second. 'All the touristy things, I suppose. Anne Frank's house, a couple of art galleries and museums, windmills . . .' Then he grinned. 'And a few leather bars, of course.'

Nathan put his hand on Marco's knee. 'Now that goes without saying,' he said with a laugh.

The Royal Amsterdam Hotel was old yet beautifully maintained, with an air of luxury that came straight from a bygone age. Its tall, imposing façade was set back in a small side street, about five minutes' walk from the very centre of Amsterdam.

The driver, who had stayed silent for the whole of the journey, parked the car and then carried their bags into the foyer.

'Just wait here,' he said with just the faintest trace of an accent. 'I'll just go and sort everything out.' Then he smiled, a grin that lit up his surly, square face. 'Won't be long.'

'Helpful bloke,' said Marco.

Nathan watched as the driver sauntered over to the reception desk. Underneath his dark suit, he was probably quite a hunk, Nathan decided, and wondered briefly how far the driver's duties went. Guessing that he was another paid employee of the Elective, Nathan had a fair idea of the answer.

While they waited for the driver to book them in, Nathan looked around the foyer. It had a tall ceiling decorated with elaborate, gilded carvings, with a huge crystal chandelier just above them. Nathan took a rough guess at how much it was costing the Elective to put him and Marco up in the hotel and whistled through his teeth: it was definitely more than he could afford.

The price of your silence, came the voice. *Blood money from the Elective.*

At that moment, the driver came back. 'I'll carry your bags to your rooms,' he informed them, before picking them up and walking off to the lifts.

'Rooms?' asked Marco. 'In the plural?'

In the plural. They were staying in a suite on the tenth floor, with two interconnecting bedrooms, a lounge, and two huge bathrooms. From the heavy velvet curtains to the antique furniture, everything simply dripped money. Nathan's eyes were drawn to the Emperor-sized bed that he could just see through the connecting door to one of the bedrooms. There was undoubtedly another one in the other bedroom, but Nathan doubted that he would be sleeping alone during his stay in Amsterdam: if he wasn't with Marco, there were plenty of candidates in the many leather bars down the Warmoesstraat and Regulierdwarsstraat.

'Rooms,' repeated Nathan. He had to admit that, even he was impressed: in the course of his career, he had stayed in more hotels that he cared to count, but he had never stayed in anything quite approaching this amount of luxury. It was actually quite overwhelming.

'Will that be all?' asked the driver, having placed their bags against the wall.

For a second, Nathan wondered whether the man was

168

waiting for a tip, before remembering the question he had asked himself earlier. He smiled. 'I don't suppose that you'd like to stay for a little bit longer, would you?'

He caught the slightly shocked expression on Marco's face and had to stop himself from laughing. Perhaps he was being a little bold, but what the hell? He was on holiday.

The driver shrugged. 'If you want, sir,' he replied, taking off his jacket and laying it on the bed. He was wearing a plain white shirt with a blue tie. As Marco and Nathan watched, he undid the tie and began to unbutton the shirt. Seconds later, he was standing there topless, revealing a good-looking, thickset body. He was broader and more muscular than Nathan, without an inch of fat. A light dusting of black hair covered the upper part of his chest and his flat, solid stomach.

'Want me to carry on?' the driver asked.

Nathan nodded. 'If it's OK with you,' he added. No harm in being polite, he decided.

'I'm completely at your disposal, Mr Dexter,' said the driver as he unbuckled his belt and pulled his trousers off. 'My employers want to make your stay in Amsterdam as pleasant as possible.'

And it looks to be very pleasant indeed, thought Nathan, looking at the stocky, muscular man who was now wearing only his blue boxer shorts. He glanced round at Marco, and was surprised – and delighted – to see that he was taking off his clothes. Nathan wasted no time in following suit, taking off everything apart from his own boxers.

Seconds later, all three of them were standing in the centre of the lounge, stripped to their underwear. Nathan could see Marco's erection through his briefs, and was aware that his own hard-on was poking through the gap in his boxers.

The driver walked over to him and sank to his knees, pulling Nathan's boxers down and taking his moist helmet in his mouth. Nathan trembled with pleasure as the stocky man's tongue lingered over the end, before probing his dick slit.

Nathan put both hands on the man's shoulders to steady himself as the driver took all of his cock in his mouth and ran his lips up and down the thick shaft.

Then Marco came over and knelt behind Nathan. For a moment, Nathan wondered what he was up to, but a couple of seconds later he had the answer: he felt the cool wetness of Marco's tongue, probing between the cheeks of his arse until it quickly found its target. Marco ran his tongue around Nathan's ring for a moment, before forcing it inside. Marco's hands grabbed Nathan's firm, hairy thighs and started to massage them.

Nathan sighed with pleasure. Now this was how to begin a holiday in Amsterdam! He gave an involuntary shudder of pleasure as the driver ran his tongue around the rim of his helmet. Looking down, he saw the driver looking up at him with an expression of enjoyment on his face, and that excited Nathan even more: the driver may have been in the pay of the Elective, but he was now doing this because he wanted to.

Nathan pulled his dick out of the driver's mouth and urged him to stand up. Then he turned to Marco, who stood up. 'I wouldn't mind sucking that dick. He gestured at the thick cock that was just visible through the driver's boxer shorts.

'Sounds good to me,' said Marco.

'Want us to suck your cock?' he asked the driver.

The driver nodded. 'Hasn't been sucked for a long time, sir,' he replied.

Nathan knelt in front of the driver and beckoned for Marco to do the same. Reaching out, he pulled the driver's dick from his boxers and was impressed. Although it was shorter than either Marco's or Nathan's, it was almost twice as thick; circumcised, with a wide red helmet, wet with pre-come.

Greedily, Nathan took it first, forcing his mouth round the broad cock with some difficulty. He started to lick the helmet and relished the salty wet taste. The driver let out a short cry of pleasure as Nathan's tongue continued to explore the moist thickness, running up and down the dark, veined shaft.

Marco was getting impatient: Nathan could sense it. He released the driver's cock and allowed the Australian his turn. He watched for a second as Marco attempted to get all of the dick into his mouth, before lying down on the floor so that Marco's own dick was only a few inches from his mouth. Then he began to suck Marco's helmet, which was leaking vast amounts of clear wetness.

Suddenly he was aware that the driver was moving: without taking his cock from Marco's mouth, he was lying down on the floor, and Nathan didn't have to be a genius to know what he was planning. Marco obliged by moving as well; moments later, the driver was on the carpet, forming a triangle with Marco and Nathan.

Still sucking Marco's big Australian cock, Nathan gasped as the driver once again started running his tongue over his helmet. Then he felt a sharp pain that immediately became pure pleasure as the driver tightly squeezed his right nipple, pinching it until Nathan didn't think he could take any more. Then he moved across to the other nipple and repeated it, and it was only the presence of Marco's dick in his mouth that prevented Nathan from crying out with the combination of ecstasy and pain.

The driver's actions were bringing Nathan to the very brink of orgasm, but he decided that he didn't care. He just wanted to flood the driver's mouth with his come, and hoped that Marco wasn't too far off: he desperately wanted to taste the Australian when he shot his load.

A grunt from Marco made it clear that this wasn't going to be a problem: Nathan felt Marco convulse, and felt the thick shaft of his dick grow suddenly thicker. Then Nathan's mouth was filled with the warm salty taste of Marco's load, and that was all it took for Nathan to come. He thrust his groin into the driver's face, forcing even more of his cock into his willing mouth as load after hot load shot against the back of the driver's throat. As Marco's subsiding dick slipped from Nathan's mouth, Nathan let out a groan of pleasure, of release, before finally sinking back on to the carpet.

Marco knelt over him, a telltale dribble of white in his moustache proof that the driver had also succumbed to Marco's actions.

'I'll tell you what, Nate,' said Marco breathlessly, 'if this is Amsterdam, I think I'm going to enjoy it.'

Nathan grinned, but a dark thought entered his mind. That sex had been brilliant, but it had been courtesy of the Elective. Was he in danger of falling prey to their plan? By the time he got back from Amsterdam, would he be a willing convert to the Elective's cause?

The worst thing was, Nathan just didn't know. No, he corrected himself. The worst thing was that he hadn't thought of Scott since arriving in the hotel.

With a shudder, he wondered if conversion to the Elective's corrupted ways had already started.

Ten

___

'Smart hotel,' said Scott, sitting down on the soft bed. 'Must be costing a packet.' The hotel was in the very centre of Manhattan, a brand-new glass-and-chrome skyscraper which combined elegance with clean, stylish functionality. Scott's only previous experience of staying in a hotel was a run-down bed-and-breakfast in Blackpool and a dirty, overcrowded concrete monstrosity on the Costa Del Sol, so the Manhattan Regency was something of an eye-opener for him.

The room itself was enormous: more of a suite than a room. Scott thought about his cramped room in the halls of residence, and guessed that the hotel room was at least four times as big. It was luxuriously carpeted in deep, cream shag pile, with a huge television in one corner, a fully stocked bar – not a minibar, a real bar – in another, and various items of predominantly chrome furniture dotted around. One wall of the room was taken up with a single sheet of glass, a window which offered a stunning view of Manhattan. All in all, Scott was standing in the middle of more luxury and more wealth than he had ever encountered before.

For the briefest of moments, he wondered about Nathan:

where was he staying in Amsterdam? What was his hotel like? Then he thought about this mysterious Australian, and felt a stomach-churning feeling of jealousy, combined with anger: anger at Nathan for what he had done to him, but also anger at himself for falling for it in the first place.

Adrian shrugged. 'Let me worry about money,' he said. 'You're here to have a good time – a break. Talking of good times, you might want to have a look in the wardrobe.' He gestured to a set of mirrored doors across the huge room on the opposite side from the window. Scott hopped off the bed and walked over, pulling the doors wide open.

The wardrobe was full of clothes. There were jeans, shirts, T-shirts, boots, shoes – a complete set of everything Scott could want for a holiday in New York.

'These are for me?' he said, rather redundantly. Who else would they be for?

'Of course. I'm pretty sure that I've got the size right.'

Scott was overwhelmed. When Adrian had mentioned that he was going to buy Scott some clothes, Scott had assumed he meant a shirt and a pair of trousers. The contents of the wardrobe in front of him represented more clothes than Scott had back in London.

He went over to Adrian and gave him a warm hug, but Adrian didn't seem as responsive as he had been in his flat in London. If anything, there was a coldness, a restraint about him, which reminded Scott of how Adrian had been when they had first started their business arrangement.

'Is everything all right?' he asked.

Adrian walked away and stood by the window. It was early afternoon in New York, and the thin winter sunlight could only just crawl into the room.

'As I said, Scott, I've got some business to sort out over here. The American end of one of our . . . operations isn't going as well as my superiors would like. I need to find out why, and rectify the situation. So I'm a bit preoccupied at the moment.'

Scott wanted to believe him, but there was something about Adrian's manner that worried him. For a second, he wondered if he was being too trusting: the way that Adrian had virtually come to the rescue when he and Nathan had split up was almost too good to be true. Had he walked out of one relationship based on lies and half-truths, only to become trapped in another?

You're being an ungrateful little bastard, Scott, his conscience told him. *Adrian's probably the only thing that's kept you going over the last couple of days, and you're in danger of throwing it all back in his face. Get a grip, and don't look a gift horse in the mouth.*

'So, are you going to have any free time while we're here?' According to Adrian, they were flying back in three or four days, once he had attended to business. Scott hoped that he wouldn't have to wander around New York on his own.

Adrian seemed to snap out of his brown study. 'Of course I am. In fact, I think we've got time for dinner.' He frowned in concentration for a second. 'Actually, I know a really nice little restaurant on Fifth Avenue. Do you like Italian food?'

Scott smiled. But the faintest trace of unease remained.

Marco and Nathan stood in front of the mirror and admired their reflections. They were dressed virtually identically, with black leather jeans, biker's boots, denim shirts and heavy leather biker jackets. The only difference was the set of handcuffs which hung down from Nathan's waistband.

'Dressed to kill,' said Marco. 'We're going to knock them dead tonight.'

Nathan laughed. 'I have to admit, we do look pretty good.' He moved over to Marco and gave him a hug. 'Now remember: don't feel obliged to stay with me all evening. If you want to go off, feel free. Just let me know, so I'm not waiting around.'

Marco raised an eyebrow. 'Sounds to me like you're the one

who's going to go off,' he laughed. 'Come on: Amsterdam's not going to know what's hit it.'

As they walked out of the hotel room, Nathan pondered the relationship between himself and Marco. They weren't partners: Nathan was very fond of the big Australian, but he didn't love him. After what happened with Scott, it would be a long time before he felt able to open up to someone again, to trust him the way that he had trusted Scott. In Nathan's experience, trust meant dropping your defences, and that was how you got hurt.

But Marco offered friendly, fun companionship, with some good sex thrown in. Nathan couldn't take away the pain that he felt over Scott, but he could temporarily take his mind off it, replace it with purely physical pleasure.

Perhaps the way of the Elective was right, after all.

Night was beginning to fall when Scott and Adrian left the restaurant. The meal had been excellent, but Adrian's distracted mood had returned; throughout the meal, he had been constantly looking at his watch, as if he desperately wanted to be somewhere else.

Standing in the chilly New York evening, Adrian turned to Scott. 'I'm afraid I'm going to have to deal with that business affair now.' He handed Scott a black leather wallet. 'There's about two hundred dollars in there. That should keep you amused for the evening. Don't come back to the hotel room before about two o'clock.'

With that he hailed a taxi. Scott was so shocked by his brusque dismissal that he was unable to reply, and simply watched as the yellow cab sped off down the street.

He really couldn't figure Adrian out. One minute he was flying him to the States, buying him new clothes and taking him to expensive restaurants; the next, he was treating him like a little boy, giving him money for sweets to keep him occupied.

Scott sighed and looked at his watch. After getting ready –

now he realised why Adrian had insisted that he have a shower and put on some of his new clothes, since he wasn't going to be going back to the hotel room – and the meal, it was now nine o'clock in the evening.

And Scott was alone in a city where he didn't know a single soul.

He sighed. Well, he was dressed for an evening out, he had two hundred dollars, and Adrian had given him a list of clubs he might want to visit and a map.

Sod it. He was in New York and he was damn well going to enjoy himself.

Choosing a club called Excess from the list, he set off in the direction of Thirty-second Street.

Nathan and Marco were sauntering down Regulierdwarsstraat, relishing the admiring glances they were getting from the large number of leathermen who were virtually parading themselves along the long street of clubs. Nathan considered himself to be something of an Amsterdam regular, but even he was surprised by how many people were out tonight.

'Check him out,' whispered Marco, nodding towards a man walking towards them. He was at least six foot three and incredibly broad, with cropped hair and an impressive black moustache. Underneath his black jacket he was wearing a rubber vest, which showed a firmly muscled, smooth chest. But Nathan couldn't keep his eyes off the bulge in the man's jeans: he was obviously hung like a horse. When the man smiled at Nathan as he walked past, Nathan's stomach did a somersault.

'You're in there,' said Marco, watching the man as he retreated away from them. 'Lucky you.'

Nathan tried to work out where the man was going. He had stopped outside Chains, which Nathan remembered as being a large, dark club with a labyrinthine back room downstairs.

Nathan grinned at Marco. 'I feel like taking a bit of a chance.'

His eyes followed the leather-clad man as he walked into the club. 'Fancy going to Chains?'

Marco shrugged. 'As long as I cop off with someone, I don't mind. You indulge yourself.'

Nathan thought about this for a second. He was very fond of Marco, but there wasn't any sort of formal contract between them: indeed, Marco had been sent to Amsterdam with him by the Elective. Even if he wasn't in their employ, he embraced their ideals. And their ideals would have agreed with Nathan following someone he fancied into a club. 'OK, let's go.'

They reached the entrance of Chains. The doorman, a surly-looking man in a black sweatshirt and jeans, gave them the once over and let them in.

Chains was exactly as Nathan remembered it: dark, crowded, and smelling of smoke and sweat. He gestured for Marco to follow him to the bar. 'Fancy a drink?'

'Why not?' said Marco. 'You're going to be busy for a while.'

Nathan was still a bit worried. 'I thought we'd agreed –'

Marco grabbed his shoulder. 'Look, mate, whatever you want to do, just do it. I don't mind – this is a holiday, and we're here to have fun. Go for it.'

Nathan shrugged. Marco was right: he was in Amsterdam to enjoy himself, and it was about time he started to do it. He bought them both a beer and looked around the dark interior of Chains to see if he could see the big leatherman, but there was no sign of him. Then again, Chains was large and dark, and there was a good chance that he had gone directly downstairs, where a network of small corridors provided more direct action.

'Is this the club with the downstairs?' asked Marco, before taking a swig from his beer bottle. 'He might be down there.'

Nathan thought for a second: much as he liked Marco, they had agreed that they were in Amsterdam for a holiday, for a bit of fun. 'I think I'll take a look,' he said.

Leaving Marco at the bar, Nathan walked over to the far side of the big, dark room until he found a curtained archway. Pushing the curtain aside, he saw the stone steps that led downstairs, and began to descend.

The downstairs darkroom in Chains was legendary: it was like a maze, with short corridors and dark alcoves. It was quite early for Amsterdam's leather scene, but there were already shapes moving in and out of the shadows. Nathan positioned himself at one of the busier junctions and waited.

After a few seconds, he spotted his quarry. The tall man was standing about six feet away. And he was staring directly at Nathan. For a moment, Nathan actually felt nervous, but his attraction, his longing, for the leatherman quickly overcame any doubts or worries. He smiled, and was pleased to receive a broad grin in return. He had been noticed: it was time to do something about it.

He slowly walked over to the man, keeping eye contact all the time. He leant against the brick-lined wall next to him and nodded a greeting. The man smiled once again.

'Hello,' he said, with the faintest trace of a Dutch accent. 'My name is Ruud.'

Nathan was a little surprised: he had expected the usual anonymity, the faceless, nameless sex. But he was also very pleased: knowing the man's name would make it more intimate, more personal.

'Nathan,' he replied, reaching out and stroking the man's denim-clad thigh.

'Shall we go somewhere a little more private?' asked Ruud. 'There is a little room over there.'

Nathan couldn't help smiling: privacy in a dark room. But he could feel his excitement rising, and he was finding it difficult not to grab the man and start kissing him, undressing him, taking his cock in his mouth and swallowing everything Ruud had to offer.

Following Ruud, he found himself in one of the alcoves, the

179

only illumination a shaft of light from a dim wall lamp. A pair of manacles were fixed to one of the walls, and Nathan hoped that they would be more than just ornamental. As soon as he was in the alcove, Ruud took hold of him, bending down slightly and pressing his face against him. His thick moustache rubbed against Nathan's beard as Ruud's tongue forced its way into Nathan's mouth, seeking out his own tongue and massaging it. Hot spit passed between them as Ruud's kissing became even more frantic, more violent. Then he pulled back, and gestured to the manacles. 'Interested?' he asked simply.

Nathan nodded. He knew he was taking a risk, being chained up by someone he didn't even know, but that only added to the excitement. His cock was already hard in his leather jeans, and he wanted Ruud to take it out, to suck on it until he came.

He moved over to the wall and allowed Ruud to roughly force his hands through the manacles and clip them shut. Seconds later, he was secured, unable to stop whatever Ruud wanted to do to him.

Ruud reached down and started to rub the bulge in Nathan's trousers, making it even harder. Nathan began to feel uncomfortable, desperate for Ruud to undo the zip and pull out his hard-on. Instead, Ruud began to kiss him again, even more roughly, while he continued to rub Nathan's groin.

The mixture of pleasure and discomfort had almost become overwhelming when Nathan felt Ruud's finger's pulling on the top of the zip. Moments later, Nathan's leather jeans were undone; since he wasn't wearing anything underneath, his cock sprang free immediately. Ruud took it in his hand and smiled. 'You've got a nice cock, Nathan.' He gently pulled back the foreskin to show the glistening red helmet, wet with pre-come. Ruud moved his thumb so that it was resting over the end of Nathan's helmet, and then started to rub. His thumb made circular motions over the end, the movement lubricated by Nathan's salty wetness.

Nathan gasped at the sensation – it was almost more than he

could bear. But Ruud had no intention of stopping; and with his hands manacled to the wall, there was nothing Nathan could do but hang there and experience the pleasure.

His breathing grew harder as Ruud's thumb rubbed the sensitive end, and he knew that he wasn't going to be able to hold out for much longer.

'Good?' asked Ruud, a mischievous glint in his eyes.

Nathan could only nod as he felt a tingling, churning sensation in his balls and above his cock. He started to tremble as the strength of his orgasm began to take him over, spreading out from his cock in wave after wave of pleasure. At the exact moment that he knew he was going to come, Ruud dropped to his knees and took Nathan's cock in his mouth.

With a cry of release, Nathan shot load after load into Ruud's mouth, and watched as the Dutchman gratefully swallowed the hot spunk. Nathan continued to come, unable to remember the last time he had had an orgasm like this, his come filling up the Dutchman's mouth faster than he could swallow it; a thin dribble of white appeared at the corner of his mouth.

Finally it stopped, and Nathan let out a deep sigh. 'That was great,' he said.

'My turn,' said Ruud, unlocking the manacles.

'Be my guest,' said Nathan with a smile. He was looking forward to it.

Scott stood at the corner of the bar, people-watching. Excess was getting busy, attracting a youngish crowd of men wearing jeans and chinos and smart shirts. Just like him.

He sipped his beer and tried to decide what to do. If he had sex, was he being unfaithful? He was feeling incredibly randy that night, and getting randier by the second. But Adrian wasn't his boyfriend, and his earlier behaviour, inexplicable as it had been, suggested that Adrian didn't see Scott in that light either. For a moment, Scott thought about Nathan, and a sharp image of him appeared in his mind. Scott's anger over Nathan's infidelities was fading rapidly, to be replaced by understanding. Nathan must have been devastated by John Bury's death: having sex under those circumstances would have been inevitable. There was still the matter of this Marco Cappiello, but that was a puzzle for a different time.

'Haven't seen you around before,' came a strong American accent. Scott looked round to see a tall, well-built man with short black hair and a healthy tan, dressed in a black-and-white-checked shirt and black trousers. Scott guessed he was in his mid-twenties.

'I'm on holiday,' explained Scott. 'Arrived today. I'm Scott.' He held out his hand and the man shook it.

'I'm Steve – welcome to New York.' He gestured around the bar. 'What do you think of the club?'

The main bar of Excess was huge, with white-tiled walls and a completely mirrored ceiling. After a cursory walk around, Scott had counted at least another three bars, and a room that he suspected to be a back room.

'It's impressive. Do you come here a lot?' Scott knew that this was almost turning into a series of chat-up lines, but he was bored. At least Steve was taking his mind off his other worries. And besides, if he did chat Steve up, where was the harm in that?

'You could say that,' said Steve with a smile. 'I run the place.'

Scott laughed. He'd been thinking of chatting up the owner! What chance did he stand with someone who could probably take his pick from all the men in the club? All he could say was 'Oh'.

'Are you here with anyone?' Steve asked nonchalantly.

'Here as in "the club", or here as in "the States"?'

'Both. Either. Whatever,' said Steve, laughing.

'I came to the States with a friend, but he had some business to attend to. So I thought I'd take a look around the club scene.'

182

'And you came here. Well, well.' Scott was suddenly apprehensive. There was something about Steve's manner that wasn't quite right. Actually, it reminded Scott of someone else's behaviour: although he couldn't explain it or rationalise it, Steve reminded Scott of Adrian.

'Fancy going somewhere a bit more private for a drink? I've been to England a few times: it would be nice to chat for a while.'

Scott thought about it for a second: at least he wouldn't be standing there on his own. A voice inside him suddenly spoke up: *Don't do it*, it said. *If you do, you'll live to regret it*.

But Scott decided it was worth the risk. What was Steve going to do – kidnap him?

Nathan returned to the upstairs bar of Chains, convinced that his satisfied grin was visible from the other side of the room. He and Ruud had each come three times, and each time the feeling had been more and more intense until Nathan had decided that he'd better stop before he was totally drained. Ruud had seemed disappointed, but had insisted on giving him his phone number. Nathan fully intended to call him – once he got his strength back.

Marco appeared out of a throng of people. 'You look happy with yourself,' he said. 'Mission accomplished?'

Nathan nodded. 'More than you could possibly imagine,' he laughed. 'What about you?'

Marco gestured behind him. 'I've met this French bear who wants to take me back to his hotel room. I thought I'd better wait until you finally surfaced. Would you mind?'

Nathan laughed. 'I'm hardly in a position to mind, am I?' He looked over Marco's shoulder, and saw a handsome-looking man with a black flat-top and well-kept beard, dressed entirely in denim. 'What's his name?'

It was Marco's turn to laugh. 'Believe it or not, he's called

Nathan. Anyway, don't want to keep him waiting any longer. See you tomorrow?'

Nathan gave Marco a peck on the lips. 'Fine. Don't wear him out too much.'

Marco raised an eyebrow. 'I'll try not to. What about you? Going back down for more?'

Nathan shook his head. 'I'm exhausted; think I'll head back to the hotel. I'll see you tomorrow.'

With that, he walked over to the exit. People were still arriving, but Ruud had taken away any thoughts of sex. Nathan just wanted to get back to the hotel and crash out. Despite his initial reservations, he was beginning to really enjoy himself once more.

For a second, he thought about Scott. Where was he? Was he safe? But these weren't questions that were going to be answered any time soon. Nathan decided he should just get on with the holiday. And phone Ruud the next morning.

Steve had taken Scott to his office, a modern room with chrome furniture and a two-way mirror which overlooked the main dance floor.

'What do you think?' Steve asked.

'Nice view.' He looked down at the desk, which was covered in paperwork; a computer was switched on, the whirling colours of its screensaver reflecting off the two-way mirror's glass surface.

'Would you like a drink?' Steve walked over to a small fridge and drew out two bottles of Bud. He opened them and passed one to Scott.

'That would be great,' Scott replied, taking the ice-cold bottle and taking a swig. He still wasn't sure where all of this was leading: did Steve want sex, or was there something else, something that Scott didn't know about?

Suddenly the phone rang. Steve answered it. After a few

seconds, he replied, 'I'll be right down,' and replaced the receiver.

'You'll have to excuse me for five minutes, Scott. I've got some business to attend to in one of the bars.' He gestured around the office. 'Make yourself comfortable.' With that, he left the office.

Scott sat down at the desk and idly looked through the papers, more for something to do than out of curiosity. But his eyes were drawn to one particular sheet, drawn by a name.

Nathan Dexter.

He frowned. Surely there couldn't be two Nathan Dexters, could there? He started reading the paper, realising that it was a printout of an e-mail which had arrived yesterday. As he read the information, a cold shudder went down his spine. Phrases leapt off the paper and hit him, phrases which, if true, meant that he had been well and truly caught in a web of deception and lies. Scott's head was spinning with the realisation of what he was reading, what he had stumbled into.

I have succeeded in splitting him up with his partner. I have taken the partner to New York to act as insurance.

Dexter is in Amsterdam with one of our operatives, Cappiello: at the very least, this will put a stop to his interference. I had hoped to convince him to join us: I believed that Dexter would prove a valuable asset to the Elective. However, he is too wilful. Cappiello has orders to dispose of him.

Scott stopped reading as he tried to make sense of it all. He and Nathan had been deliberately split up. Perhaps Nathan had been unfaithful, but Scott felt sure that, left to his own devices, he and Nathan would have worked it out. But they had never had a chance.

Somehow, he had to warn Nathan. For a second, he was at a loss: how could he contact him, when he didn't know where he was staying. *Think, Scott – what does Nathan always take with him?*

The answer was blindingly obvious: his laptop.

Scott swivelled round to the computer and gave the mouse a couple of clicks; the screensaver dissolved to reveal a standard Windows 95 desktop environment. Scott looked around for some sort of mail package, and saw the icon for one in the corner. Opening it up, he dredged Nathan's e-mail address from his mind, typed it into the address line, and then composed what was probably the most important message he had ever written:

Nathan, this is Scott. The whole thing's a trap. Marco's working for the Elective and I suspect they've caught me as well. Get out of there before they kill you.

Then he added the words that he desperately wanted to say in person:

I love you.

He looked down the printed e-mail and saw the name at the bottom.

The name of the sender. The name of the person responsible for this whole mess. Scott suddenly felt sick.

Oh my God, thought Scott, taking deep breaths to try to calm himself. He'd been in the hands of the Elective all along and hadn't realised it. Suddenly he heard footsteps outside the office, and realised that there wasn't time for anything else before Steve came back. Frantically, he sent the e-mail, and sighed with relief as it vanished from the screen.

Then the door opened. But it wasn't Steve standing in the doorway.

It was the person whose name lay at the bottom of the e-mail. The Comptroller of the Elective.

186

Adrian Delancey.

Adrian stepped over to the desk, snatched the printed e-mail from Scott's hands and read it. Then he raised an eyebrow. 'So, you've uncovered my little secret, have you, Scott?'

'You bastard,' was all Scott could say.

'Steve – who is my opposite number in New York, by the way – suspected who you were. When he heard I was in the club, he came to tell me. Not that I was particularly bothered,' he added.

'I thought you cared about me,' said Scott lamely. However, it was the one question to which he still wanted – needed – an answer.

'Cared about you?' said Adrian, incredulity in his voice. 'Cared about you? You're nothing more than a bit of rent, Scott, a bit of trade that has been bought and paid for. A slave in the service of the Elective. But you've served your purpose. Dexter will stop his prying, and the Elective can continue as it has always done: in secret, away from people who couldn't possibly understand our higher purpose.'

'You're sick, Adrian,' Scott snapped. 'You killed John Bury.'

'Bury was a failure, and the Elective doesn't tolerate failure. But that still leaves you. What I am going to do with you? I wonder.' There was an icy streak of cruelty in Adrian's voice. Scott didn't doubt for a second that he could arrange for Scott to go the same way as John.

Scott swallowed. But whatever happened to him, Nathan had been warned. Scott just hoped it was in time.

Nathan sat on one of the beds and sighed. He was exhausted, but somehow sleep was eluding him. Deciding that he had to do something, he retrieved his laptop from on top of the table and plugged it in to the mains and the phone socket. Perhaps reviewing his e-mails would send him to sleep.

Thanks to the machinations of the Elective, Nathan hadn't attended to the mundane tasks of life for far too long: it was time to bring a little order back into his life. If he was to fight the Elective when he returned to Britain, he needed stability in his life.

He looked at the incoming e-mail log, and saw that he had about fifty new messages. He scanned the list of senders, and was able to mentally dismiss most of them; then his eyes caught an unfamiliar e-mail address, somewhere in the States. Curious about who it was, he opened it up.

And read Scott's message.

Seconds later, Nathan had started to pack. Hopefully he would be long gone before Marco got back. Although he couldn't imagine Marco hurting him, Nathan knew too much about the Elective to be taken in by surface appearances. He had to get back to England and attack the Elective now, while he still had a chance. He just hoped that he could save Scott as well.

Suddenly the door opened. Before Nathan had a chance to react, Marco was standing there, a cold, hard expression on his face. He walked over to Nathan.

'I'm sorry, Nathan. I wish you knew how hard this is for me.'

Nathan swallowed. Was this how it was going to end, finally trapped in the Elective's chains of deceit?

Eleven

The flight back to London had probably been the longest eight hours of Scott's life. Although Adrian hadn't been forthcoming in what he planned for Scott, it had been made quite clear that any attempt to escape, any attempt to warn the authorities, would result in the harshest of penalties. And John Bury was evidence of what those penalties were.

When they reached Heathrow, there was a car waiting for them. Adrian ordered Scott into the back and then got in after him.

As the car drove off, Scott glanced at the driver, and realised that he probably doubled up as Adrian's bodyguard: he was massive, with a bullet head and almost no neck to speak of. Not that Scott had any intentions of trying to escape: he didn't know where to go or who to go to. The Elective was everywhere – that was what Nathan had said. If only he had listened to him, believed him . . .

Scott just hoped that, in sending the message, he had helped to redress the balance.

★ ★ ★

189

'Deputy Comptroller?' said Nathan. 'I wasn't aware that there was one.'

'There's still so much about the Elective that you don't know, Nathan,' said Marco. 'But that's about to change.' He put a big hand on Nathan's thigh and squeezed. 'You're the person who can help me do that. With the evidence you've amassed, we can expose Delancey as the incompetent failure that he is. Buried in those coded e-mails is proof that he's been defrauding the Elective to feather his own nest. When the Director hears about this, he won't be pleased.'

They were sitting in Nathan's front room, drinking coffee. Nathan still found it difficult to believe: Marco had been working for the Elective, that was true. But his motives were far more complex than they first appeared. And it did seem that Nathan had found the ally for whom he had been desperately searching. 'What happens then? Do you become Comptroller?' There was still the possibility that this was nothing more than an internecine power struggle between different factions of the Elective.

Marco shrugged. 'Whether I become Comptroller or not isn't important at the moment. This whole slave ring was Delancey's idea, and it's been a fiasco. I didn't like the idea in the first place: the Elective was set up to help gay people, believe it or not. Delancey has corrupted its ideals, turned it into a sick and twisted version of what it's meant to be. All I want to do is bring Delancey down. And yes, I do want revenge. There's a perfectly decent person out there, confined to a wheelchair because of Delancey's greed.'

Nathan realised that Marco was talking about his boyfriend. Or, rather, ex-boyfriend.

'OK, OK, you've convinced me. I just want to make sure that Scott is safe.'

Marco glanced at his watch. 'Delancey's plane has just landed. He'll probably go straight to his office in the Harness. Now,

I've put in a call to the Director: he'll meet us there in two hours. From what I can gather, Scott will be with him.'

Nathan breathed a sigh of relief. As long as Scott was OK, that was all that mattered.

Marco moved his hand to Nathan's groin and squeezed gently. 'Look, we can't do anything till then. What do you say?'

Nathan hesitated for a second. With everything hanging in the balance, how could he have sex? But his body had different ideas, and he felt his cock stiffen under Marco's hand.

Marco was right. There wasn't anything that he could do until they confronted Delancey with the Director. He stood up and pulled Marco up with him. He started to take Marco's shirt off: not gently, but roughly, violently, as if the stresses and tensions of the last few days were all coming out, all being channelled into one desperate act of sex.

The shirt ripped from his back, Marco grinned. 'Just how I like it,' he growled. Reaching out with both hands, he tore Nathan's denim shirt apart, buttons flying across the room, before leaning forward and nuzzling into the thick black hair. His teeth sought out each nipple in turn, biting them hard and causing that mixture of pleasure and pain that Nathan craved. Nathan grabbed the back of Marco's head and forced him towards him, urging him to bite even harder. Soon the feeling was too strong for even Nathan to handle, and he roughly pushed him away, before sinking to his knees and pulling down Marco's zip. The Australian's erection was already free of his boxer shorts, and Nathan took it greedily, allowing the full length of the big cock into his mouth. Then he pulled back to concentrate on the helmet, licking the sensitive ridge and the wet dick slit, while one hand came up and started to wank him with hard, brutal strokes.

Marco let out another growl as Nathan continued to wank and suck him; he put one hand to the back of Nathan's neck to push him even further, to make him take even more of his cock.

Then Nathan stopped.

'Fuck me,' he said. That was all he wanted.

Marco said nothing: he undid Nathan's belt, pushed his jeans and briefs to the floor, and turned him around, forcing him to lean over the sofa. Nathan's hands lay on the back of the sofa to steady himself as Marco pulled Nathan's cheeks open and began to greedily lick at his ring, his tongue flicking in and out and making Nathan gasp with the hot, wet feeling.

'I've wanted to do this for a long time,' said Marco. 'I've been watching you for months, Nate. I've always wondered what it would be like to be inside you.' He reached into his pocket for a condom.

He smeared lubricant around and inside Nathan's ring, and then applied some to his cock.

Echoing what Marco had said to him when they had first had sex, Nathan called over his shoulder. 'Be rough, Marco. Force it inside me.'

Marco didn't hesitate. Nathan felt the Australian's helmet touch his ring, and then Marco was inside him, forcing his way into Nathan's arse. Nathan almost cried out with the pain of penetration, but managed to relax himself enough to turn the burning into total pleasure, a feeling of fullness and contentment that threatened to overwhelm him.

Marco withdrew what felt like half of his length, before entering Nathan once more with a hard thrust. Slowly he began to build up a rhythm, pulling out and then sliding back in with all of his body behind it. Nathan grabbed his own cock and began to wank himself off in time with Marco's strokes, drops of pre-come falling from the wet helmet and landing on the leather of the sofa. Nathan was getting close, and Marco's frantic breathing against Nathan's neck suggested that it wouldn't be long before the Australian exploded inside him.

Nathan suddenly gasped: his whole body suddenly felt as

sensitive as his cock, and he totally lost control. With a long, deep cry of pleasure and relief, he shot a stream of white against the back of the sofa, and then another and then another. As he did, Marco yelled out and forced all of himself into Nathan, his body shuddering with the effort. Then, satisfied and drained, he pulled his cock out and sighed.

Nathan turned round and grinned at him. 'That was . . . unbelievable,' he gasped.

Marco kissed him deeply for a few seconds. Then he shrugged. 'I'm not going to argue with you.' He looked at his watch. 'Anyway, time to get ready. We've got a Comptroller to depose.'

Scott sat in Adrian's office: he had been surprised to discover that the Comptroller of the Elective was based in the Harness. Then again, Scott thought, was that really all that unexpected? It was where he and Adrian had met. Going to the darkroom was probably the Comptroller's idea of a tea break.

He looked round, and saw that the chauffeur-cum-body-guard was still at the door, watching him intently. There hadn't been a single moment since the confrontation in the Excess club when Scott hadn't been watched like a hawk, not a single opportunity for him to escape.

The door opened, and Adrian came in. He gave Scott a look of utter contempt before going over to his desk and grabbing some paperwork.

'When are you going to get round to me, eh?' snapped Scott. He had nothing to gain by being polite.

'I told you, Scott: you're nothing. Something's cropped up, something important – and unexpected. Dealing with you is going to have to wait until I've seen the Director.'

'The Director?' Scott knew from Nathan that the Director was the overall power behind the Elective. Why was he coming to see Adrian? More importantly, would it help Scott to get away from this nightmare?

'Yes. And it's all very inconvenient,' he added. 'I've got better things to do than kowtow to him.'

'Really, Delancey, is that any way to talk about our superior?' A thick-set man with a moustache stood in the doorway. From the Australian accent, Scott guessed that it was Marco. Had he succeeded in 'disposing' of Nathan?

'Ah, Cappiello. Back from Amsterdam, I see.' Adrian raised an eyebrow. 'I trust you were successful?'

'Not exactly,' came another, more familiar voice. Scott's heart leapt at the sound, and he felt tears in his eyes.

'Nathan!' he yelled, jumping from the seat and running over to the doorway. The person Scott had feared he would never see again was standing there. Neither of them said anything – there was no need for words. Nathan reached out and hugged him, hugged him as if he never wanted to let him go again.

'How very touching,' spat Adrian. 'Cappiello – what the hell is going on here? You were ordered to get rid of this . . . this nuisance.'

Marco shook his head. 'It's all over, Delancey. The slave ring has been a disaster – you could have blown the whole Elective wide open.'

Adrian laughed. 'That's your opinion. I'm sure the Director will have other ideas.'

'What will he think about the three million pounds that you've taken from Elective central funds and stashed away in a Swiss bank account? Will that impress him, do you think?' said Nathan.

'What have you been telling him?'

'I didn't need to, Delancey. Nate's a good journalist. The best. He's got all the evidence that we need.'

'You've still got to get that evidence to him. Remember: I am a Comptroller of the Elective, and you are nothing more than a deputy. I think I know who he'll believe.'

'Are you quite sure of that, Delancey?' A deep commanding voice came from behind Marco. The Australian stepped aside to let a stranger into the office. He was huge: about six foot four, with cropped grey hair and a bushy grey moustache. He was dressed in a business suit, but Scott could imagine him in full leather very easily. It was even easier to guess who he was.

The Director.

'Marco and Mr Dexter have been most forthcoming with their evidence.' He stepped forward and towered over Adrian. 'You're finished, Delancey.'

Adrian's face fell as realisation dawned. 'You're kicking me out of the Elective?' he said quietly.

'Not exactly. You'll still serve the Elective. I'm shutting the slave ring down, Delancey, but the Elective is going to recruit one last slave.' He smiled. 'You.' With that, he gestured at the bodyguard. 'Take him to my car and keep an eye on him. There's a flight leaving for Morocco in about two hours.'

Adrian's eyes opened in shock. 'You're sending me to Morocco?' he whispered.

The Director ignored him. 'Get him out of here.'

The fight seemed to drain from Adrian. Without another word, he walked out of the office. And out of their lives.

'Now,' said the Director. 'On to business. Mr Cappiello, I'd like you to become the new Comptroller. And you, Mr Dexter . . . I'd like you to help him.'

'Me?' said Nathan, the surprise clear in his voice. 'But the Elective stands for everything I despise.'

'It may do now, after all the damage Delancey's done. I want you to put that superb investigative brain to good use: I want you to help Marco to root out the corruption in the Elective. I want it to become the organisation I originally set up, using its influence to help gay people, not to enslave them.' He smiled. 'No more deceit, Mr Dexter.'

Twelve

Christmas Day was upon them almost before they realised it: the days that followed the fall of Adrian Delancey had been a blur of recriminations, pain and ultimately forgiveness, leaving Christmas Eve a frantic round of shopping that had left Nathan and Scott breathless. But they had managed it. Nathan wanted to make this Christmas one to remember, and had left out nothing: the food, the decorations, the presents. This Christmas marked the beginning of a new phase in his life, and he wanted to celebrate it. More importantly, he wanted to celebrate it with his friends.

Now it was late afternoon, and the four of them were sitting in Nathan's living room, all feeling very full from the lavish Christmas dinner that Nathan had prepared for them. Nathan and Scott's guests had been pleasantly surprised to learn that Nathan wasn't just an investigative journalist; he was also an accomplished cook, and Nathan had thoroughly enjoyed spending a couple of hours in the kitchen while the others sat around, drinking, laughing and opening their presents. Anyone who saw them would have found it hard to believe that they had been through the sheer hell that recent events had caused.

Nathan had laughed in embarrassment at the compliments that he had been given, but he knew – immodestly – that they were well deserved. Even he had to admit that he had surpassed himself. The scallop and smoked salmon parcels had come out perfectly, and when they were followed by the moist, tender roast duck in a rich orange sauce, everyone was taken aback.

After the cheeseboard, they had retired to the sofas, enjoying a reflective moment that they all deserved. A melodic ballad played softly in the background as the four of them sipped their wine and looked back over the last few months, realising what they had lost – and, more importantly, what they had now gained.

Marco patted his stomach and smiled. 'One hell of a meal, Nate. The Elective could do with a head chef for one of its London restaurants. Fancy it?'

Nathan raised an eyebrow. 'Hardly a job for the new Deputy Comptroller, Marco.'

Deputy Comptroller. Nathan still had trouble believing that. Over the course of the last couple of days, he, Marco and the Director had thrashed out a recovery plan for the Elective, one that would remove the corruption which Adrian Delancey's time as Comptroller had introduced. The Director was fairly sure that he could identify most of the areas which needed attention, but he wanted Nathan's analytical skills to help him find them all. Marco would co-ordinate it: as the new Comptroller, that was his first task. But Nathan would be his right-hand man: together, they would return the old values to the Elective, turning it back into the philanthropic organisation that the Director had always intended it to be. Then the Director had offered Nathan the role of Deputy Comptroller.

Nathan had initially argued against it, but the Director's logic couldn't be faulted: the position would give Nathan the access to the Elective that he would need to accomplish the task. As Deputy, he would have access to the inner workings of the Elective; no door would be closed to him.

The irony wasn't lost on Nathan: for months, he had been trying to uncover the truth behind the Elective, lifting up the stones to see what crawled out. And now? Now he was part of the organisation, installed at one of the highest levels of its hierarchy, with complete access to its inner workings. Sometimes, life wasn't just odd – it was plain crazy.

But today was Christmas Day, a time to put any worries or concerns aside for a while and enjoy life. A good meal with good friends: number one on Nathan's list of favourite things. Then he glanced at Scott, who noticed the attention and put his hand on Nathan's knee. OK, perhaps it's number two, he thought.

'That really was an excellent meal, Nathan. Then again, after the last month, it's just good to be back among friends again.' Leigh smiled, but there was still a trace of pain in his face, pain caused by what he had endured over the last couple of months. 'How can I ever thank any of you enough for what you've done?'

When the Director had offered Nathan the post as Deputy Comptroller, Nathan had thought about it long and hard. But he could see the benefits that it would bring, both to himself and the Elective. So he had accepted – but with conditions. Or rather, one condition. All the people who had been caught in Adrian Delancey's web of slavery were to be released – all of them.

Two days ago, Leigh had arrived at Heathrow Airport, having been flown back from Germany. Scott and Nathan had met him there, and then brought him back to their house – yes, *their* house – where he had told them the horrifying story of what had happened to him after he had met the leatherman with the jaguar tattoo in the Brave Trader.

The leatherman – one of Delancey's personal army of recruiters – had drugged him, slipping something into the coffee when they had got back to Leigh's flat. The drug had initially made him susceptible to suggestion for a couple of days

– hence the phone conversation with Nathan – before another dose knocked him unconscious.

The next thing Leigh remembered was waking up to discover that he was in Germany, in a small town called Sindelfingen, just outside Stuttgart.

And he was a slave.

His masters had been good to him: two big German bears, very good looking and extremely rich. But the lack of freedom, and the fact that they regarded him more as a plaything than a human being, had been the worst experience of his life. He had tried to escape, but the bears took that as part of the game they were playing. They punished him, and obviously took a lot of pleasure from that punishment, tying him up, making him eat from a dog bowl, treating him as something less than human.

Now he was free, although events of the last couple of days suggested that he wasn't going to be free for very long. Nathan looked at Marco and Leigh on the sofa opposite him and couldn't help smiling. If they thought that the clandestine looks and seemingly accidental touching was fooling him, they underestimated his powers of observation. It was clear that there was a strong bond of attraction forming between the stocky little Northerner and the big Australian.

How did he feel about that? Both Marco and Leigh had played important roles in his life, and he was very, very fond of both of them. But Nathan searched himself, and couldn't find anything apart from a heart-felt hope that a solid relationship would develop between the two of them. There was a certain symmetry in it, he had to admit. And looking at them, at the almost tangible attraction between them, it did feel good. It felt right. Marco would be able to help Leigh, help him to get over what had happened and start again.

Nathan sighed with contentment. 'It's good to have you back, Leigh. It's good to have everyone who was kidnapped back.'

But he knew that not everyone had escaped the consequences of the Comptroller's sinister and perverted plot, and allowed himself a moment's sad reflection. According to the Director, three people wouldn't be coming back, including someone that Nathan had known quite well, a lanky leather man that everyone knew simply as Ledge. His new masters in Sweden had taken their little games just a bit too far, and Ledge had paid the price for it in his blood.

'Poor Ledge,' sighed Nathan. 'I just hope that everyone who survived this ordeal recovers as well as you have, Leigh.'

Leigh couldn't help himself, and squeezed Marco's hand – more proof of their developing relationship. 'I'm getting there,' he said almost wistfully.

At that moment, the CD changed disks; as the first track on the Celine Dion album burst into the room, Nathan couldn't help grinning at the irony of the song, and how it summed up the last few months.

There had been a point in his life, after his encounter with Adrian Delancey, when he thought he had lost everything: Scott, his career, his reason to carry on with life, all of it stripped away. But sitting here, with Scott beside him and two of his best friends opposite, with a new career – one which would really help people – waiting just around the corner, he couldn't help but echo the sentiments of the song that came from the hi-fi.

It's all coming back to me now, thought Nathan. *And this time I'm going to keep hold of it – all of it.* He picked up his wine glass, still full of a wonderful burgundy. 'I'd like to propose a toast.'

Marco frowned. 'To what?'

'Isn't it obvious?' asked Scott. Over the last couple of days, it had become clear that Scott understood Nathan better than Nathan had ever realised – in many ways, better than Nathan understood himself.

Nathan laughed. 'A toast I never thought I'd hear myself making, Marco. But with you there to put things to rights, and me to keep an eye on you,' he added mischievously, 'I honestly mean this.' He raised his glass. He did mean it. It had once been his arch-enemy, something which stood against everything he believed in, but now he could see it as a force for good – if he and Marco did their jobs properly.

'To the Elective.'

As the others echoed his words, Nathan laughed. He was looking forward to the future. His future with Scott. The best future he could hope for.

Hours later, the inevitable happened: Marco and Leigh were in the spare room, and you didn't have to be a genius to work out what was going on there. At about two in the morning, they had both complained of being tired, and Nathan couldn't blame them: supper had been late, and the wine and whiskey had been flowing freely all day. But he still raised a knowing eyebrow as they ascended the stairs together, Marco claiming that it saved Leigh having to sleep on the sofa.

Yea, right, thought Nathan. Who do you think you're fooling?

Once he heard the bedroom door close, he sank back into the sofa, his arm around Scott. 'How are you feeling?' he asked.

Scott smiled. 'Happy. Best I've felt for a long time, actually.'

Nathan gave him a kiss on the lips. 'I know what you mean.'

After Adrian had been dragged off to Morocco, Nathan and Scott had taken themselves away for a while, spending the night on neutral territory: Nigel, manager of the Brave Trader, had given them exclusive use of the upstairs bar – and the flat above it. They needed space, and time, to repair the damage, to see where they would go next, and Nigel had been only too pleased to help out.

They had talked. They had talked until they didn't think that there was anything more to say, but still they had carried on talking. Nathan had begged Scott to forgive him for being unfaithful, only to discover that Scott had already forgiven him, having understood the reasons why. Then Scott had told him about his business arrangement with Adrian Delancey, a fact greeted by a stunned, incredulous silence from Nathan.

Nathan had been devastated: all the time that Nathan and Scott had been together, Nathan had been sharing him with the Comptroller of the Elective! But it didn't take him long to come to terms with it: Scott had been manipulated by the Elective, just as Nathan had been. How could Nathan blame Scott for falling victim to their sick and twisted schemes?

At that moment, the forgiveness was total, and mutual: they loved one another, and that was the most important thing. They didn't have to agree to go back out with one another; it was almost as if that were a given, as if it were inevitable. With that understanding, they had gone upstairs to the flat, and sealed their friendship with a night of love-making in which they pushed the boundaries of their sex life to the limit, doing things to one another that they had only dreamt of. The honesty that they had found between themselves in their relationship was applied to their sex life. There was nothing that they wouldn't tell one another, nothing that they wouldn't ask of one another.

And in that, something else fled their relationship: jealousy. Both Nathan and Scott knew that there would be other people; it was the way that the world went, and both of them were far too intelligent to expect complete fidelity. But both of them also knew that any sex which they indulged in outside of their relationship would be nothing in comparison to what they felt for one another, what they could do with one another. They would always be there for one another, and that was what mattered.

And now they were in Nathan's house, in the quiet hours of Boxing Day. Or rather, they were in Nathan *and* Scott's house: the morning after their reconciliation, Scott had moved into the house in Docklands – it was what they both wanted. It was what they both needed.

Stability. Love. Each other.

'Thanks for making this Christmas so special, Nathan,' said Scott.

Nathan shrugged. 'The first of many, Scott. Over the last month, I'd been so obsessed with the Elective that I'd started to shut you out of my life, to create areas in it that you weren't welcome in.

'That's going to stop – if we're going to be together, then I'm going to share all of my life with you. No more secrets, no more deceit.' He smiled. It was time for one last surprise. He reached down the side of the sofa to the spot where the little box had been hiding, away from prying eyes.

'One last Christmas present, mate.' He handed it over.

Scott opened the box, looked at the contents, and then looked back at Nathan.

'A ring?'

'Call me sentimental, but I thought it was the right thing to do.'

Scott took the plain gold band from the box and put it on the correct finger. 'A perfect fit,' he added.

Nathan coughed. 'One thing that you should have realised about me now, Scott: I do my research.' He reached over and gave Scott a tight, breathless hug that lasted for ages. Finally, Nathan released him. 'I know that it's what's inside that matters, but I wanted something that would show everyone how much you mean to me.'

'You big softy,' Scott laughed, but it was clear from the way he was blinking rapidly that the gift had really moved him. Scott stood up. 'Then I suppose I'd better give you your Christmas present as well.'

Without saying another word, he pulled Nathan from the sofa and led him up the stairs. Scott walked into the bedroom and switched on the bedside lamp. The light glittered off the corners of the bed, and Nathan realised what Scott was intending.

Four sets of handcuffs were attached to the bedposts. He found himself grinning widely.

'I've never let you chain me up before, have I?' asked Scott.

Nathan had to admit that Scott was right: whenever Nathan had broached the subject, Scott had been reticent. Indeed, Nathan had actually started to get a bit frustrated that Scott wouldn't share Nathan's favourite fetish, and he had often wanked himself off while fantasising about his boyfriend, chained to the bed and unable to stop whatever Nathan wanted to do to him.

Without another word, Scott began to remove his clothing. He first took off the blue polo shirt, revealing his muscular chest with its thick covering of wiry brown hair: a chest restrained by the upper part of Nathan's leather body harness. Nathan raised an eyebrow in surprise; this was something else that Scott had always refused to do. At the sight of his boyfriend in the harness, Nathan felt his erection spring to life, pressing against his jeans – but he refused to touch it, refused to release it. The way he felt at that moment, he wanted this to last.

Scott then unbuttoned his own jeans and let them fall to the floor. He wasn't wearing any boxer shorts, which showed off the way that the leather strap of the harness followed the solid muscle of his stomach down to his thick hard-on, where the studded leather cockring was fastened tightly around his cock and the base of his balls.

Scott looked down at the obvious bulge in Nathan's jeans. 'I take it you approve?' he asked.

'What do you think?'

'Then chain me up, master.' Scott's whole bearing and manner suddenly changed. He was now subservient, there only to please his master. He would only do what Nathan asked – no, *told* – him to do.

For the briefest of moments, Nathan hesitated: the games of power and pleasure that he enjoyed, that he fantasised over, had always been between him and strangers. The idea of enacting his love of bondage and domination with his boyfriend was strange, alien even. But suddenly he realised that it was turning him on even more than normal. Scott knew him, knew what he liked to do and how to respond.

In that second, Nathan knew with certainty that this would be the best session he had ever had.

'On the bed,' he ordered. Scott got onto the duvet and moved his arms and legs so that they were brushing against the open handcuffs.

Nathan pulled off his own shirt and slipped off his jeans in seconds; his erection freed, it sprang out of his boxer shorts and stood proudly against his stomach. He leant over Scott, and his dick brushed the boy's chest. An electric thrill ran through his body at the sensation, but he refused to act on it. He glanced at Scott's face, and saw him staring at Nathan's cock with a greedy look of desire. Nathan knew that he was going to take full advantage of that.

He fastened the handcuffs around Scott's wrists, then moved further down so that he was crouching over him. Then, roughly, with no concern for the boy's comfort, he kissed him on the mouth, deeply, forcefully, his tongue entering Scott's mouth and probing it, exploring it, without mercy.

Pulling away, he allowed his tongue to trace a line down Scott's neck until he was licking the hairs on his chest. He moved across so that his mouth was above Scott's left nipple, and then took the stiff pink bud between his teeth and started to bite. Glancing up at Scott, he saw him begin to breathe heavily, obviously feeling the mixture of unbearable pain and pleasure that he was causing. He took Scott's other nipple between his fingers and squeezed, applying the same amount of pressure as his mouth was doing. Scott gasped, and that drove Nathan on. Hungrily, he bit and teased Scott's nipples until he had brought Scott as close to orgasm as he dared. It was time to move on.

His tongue carried on its descent, reaching Scott's flat, hairy stomach and spending a few seconds licking his navel, while his hand gently stroked Scott's chest, a contrast to his roughness earlier. Then it was time for the main course. Nathan's tongue lingered for a moment on Scott's thick, solid thighs, before darting downwards to his balls. He took each one in turn, applying enough pressure to cause Scott to gasp.

Although he desperately wanted to take Scott's rigid, waiting hard-on in his mouth, he refrained: he didn't want it to end too quickly, and he knew Scott well enough to know that he wouldn't last long – he was too excited, too desperate for that.

Crouching between Scott's legs, he forced the boy to lift them to give him access to his desired target: Scott's hot, hungry arse. Lubricating a finger, he forced it inside Scott's hole – roughly, taking no notice of the sharp cry of pain which resulted.

'Quiet,' he snapped. 'You're going to take all of this, boy.' He smeared some more lubricant over his condom, and then lifted Scott's legs even further into the air, keeping hold of them to support himself as he guided the end of his cock towards Scott's ring.

'You're going to take all of this cock, aren't you, boy?' he repeated.

'Yes, master,' said Scott, and the tone of genuine obedience in his voice made Nathan even more excited, more eager. As his helmet touched Scott's hole, Nathan forced himself forward, shoving his cock deep inside Scott. Scott cried out with pain, but Nathan didn't care: the pain wouldn't last long, and soon Scott would feel the pleasure that his master was bringing him. Once his dick was fully enclosed by the warmth of Scott's body, he slowly pulled it out until only the helmet was still inside. Then he thrust it back inside with a forceful shove. Scott groaned, and Nathan couldn't tell whether this was out of pain or pleasure. Nor did he care: Scott was there to please him. If he did a good job, Nathan would reward him. If he didn't, well – he would punish him instead.

'You like this, don't you, boy? You like to have your master inside you,' Nathan growled, pulling his cock almost all the way out again before sliding it back.

'I want you to fuck me,' groaned Scott. 'Please fuck me hard,' he begged. The look of utter subservience in his eyes drove Nathan on, and he knew that it wouldn't be long before he came. He built up a rhythm, repeatedly entering Scott before sliding his cock almost all of the way out.

Scott's cock was stiffer than Nathan could ever remember, a combination of the cockring and the excitement he was feeling. But Scott was unable to touch it without his master's permission. When Scott came, it would be at a time of Nathan's choosing.

Nathan started to breathe heavily, and knew that another few strokes would bring him off. He started to fuck Scott even faster, and felt the warmth in his groin increase, turning into a hot, trembling sensation that expanded from his groin to flow throughout his whole body. At the same time, the end of his dick became so sensitive that he gasped with the overwhelming feeling. With one final thrust, Nathan came, grunting with the exertion and the relief, a feeling of total satisfaction enveloping him.

'Good boy,' he gasped, pulling his cock from Scott's arse. 'You've been a good boy, so it's time to reward you.' Still breathing heavily, Nathan took Scott's stiff, red cock in his mouth, and grabbed it with one hand as he did so. Scott shivered with the sensation, and Nathan knew that it wouldn't be long before Scott's come was hitting the back of his mouth.

He started to wank Scott with measured strokes, running his tongue over his engorged helmet as he did so. He put his other hand between Scott's legs, and quickly reached for his arse, still relaxed and wet from the pounding it had just received. Nathan's fingers began to probe Scott's open ring, while his tongue flicked over the helmet and the dick-slit before he ran it around the sensitive ridge revealed by the pulled-back foreskin.

He suddenly sensed the tightness in Scott's balls, and knew that the boy was close. He wanked him even faster, sucked him even harder, and stuck his fingers even further up Scott's arse.

With a deep, heartfelt groan, Scott came, his dick expanding and contracting with each warm, salty jet. Nathan tried to swallow every gout, but even he had difficulty, and he felt a trickle of Scott's come dribble down the side of his beard.

Finally, Scott was drained. Nathan let Scott's cock fall from his mouth and sat up on the bed.

'Did you like that?' he asked, putting his arm around Scott's shoulders.

Scott grinned. 'I wasn't sure whether I would – I thought it might be difficult with someone I love. But . . .' He nodded. 'It was great. I can't wait to do it again.'

Nathan laughed, realising the endless possibilities that were now opening up for him. Then he looked at the handcuffs and had an idea.

'What about the other way?' he asked.

'The other way?'

'How d'you fancy bossing me about for a change?'

Scott laughed, and then his voice hardened. 'Unlock these handcuffs and get on the bed,' he ordered.

Nathan looked at Scott and smiled. It was going to be a long and enjoyable night.

The first of many.

IDOL NEW BOOKS

Also published this month:

THE VELVET WEB
Christopher Summerisle

The year is 1889. Daniel McGaw arrives at Calverdale, a centre of academic excellence buried deep in the English countryside. But this is like no other college. As Daniel explores, he discovers secret passages in the grounds and forbidden texts in the library. The young male students, isolated from the outside world, share a darkly bizarre brotherhood based on the most extreme forms of erotic expression. It isn't long before Daniel is initiated into the rites that bind together the youths of Calverdale in a web of desire.

ISBN 0 352 33208 5

THE KING'S MEN
Christian Fall

Ned Medcombe, spoilt son of an Oxfordshire landowner, has always remembered his first love: the beautiful, golden-haired Lewis. But seventeenth-century England forbids such a love and Ned is content to indulge his domineering passions with the willing members of the local community, including the submissive parish cleric. Until the Civil War changes his world, and he is forced to pursue his desires as a soldier in Cromwell's army – while his long-lost lover fights as one of the King's men

ISBN 0 352 33207 7

WE NEED YOUR HELP . . .
to plan the future of Idol books –

Yours are the only opinions that matter. Idol is a new and exciting venture: the first British series of books devoted to homoerotic fiction for men.

We're going to do our best to provide the sexiest, best-written books you can buy. And we'd like you to help in these early stages. Tell us what you want to read. There's a freepost address for your filled-in questionnaires, so you won't even need to buy a stamp.

THE IDOL QUESTIONNAIRE

SECTION ONE: ABOUT YOU

1.1 Sex (*we presume you are male, but just in case*)
Are you?

Male ☐
Female ☐

1.2 Age

under 21 ☐ 21–30 ☐
31–40 ☐ 41–50 ☐
51–60 ☐ over 60 ☐

1.3 At what age did you leave full-time education?

still in education ☐ 16 or younger ☐
17–19 ☐ 20 or older ☐

1.4 Occupation _____

1.5 Annual household income (if you don't mind telling us)

under £10,000 ☐ £10–£20,000 ☐
£20–£30,000 ☐ £30–£40,000 ☐
over £40,000 ☐

1.6 We are perfectly happy for you to remain anonymous; but if you would like us to send you a free booklist of Idol books, please insert your name and address

_____

_____

_____

_____

SECTION TWO: ABOUT BUYING IDOL BOOKS

2.1 How did you acquire this copy of *Chains of Deceit*?

I bought it myself (from a bookshop)	☐	My partner bought it (from a bookshop)	☐
I borrowed/found it	☐	It was bought through mail order	☐

2.2 How did you find out about Idol books?
I saw them in a shop ☐
I saw them advertised in a magazine ☐
I read about them in _____
Other _____

2.3 Please tick the following statements you agree with:
I would be less embarrassed about buying Idol
books if the cover pictures were less explicit ☐
I think that in general the pictures on Idol
books are about right ☐
I think Idol cover pictures should be as
explicit as possible ☐

2.4 Would you read an Idol book in a public place – on a train for instance?
Yes ☐ No ☐

SECTION THREE: ABOUT THIS IDOL BOOK

3.1 Do you think the sex content in this book is:
Too much ☐ About right ☐
Not enough ☐

3.2 Do you think the writing style in this book is:
Too unreal/escapist ☐ About right ☐
Too down to earth ☐

3.3 Do you think the story in this book is:

      Too complicated   ☐   About right   ☐

      Too boring/simple   ☐

3.4 Do you think the cover of this book is:

      Too explicit   ☐   About right   ☐

      Not explicit enough   ☐

Here's a space for any other comments:

SECTION FOUR: ABOUT OTHER IDOL BOOKS

4.1 How many Idol books have you read?

4.2 If more than one, which one did you prefer?

_____

4.3 Why?

SECTION FIVE: ABOUT YOUR IDEAL EROTIC NOVEL

We want to publish the books you want to read – so this is your chance to tell us exactly what your ideal erotic novel would be like.

5.1 Using a scale of 1 to 5 (1 = no interest at all, 5 = your ideal), please rate the following possible settings for an erotic novel:

      Roman / Ancient World   ☐

      Medieval / barbarian / sword 'n' sorcery   ☐

      Renaissance / Elizabethan / Restoration   ☐

      Victorian / Edwardian   ☐

      1920s & 1930s   ☐

      Present day   ☐

      Future / Science Fiction   ☐

5.2 Using the same scale of 1 to 5, please rate the following themes you may find in an erotic novel:

       Bondage / fetishism ☐
       Romantic love ☐
       SM / corporal punishment ☐
       Bisexuality ☐
       Group sex ☐
       Watersports ☐
       Rent / sex for money ☐

5.3 Using the same scale of 1 to 5, please rate the following styles in which an erotic novel could be written:

       Gritty realism, down to earth ☐
       Set in real life but ignoring its less pleasant aspects ☐
       Escapist fantasy, but just about believable ☐
       Complete escapism, totally unrealistic ☐

5.4 In a book that features power differentials or sexual initiation, would you prefer the writing to be from the viewpoint of the dominant / experienced or submissive / inexperienced characters:

       Dominant / Experienced ☐
       Submissive / Inexperienced ☐
       Both ☐

5.5 We'd like to include characters close to your ideal lover. What characteristics would your ideal lover have? Tick as many as you want:

Dominant	☐	Caring	☐
Slim	☐	Rugged	☐
Extroverted	☐	Romantic	☐
Bisexual	☐	Old	☐
Working Class	☐	Intellectual	☐
Introverted	☐	Professional	☐
Submissive	☐	Pervy	☐
Cruel	☐	Ordinary	☐
Young	☐	Muscular	☐
Naïve	☐		

Anything else? _____

5.6 Is there one particular setting or subject matter that your ideal erotic novel would contain:

_____

5.7   As you'll have seen, we include safe-sex guidelines in every book.
      However, while our policy is always to show safe sex in stories with
      contemporary settings, we don't insist on safe-sex practices in stories with
      historical settings because it would be anachronistic. What, if anything,
      would you change about this policy?

      _____

      _____

SECTION SIX: LAST WORDS

6.1   What do you like best about Idol books?

      _____

6.2   What do you most dislike about Idol books?

      _____

6.3   In what way, if any, would you like to change Idol covers?

      _____

6.4   Here's a space for any other comments:

      _____

      _____

      _____

      _____

*Thanks for completing this questionnaire. Now either tear it out, or photocopy it, then put
it in an envelope and send it to:*

> **Idol**
> **FREEPOST**
> **London**
> **W10 5BR**

*You don't need a stamp if you're in the UK, but you'll need one if you're posting from
overseas.*